Serafino da Ferrara

Paolo G. Grossi

Also by Paolo. G. Grossi *The Tiergarten Tales*

Serafino da Ferrara

Published by The Conrad Press in the United Kingdom 2023

Tel: +44(0)1227 472 874
www.theconradpress.com
info@theconradpress.com

ISBN 978-1-915494-29-0

Typesetting and Cover Design by:
Charlotte Mouncey, www.bookstyle.co.uk
Images Courtesy National Gallery of Art, Washington - *Bindo Altoviti* by Raphael and The Metropolitan Museum of Art, New York - *Fantastic Landscape* by Francesco Guardi.

The Conrad Press logo was designed by Maria Priestley.

Printed and bound in Great Britain by Clays Ltd, Elcograf S.p.A.

To Silvio G.

Contents

Here vigour failed the lofty fantasy:
But now was turning my desire and will,
Even as a wheel that equally is moved,
The Love which moves the sun and the other stars.

Paradiso - Canto XXXIII

Italian, Italians, and *Italics*

As with my previous work, *The Tiergarten Tales*, I have been parsimonious with the use of italics.

Both books are set in continental Europe through various historical contexts. The number of terms and expressions which should be set in italics is perhaps too extensive.

I might have broken a few rules in doing so, but I was worried about pages ending up looking like the tiled walls of the Topkapi Palace.

As for some Italian terms and expressions, most of them (if not all) are Latin-based, hence easily recognisable. We live in the age of Kindle and Google Translate after all.

Some idioms are colloquial or outright slang and it might be more complicated to understand their exact meaning, though the characters conveniently do some of the explaining for me.

For example, Italian students use the word 'Prof' as an abbreviation for Professor (male or female). It is, however, a kind of vernacular used mainly between pupils, not to address the teacher (at least in my times, nowadays students might be less deferential).

To avoid misunderstanding, a *Liceo Artistico* is not, despite the name, an 'Art' school in the strict definition of the word. It isn't an Academy of the Arts, but one of the four *Licei* (roughly the equivalent of American High Schools) where boys and girls with artistic tendencies and/or talent are generally (but not always) sent between the age of fourteen and eighteen. In theory - a very loose theory - pupils with a passion for sciences and maths should attend the *Scientifico*, the ones who are fond of literature the *Classico*, and those versed in foreign languages the *Linguistico* (though Ancient Greek and Latin are taught in the latter, more 'no-longer spoken' than 'foreign', but there you are).

In reality, quite frequently (too frequently) parents pick the more convenient Liceo because of distance from home, reputation and so forth, blithely ignoring the vocations of their children.

For anyone not wholly familiar with the Renaissance period, leading and less leading artists would gain, at some point in their careers, nicknames associated with some sort of quirk in their lives.

Agnolo di Cosimo was known by the sobriquet *Il Bronzino* due to his dark skin and reddish hair.

Tommaso di Currado di Doffo Bagordi became known as *Il Ghirlandaio* because his father was a garland-maker, crafting head-dresses for Florentine ladies.

Giovanni Francesco Barbieri was nicknamed *Il Guercino* because he was cross-eyed, though it didn't seem to prevent him from producing masterpieces.

The fictional character of Jacopo da Cremona earns the appellative of *Il Formaggiaro* as he is the son of a rich cheese merchant from that city. Trust me when I say that it doesn't sound very complimentary in Italian, never mind how delicious the cheese might have been.

Almost invariably they became known by the first name followed by 'da' (from), and the city of provenance.

If you are Italian you might not recognise yourself in some of the characterisations depicted in modern day Florence. And some are admittedly slightly exaggerated for dramatic effect.

But I was born and bred in Milan, where I attended a Liceo Scientifico, despite believing Maths and Physics to be Satan's revenge on humankind.

Uniquely among European countries, Italy has never been - and never will be - a homogenous entity. Even cities and regions next to each other have at times very little in common or, in some cases, thoroughly despise and revile their neighbours on a regular basis. In the past, of course, the disdain and the offensive language were skipped in favour of a good old reciprocal slaughter on the fields of this cantankerous land.

Furthermore, in some cases we can barely understand each other as our dialects are more or less different languages altogether. It doesn't help.

I. *All happy families...*

He hears the final bell. The school erupts, classroom doors slam open barely holding on to their hinges, the metallic noise of lockers being opened and shut again is deafening.

Summer break is here. A torrent of students regurgitates into the street causing an almighty traffic jam. SUVs with mothers or nannies at the wheel vie for space, right of way, and ultimately a not-too-subtle parade of the best four wheels in Georgetown.

This is no cheap suburbia, most of their husbands or employers are toiling at some desk or chairing important meetings at Foggy Bottom, on Capitol Hill or the White House. Most often all three.

Parker walks out of the front door with his hands in the tight pockets of his slacks and his rucksack on his shoulders. A few hugs with the girls and some high-fives with fellow boys ensue. His older brother is already waiting at the bike stand. When he gets there the high-five is followed by a manly hug.

'Dude, summer break and birthday tomorrow. Lucky little bro.'

'Bet you know what the old folks have got me.'

'Sure I do.'

They start cycling. When Parker reached the age of

fourteen, their parents went out and bought a cheap bike for his growing frame. The Hendersons' pristine drive sports the standard two SUVs parked neatly by each other, yet their mother wasn't fond of school runs. In their opinion he was still a bit too young to cycle all the way to school by himself but the city had finally built some decent bike lanes and Tommy was now seventeen so they made them promise to stick together on the journey.

Tommy, who finds cycling by himself rather dull - he's not much of a loner, any activity has to involve other people - had gone out of his way to promise to look out for his little brother at traffic junctions.

They had also promised never to set off without their helmets, though Tommy had swiftly pointed out to Parker that "setting off" with them was not the same as "wearing them". Parker, the more academic of the pair, had found the distinction clever though he had laughed while retorting that it was still cheating.

So when they are a couple of blocks away from home they stop, unlock their helmets from their rucksacks' straps and don them before reaching the driveway. A few times Parker had remarked that one day they might get caught by their mother driving by.

He walks to the garage door to open it but he's shouted down by Tommy who parades himself in front of it.

'Off-limits until tomorrow, bro.'

A smiling Parker leaves his bike with his brother and heads for the kitchen door. Tommy has just narrowed down his guesses for his present. One doesn't need a garage to hide a watch or a pair of trainers.

To his surprise he finds them both at home, sat at the kitchen table with two mugs of coffee in their hands. After kissing his mother on the cheek (Tommy is starting to cringe at that, but Parker still likes it. Tomorrow's birthday might change that), he meets his father's closed fist with his; they have gradually stopped hugging.

'Why are you home?' Parker's face frowns in suspicion. 'You've got the day off tomorrow, haven't you, Dad?'

"No worries. All free tomorrow. Left office early, not much to do at the moment. There might be a few changes in my career; new President, new direction.'

Tommy comes in. His parents are resigned at getting neither hugs nor kisses from him. Apparently at some unspecified date he had decided that he had become a man and those are for little boys. The Hendersons are uber-liberal and just shrugged at that.

'Dad, you home? What's up? You are free tomorrow, are you?'

'Why does everyone think I'm going to miss out on my son's birthday?'

Parker winks at Tommy.

'Obama is promoting Dad to Secretary of State.'

They all laugh though Elizabeth is slightly reproachful.

'Stop mocking your father's career. It's paying for all of this.' She showcases the the faux-Georgian house with her hand and points her finger at Parker. 'And your present.'

Larry is already in his shorts, trainers and vest. Tommy is heading upstairs.

'Change in a second and back for a game, Dad. Parker, you coming?'

Tommy and his Dad built a good size basketball court at the back of the house. Elizabeth did not like the view ruined by a metal post with a net attached to it but she came around when Larry pointed out that the two boys were doing well at school (Tommy at sports and girls and Parker at everything else) and their elder sister had just been admitted to Princeton.

'Basketball is healthy', he had remarked while kissing her, 'Would you rather prefer them to do drinks, drugs and sex?'

At which point Mrs. Henderson couldn't help observing that they must do some sex at least.

The men of the house like their game and at around five Olivia is sent to holler at them to get upstairs, shower and get ready for dinner.

The fare is never fully American. The Henderson are mid-atlantic urbanites and Elizabeth never tires of shopping for overpriced food items at Gennaro's, the Italian deli conveniently located a few blocks away. Tonight she has laboured intensively on a mushroom risotto; whatever the result, everyone knows better than to make cringing faces. Larry and Parker actually like the European taste, Tommy is resigned to it (he goes 'all-American' with his team pals at the hamburger bar near the school), and Olivia eats like most eighteen-year girls who are thin and beautiful and want to stay that way.

Parker is always inquisitive at the table and everyone likes that. Dinners are never boring.

'Why do we eat so early?'

Elizabeth is pouring the risotto.

'We always eat at six, Parker.'

'That's what I mean. I read that in Spain they eat at eleven at night.'

Larry smells the risotto.

'That smells delicious. Every country has different traditions, buddy.'

'Why do we have this one?'

That's the only drawback of Parker's curiosity: it's entertaining but it never ends.

'Bro, that's nuts eating at eleven. We have to be in bed at that time.'

'Obviously Spanish kids don't.'

Elizabeth, strokes Parker's spiky brown hair.

'They do. When it's summer holiday they stay up late as it can get very hot out there.'

Parker takes a forkful of the risotto. They don't say grace as Europeans don't, not even the most religious ones.

'Mom, it's awesome. It gets very hot here. We still eat at six.'

Olivia throws a sardonic smile.

'You'll never get away with anything with him.'

They have learnt how to curtail the machine-gun-like inquisition by now. They precipitously change subject though they are convinced that Parker keeps ruminating more questions in his mind. Larry volunteers for the task.

'Well, looking forward to the party tomorrow. Now, I understand it's your friends in the afternoon and you're not going to want your old folks around at that time but we can have a "tail" later on when they are off.'

'Why?'

'We just stick around discreetly, that's all.'

Parker frowns.

'You're not a hundred years old, I'm not embarrassed by you. When do I get my present?'

'Do you want it at the garden party in the afternoon?'

'Yes, Dad.'

'You got it. Now, your mother and I have been thinking. The spare room on the top floor is full of junk; boys, what do you say if we clear it up and you can have a room each?'

The sudden silence is not one which usually follows the bearing of good news and both parents detect that. Tommy throws an inquisitive look at his brother. They both lift a forkful of risotto while staring down at the plate. Elizabeth is the first to acknowledge the lack of enthusiasm.

'I thought that you two might want a bit of independence.'

The pair looks at each other again, then Tommy speaks directly to Parker.

'Do you, bro?'

Parker just shakes his head. Tommy turns to his father.

'Do we have to?'

'No, of course not. Usually it's the opposite but glad that you get on fine.'

'Well, it's not that I can take girls back here anyway, can I? Little bro is cool, even with all those damn drawings of his everywhere.'

Larry and Elizabeth smile at each other, fully aware of Tommy's phobia of being alone. They hadn't thought this through.

Olivia's lips widen in a sneering smile.

'I bet they still do those disgusting things boys do.'

Tommy sneers back.

'At least he keeps his mouth shut while we jerk off. As if Jack doesn't do it. Yeah. Right.'

Larry points his finger at his son.

'Tommy, we are very liberal but swearing is still not allowed. Apologise to your mother and your sister.'

'Sorry Mom, but Olivia started it. It's none of your business. And your boyfriend totally does it with his pals.'

'Tommy, enough. Olivia, there is no need to poke fun.'

Parker has listened to all of this in silence, then he looks at his Dad.

'Are you sure that it is swearing?'

They all burst in a loud laugh, Tommy almost crying in his plate.

'Man, you're funny, bro.'

They are in bed now. Tommy playing Nintendo, Parker drawing on a notepad with a pencil.

Their room is spacious and it has been transformed into a tale of two cities. On Tommy's side basketball posters, sport cars and a typical cataclysmic chaos, his bed never made up. On Parker side the atmosphere is more refined. There are indeed drawings everywhere, much less untidiness and hardly any computer games paraphernalia except for the laptop on his desk. He doesn't quite make his bed up but he tentatively pulls the duvet over in the morning, a bit conscious about his mom discovering the mess. Tommy seems not to care a jolt.

There haven't been many fights in the years they have shared the room and mostly only about Parker taking too long in the bathroom with Tommy shouting: 'Hurry up, you damn girl!'.

'Show me.'

Parker hands the notepad over.

'You're drawing Olivia?'

'She's a good model.'

'Yeah, but girls never shut up. You're lucky, bro.'

Parker is unsure what his brother means. In any case Tommy's underwear has gone and he can already hear the thrusting sound. He lowers his pants and silently joins in. Tommy is right, they do it in silence, he thinking about girls' body parts and Parker not yet sure what to think about while he does it. He likes it and his brother is at it every night without fail so, why not?

They never bother to clean the mess up, they just pull their duvets over. Tommy once remarked how disgusted their sister would be if they told her (something they were very tempted to do). He turns the lights off.

'You sure you don't want your own room?'

'Yeah.'

'Night, little bro.'

'Night, big bro.'

* * *

Tommy is a boy of few words, no hugs, no kisses (definitely no kisses) and has never in his short life told anyone in the family that he loves them. Not that he needs to: everyone knows that he does. They also know that schmalz is anathema to him so they all steer very clear of it. When his mother started crying while watching The Hours on television, he got up, hauled a box of Kleenex from the downstairs bathroom and held it for her to help herself while shaking his head, wondering what it was all about, blissfully unaware that his silent action had spoken a thousand words.

When Jack was invited for lunch for the first time as Olivia's official new boyfriend, he was, like every boy meeting his girlfriend's parents, a nervous wreck.

That changed quickly upon meeting Tommy who, despite the two of them being dressed up for lunch, lured him on the basketball court for a long afternoon game and loud banter leaving Elizabeth holding her daughter's shoulders and kissing her hair while looking at the pair now wrestling on the floor.

'I'm sure Jack loves you. But boys are like that.'

Parker genuinely wants to keep sharing the room with his brother and, being the sensitive boy he is, he also noticed the veil of panic on Tommy's face when their father had proposed to split them. Tommy does not do loneliness.

And he probably never will. Blond, athletic and impossibly handsome in the boy-next-door fashion, he is way too popular with almost every girl at Georgetown High. Parker is often used as a go-between, something he thoroughly enjoys. He also wallows in reflected glory as he often remarks to boys in his year how awesome with the ladies his brother is.

His dates don't last much though and when Parker enquiries about why the latest one has been dumped, the reply is always the same.

'Man, she wouldn't shut the fuck up.'

To which Parker usually responds with raising eyes to the sky.

'Well, all girls want to talk, big bro. What you gonna do about it?'

When Parker joined the same school, he knew bullying wasn't far away. He was resigned to the rite of passage. He wasn't exactly weedy but a bit skinny and a little too gentle. More of a European. His look was elegant preppy cool, his round spectacles way too intellectual, and his passion for drawing anything that moved was honey to any bullying bee. It only took a few days before he got smashed against his locker by Logan, a boy three times his size in Tommy's year and basketball team. Parker knew it was only a matter of time before he would be beaten up and he was kind of preparing to defend himself the best he could, which was just about zero.

He had decided against telling Tommy. That would have been dead slimy and he wasn't a snitch.

But Tommy was also the star of the team and some of his loyal teammates reported to him about Logan's pestering his little bro while proposing to teach him a lesson. Tommy just said no.

At the end of a spectacular win, the coach had walked down to the changing rooms and given a satisfied talk to his boys.

'Guys. Awesome win. Henderson, man of the day.' He went on to high-five Tommy who coolly replied while throwing his towel on the bench.

'Just as well. Because I quit.'

That dropped like the proverbial lead balloon. The silence was broken almost immediately by a shouting hail of 'What?', 'What's the matter, man?', 'Are you crazy, dude?'.

The coach struggled to restore some order but he finally managed to sit them all down on the benches, Tommy standing by him.

'Ok. Ok. Can you just all shut the fuck up. Tommy, what's this crazy stuff?'

'You see coach, I don't want to play with cowardly assholes who take it out on boys half their size.'

His eyes turned on Logan.

'I say, come and take it out on me, if you have the balls.'

The trainer was coaching Parker's junior team too and instantly knew what it was all about.

'Well. I guess someone here must apologise.'

Some of the boys started to nudge Logan and hit him with their towels.

Logan stood up.

'Ok. Ok. I'm sorry. I'll leave him alone. Sorry.'

'Cool. By the way, my little bro is no snitch. He told me nothing. Just start hitting on the girls, man, and quit being a jerk, it ain't cool.'

Tommy couldn't fend off the hugs and the high-fives. Parker was met by Logan in an empty corridor and closed his eyes, waiting for blows which never landed.

'Hey. You're no snitch, little one. That's cool.'

* * *

All happy families are alike and the Hendersons would make Tolstoy proud. Larry and Elizabeth met at Princeton, he on his way to a law degree, she shining in Freudian essays towards her masters in psychiatry.

Larry had been a confident and sporty young man,

sensitive and polite. Their upper-middle-class origins hadn't taken long to converge in an all-American happy ending and the beginning of a new chapter.

Cosseted by east coast parental financial power, a lavish but tasteful wedding came first, followed by a well-paid starter job at a Boston law firm, the purchase of a brownstone downtown and a fragrant and slender Elizabeth expecting Olivia. She never bothered to use her degree for any work. Larry's salary and perks were more than enough to conduct a comfortable yet restrained eastern seaboard existence: some occasional dining out, entertaining friends and sporadic evenings at the Boston Symphony Hall of which Elizabeth became a patron.

At a dinner party a rather brazen acquaintance had once remarked how the Hendersons could stand in if the Kennedys were ever to be fully exterminated. The word 'extermination' in conjunction with Massachusetts royalty had caused a mild unease at the table until the hapless guest with an importune sense of humour had remarked that it was a 'goddam' joke.

Yet a silly quip had got Larry thinking. Standing by the bed in his dressing gown he had tested the waters with his wife.

'Well, why not?'

Elizabeth, brushing her long, silky hair at the vanity desk, had turned with a frown.

'Why not what?'

'Politics? You know, that stupid joke about us looking like the Kennedys?'

Elizabeth turned back to face the mirror.

'Bobby can be such an idiot when on far too much Chianti. I'm not sure whether I cared for that. At least they are a good-looking family to be compared to.'

Larry's silence became suspicious. She had turned again.

'You mean it, don't you?'

'The guys at the party would be over the moon.'

She had faked a pensive pose.

'I've heard the White House is rather uncomfortable to live in.'

Larry had laughed.

'I was thinking about a position at the State Department rather. Let's not get carried away.'

'This is America. You are supposed to be carried away with this kind of dream.'

And it happened. Larry's record at Princeton and his CV had impressed Foggy Bottom no end and his affable yet professional demeanour had done the rest.

Thus Tommy and Parker were born with fewer voting rights then their fellow Americans and grew up in the capital, with only Olivia at times missing the gentler and more European scent of the north east.

They still took their vacations in Nantucket as Larry's parents were happy for the whole family to come and visit, complaining when the time lapses between trips were too long.

The boys had never disliked Georgetown. Tommy had plenty of friends, Parker fewer still but neither had ever been unpopular over their school career.

* * *

Parker wakes up first, the excitement of his fifteenth birthday having the better of him. He parts the curtains of his window and stalls, smacking his forehead with his hand.

'Dad is at it.'

Tommy hears him and gets out of bed in his pants while awakening his blond hair with long strokes of his hands. Squinting his eyes he approaches the window. There is a giant red and blue "15" balloon floating and intermittently banging against the glass. From close inspection an extensive display of more balloons is being arranged by Larry who is on a ladder trying to reach the gutter with a string of little stars and stripes flags.

'Happy birthday, little bro.'

Parker nods. They slide into their dressing gowns and rumble down the stairs barefoot.

Elizabeth and Rose, the day-maid-cum-cleaning lady are assembling dishes arranged around a cluster of cards.

'Happy birthday, Parker.'

He kisses his mother and both the boys sit at the table, Tommy gorging down his glass of milk.

'Dad is going nuts with balloons.'

'Well, he's doing it for you Parker and you Tommy should help.'

'He loves doing it by himself.'

Parker inspects the cards.

'Shall I open them now?'

Elizabeth is shuttling between the table and the kitchen counter.

'As you like.'

The bell rings, Rose proceeds to the hallway to open the

door and reappears with an elegantly dressed lady holding a card in her hand.

'Parker, Miss Moore is here.'

Parker gets up and walks towards the lady.

'Good morning, Miss Moore.'

'Good morning, Parker, and happy birthday.'

'Thank you, Miss Moore.'

Elizabeth joins them and grabs Parkers' shoulders.

'Good morning, Miss Moore, would you like to have a coffee with us?'

'No thanks, very kind of you. I briefly came by to bring Parker's present.'

Parker widens his big brown eyes.

'A present for me? That's very kind, Miss Moore.'

'Well, here it is. It's all in this card. Hope you'll enjoy it, Parker.'

'I'm sure I will, Miss Moore.'

After her departure, Parker returns to the table and sits by his brother who gives him such a big shove that he falls on the floor laughing out loud.

'Teacher's pet...'

'Tommy, don't shove Parker on the floor. Miss Moore is very proud of his grades in her art class, if only you could say the same.'

Their three children are popular and the crowd is on the unmanageable side. The catering is a mix of homemade cakes and Gennaro's Italian pastries, the fridge stuffed with cannoli siciliani. A balmy southern spring allows everyone to be in polos, shorts and t-shirts. Larry, Elizabeth and the maid circulate discreetly as they try their best not to embarrass their children.

What they fail to comprehend is that their charming beauty has actually the opposite effect, sometimes with embarrassing developments.

Elliott, a boy in Tommy's class, became his best mate a few months earlier and the pair often came back for a basketball game or, less often, to study together.

Elizabeth, who always spends the afternoons at home to look after her three children and make sure there is no slacking on the homework front, is equally attentive and motherly with their mates too. Drinks and snacks are always at the ready together with words of encouragements.

Elliott was polite, sensitive and very grateful for the attention. Among the various thanking phrases, he thought nothing of dropping the casual compliment for her 'beautiful dresses' and 'elegant hair styles'.

Needless to say, Tommy cringed at all that garbage, until he realised that his mate meant it. When she discussed it with Larry, her husband smiled.

'Not surprised to have a rival, you are still so gorgeous.'

'Don't make fun, you know it really hurts at that age.'

'Yeah. Well, if I had a dollar for every seventeen-year-old having a crush on their friends' mothers... I wouldn't worry, it usually goes away.'

One day, while confronting an essay on the kitchen table, Tommy had lifted his head from the laptop for a casual observation.

'Not inviting Elliott around anymore.'

His mother had turned from the window with a sigh.

'Tommy. Don't cut him off. It happens. Some boys lose it a bit with older women. It will go away.'

'You're my Mom. It's gross.'

'Well, he's not going to get any encouragement.'

In the end, Tommy had confronted him and had made it clear that he wasn't cool on the idea of his best friend flirting with his mother. Like all teenage crushes it duly melt away and it wasn't long before a girlfriend appeared from the blue.

Larry's athleticism, handsomeness and elegance cause equal stirs among the girls in both Parker and Tommy's class.

Parker, who doesn't have the squeamishness of his brother, had once made everyone at the table choke on their pasta alla Carbonara.

'Emma Myles really fancies the pants off you, Dad.'

Parker adores being the centre of attention and the party is a success. When he bumps into Olivia and Jack, he stalls them with his open hands.

'Wait, I have something for you.'

He runs upstairs to his bedroom and swiftly returns holding a brown A4 envelope. He pushes it into Jack's hand.

'For you, Jack.'

'For me? It's your birthday.'

'Yeah, I know, but I finished it yesterday.'

'Finished what?'

'Well, open it.'

Jack looks inquisitively at Olivia who shrugs. She's used to her brother's weirdness. He opens the envelope and looks at the paper. Olivia cocks her head to have a peep and shrieks.

'Parker! When did you do this? This is so embarrassing.'

But Jack stops her in her fretting tracks.

'What? Why is it embarrassing? It's beautiful. Man, did you do this all yourself?'

'Yeah. Had to memorise all angles as sis wouldn't pose for me.'

Olivia is having an unnecessary tantrum.

'I can't believe you did this. Sorry about my brother.'

'Why are you sorry? For what? It's an amazing portrait. Parker, I'll hang it on my bedroom wall.'

Olivia melts in that ocean of insecurity where girls of that age usually drown.

'Really?'

Jack, who is the most matter-of-fact boy one could think of, frowns in mocking puzzlement.

'Well, yeah. Why? Do you want me to throw it away? Not gonna do that.'

She looks again at the drawing. Parker has drawn her eyes staring aimlessly at an infinite space, melancholic yet inquisitive and mesmerising.

'I mean, really? You like it? You don't find it weird?'

'No.'

Parker, who is standing there with his hands in his pockets, smiles.

'You two must have some amazing sex.'

Jack bursts in a spitting laugh while Olivia almost screams.

'Parker!'

Between hysterical giggles, Jack manages to utter a few words while led away by his girlfriend.

'Your bro is dead weird but so funny.'

When the garage door is lifted, a bulky rectangular box is

wheeled out. It is wrapped and has a big bow on top. Parker is egged on by everyone to open the main present of the day.

Helped by his Dad and Tommy, he unwraps the box to reveal the latest model of a blue and white Bianchi-Campagnolo racing bike.

Parker is on cloud nine as everyone gathers around to check the state-of-art import. He hugs his parents, then they leave him and the rest of the young crowd to the excitement of the discovery and tiptoe to the kitchen to retrieve the cake.

He also receives a spanking new helmet from Olivia and Tommy and a flaming red Lacoste polo from his mother.

The cake is gone and so are all the guests. He is elated by the amazing day and offers to help his Dad and brother to assemble the pedals and the handle of his new toy. Larry won't have any of it.

'Nah, it's your day. Tommy and I will do it. It'll be ready for you to be off tomorrow. All you'll have to do is to adjust the saddle's height.'

They change into their t-shirts and shorts and set out in earnest to complete the task. They also start to clear the party debris, surveyed with satisfaction by Elizabeth through the kitchen window. Jack has just texted Olivia with a picture of her portrait hung on the wall of his bedroom, sending her in a state of loving meltdown.

The Bianchi-Campagnolo is assembled and stands gleaming on the driveway in front of the garage, Larry patting his son's back.

'Good job. I'm really thirsty, I'll get some drinks.'

Tommy sits on the low wall adjacent to the driveway, drying the sweat with his t-shirt. Larry returns with two bottles and hands one to Tommy who frowns in puzzlement.

'Beer?'

'Oh, come on. You are seventeen, we are in our home and I'm here. The FBI is not going to swoop in. One more year and you will be able to legally buy a Kalashnikov but still no beer. Talk about insanity.'

Tommy laughs and they clink their bottles.

After a few sips in manly silence, Tommy stares ahead, then at the pavement.

'Dad...'

'Yeah?'

'About Parker.'

'Yeah, what about him?'

He looks away. He is a boy of few words and the ones he is about to utter are momentous.

'Little bro is never going to like girls, is he?'

Larry doesn't move. He doesn't need to ponder his answer but it needs to be slow and calm.

'No. It's not going to happen. How did you know? Has he told you? Or did you find something in his desk?'

'I had my suspicions. You know, little things. And he hasn't set up a password for his laptop, together with forgetting to erase its history.'

Larry smiles.

'He's the daydreaming type. Nothing too hard I hope?'

'Nah. Mostly naked boys; a bit older than him, that's all.'

Larry takes another sip.

'How do you feel about it?'

'I'm ok with it. Except...'

He finishes his beer. Larry grabs both bottles, gets up and winks.

'I think we need another one.'

Tommy puts his thumb up. When his father reappears with the bottles, he finds him pensively gazing at the pavement.

'Except?'

'Well, it's weird. It freaks me out if he's not... I don't really know how to put it.'

Larry knows he'll never be able to blurt that out.

'If he's not the "man". Is that it?'

Tommy nods.

'The thought of someone, you know... I mean, my little bro... I'd just beat the shit out of them. Sorry.'

'Tommy, that is Parker's choice. You can't be selective. And it is something which he will probably never reveal to you, me or anyone else in the family. Rightly so.'

'You seem to be dead cool with it.'

Larry crosses his legs and sits up on the wall.

'Your mother and I have known this for quite some time. She was first to come up with doubts and thoughts. You know mothers, they know everything. They feel it.'

Tommy turns with a worried expression.

'Yes, that includes you, young man. By the way, we should all wait for him to tell us. Don't put any pressure on him. I know you're very protective of Parker.'

'No probs.'

Larry gets up and stretches.

'We'll better have a wash for dinner before your mother starts yelling at us.'

He sets off for the kitchen. Tommy calls him out.

'Hey!' He lifts the bottle in a toast. 'Great chat.'

On his way through the kitchen he notices Mrs Moore's card on the table, still unopened. He places it upright against a bottle of milk for Parker to open the last of his birthday presents.

II. The boys of Ferrara

'Go and wake up the *signorini*, Beatrice, sun is up already.'

She walks up the wooden, creaky stairs and slams open the door of her brothers' room. When she pushes the rickety shutters open, the powerful rays of the blazing morning sun flood the walls causing moans and young heads to hide under sweaty pillows.

'Santa Caterina has already struck six, better hurry if you don't want father to come up.'

The threat works every morning, though she finds it strange that it has to be repeated. Serafino, Francesco and Cesarino know all too well that the alternative to their sister's wake up call is a mild beating by their father. It is actually so mild that sometimes the three boys would rather have fifteen more minutes in bed in exchange for a good slap.

Francesco and Cesarino run to the bucket of cold water in the next room, diligently prepared by Beatrice; Serafino, the middle one, is allowed to stay behind to wash a bit more thoroughly. He also has cleaner hose, polished shoes and a threadbare doublet to wear; he is allowed a bit more time to comb his wavy black hair and gather his books, papers and writing material.

Not an issue with the older and the younger. After the

usual reprimand by Beatrice for merely spraying their faces with just water and ignoring the bar of coarse soap on the small table beside it, they run down the stairs bare chested and barefoot, clumsily tying up their hole-ridden trousers.

They are never reprimanded for that. June is almost at an end and the heat of the plain has risen fast. The chores at the Osteria della Lepre are physically demanding and they will wear their white shirts only a few minutes before midday, just before the first customers make the beads of the curtain at the open entrance tinkle.

Beatrice has to tidy them up and wash the sweat away from their chests to make them somehow presentable to the clientele. She is used to their grumbles. They are good-natured boys, hardworking and kind. But not very clean.

The regulars like them and tip them handsomely, their mother apologising to her most distinguished customers that she cannot make them wear shoes to save their lives.

Don Filippo, the most revered notary in the city - notary, in fact, to no one less than Duke Alfonso himself - shrugs and laughs without fail at the complaint, tenderly ruffling the unkempt hair of Cesarino and furtively shifting a quarter of a ducat into his hand with a wink.

'Leave them alone, Signora Ippolita, they work hard and it is so hot today.'

The Osteria della Lepre sits on the side of the dusty Strada di Comacchio, a few kilometres from the Porta della Giovecca, the south-eastern gate of the city.

A thriving concern. The city dwellers and the country squires are never put off by the ramshackle exterior of the

Osteria. They gladly endure the hard wooden benches and untiled floor to savour Signora Ippolita's simple but unrivalled dishes of game and freshly cooked vegetables.

The name is no random one either. Arrosto di Lepre and Lepre alla Birra are her two strong main dishes on the one thin menu. When mother and daughter have been attending the cauldron all morning, the heavenly aroma from the kitchen window is known to halt riders and carriages on the dusty road and possibly even their horses. Hardly anyone is able to continue on their journey without dismounting and savouring the earthy lunch.

Rumour has it that from time to time even His Excellency disguises himself as a hunter in order to visit the Osteria and enjoy lunch undisturbed. Apocryphal nonsense, of course, yet one which attracts even more punters, the locals never tiring of a good gossip about their ruler and his wife. Above all, his wife.

It was witnessed that the Ducal cortege had one day halted by the Osteria. One of the footmen had trudged through the beaded curtain and enquired if the entire place could be commandeered for a private lunch. A bowing family, quickly recognising the footman's livery, had of course agreed, unaware of the apoplectic tantrum taking place in the Duke's carriage.

'Me? Setting foot in such a place?'

Her head had swung affronted towards the other side of the road, disdainfully lowering the curtain and lifting her embroidered handkerchief to her offended nose.

'Lucrezia, everyone at court has eaten here incognito. They are most complimentary. The Lepre alla Birra...'

'Then you eat here. I am a Borgia.'

Duke Alfonso had raised his eyes to the cloudless sky and signalled the footman to instruct the cortege to set on.

'And never tire of reminding me.'

Serafino is ready now. Unlike his rumbling brothers, he walks down the stairs with soft gentle steps, his bag across his shoulders, politely greeting his parents.

Francesco and Cesarino, one already on his knees scrubbing the floor, the other carrying heavy parcels of game on his shoulder across the kitchen, affectionately sneer at him.

'*Il grande testone* has arrived.'

They do that almost every morning, but Serafino knows it to be harmless brotherly banter. They are secretly proud of him, the only one in the family studying with Mastro Filargiro, one of the best regarded - and strictest - tutors in the city.

* * *

It had happened by chance. Like almost everyone - with the exception of the Duchess - Mastro Filargiro had been unable to resist the lure of a lunch or two at the Osteria and had found Serafino drawing the profiles of the most handsome customers on some papers which had miraculously found the way to him.

He had stood behind him, signalling him not to stop, attentively observing the movements of his hand, the pose of his face, the number of times he had lifted his head to memorise the contours of his impromptu models.

He had returned the following day with some good quality papers and chalks. To the puzzlement of his parents, he had politely asked their permission to set up a small stall for Serafino to sit at the optimal distance from the tables.

Gently, he had then pointed to a pretty young lady wearing a colourful veil and laid the paper on the table. He had shown a few corrections to the boy, who had registered and executed them with astonishing speed and accuracy.

Signora Ippolita had then offered a goblet of the best wine of the house to Mastro Filargiro who had spent ten or fifteen minutes carefully perusing the drawing.

Serafino, thirteen at that time, had sat composed and silent at his side, Mastro Filargiro turning his face to him with an approving smile from time to time.

'Who taught you this?'

'No one, sir. We can't afford a tutor. What did I do wrong?'

'Hard to say.'

He had pulled the drawing nearer to his eyes and placed it back on the table while tightening his lips in thoughtful fashion.

'And hard to find.'

Serafino had placed his small dirty finger on the drawing.

'Her jaw.'

'What about it?'

'She kept laughing and it kept moving up and down. I had to keep memorising it. I think it's slightly wonky.'

'Wonky?'

Serafino nodded, visibly annoyed by his own perceived failure.

'Why don't you call your mother and let me have a word with her in private?'

'Yes, sir.'

* * *

And that marked the end of Serafino's career as a floor-scrubber and the start of free teaching at Mastro Filargiro's workshop. Donna Ippolita had remarked that, despite the good business of the Osteria, they would have struggled to afford the fees - Duke Alfonso's own nephew was among the pupils - but Mastro Filargiro had informed her that having Serafino with him was of more value than a bunch of ducats. He would provide lunch and an afternoon *merenda* to the talented lad.

His wardrobe has also changed. The sons and wards of wealthy Ferrarese families have no use for their out-grown garments and Mastro Filargiro encourages them to leave silk hose, velvet blouses and bespoke leather loafers behind for the less privileged students. This is approved by their usually aristocratic parents. Despite the unpleasant hauteur of his consort, Duke Alfonso's reign is proving a benevolent one and acts of charity have become to be seen as a good way to ingratiating one's clan to the ruler.

Serafino slowly transforms into some kind of threadbare young Medici squire, inevitably provoking the mockery of his brothers.

And he is also well liked by Mastro Filargiro's wealthy young charges.

He never hides his lower status and conducts himself with dignified humility, sometimes - to his tutor's horror - offering to serve them drinks or refreshments.

Filiberto degli Aldighieri, an older boy with flaxen hair and a larger than life character - and a smaller than life talent - one day finally snaps at Serafino with a roaring laugh.

'Messer Serafino. We are all apprentices here. You are not my servant.'

He gives back the cup with a big smile and furtively peeks at Serafino's drawing on the easel.

'And I suspect you never will be. Mastro Filargiro, sir!'

'Yes, Messer Aldighieri, are you about to entertain us with one of your preposterous excuses for doing no work at all?'

Filiberto places his arm around the neck of an embarrassed Serafino and slaps a loud kiss on his cheek. Fino blushes and smiles.

'Much better than that, Mastro Filargiro. I hereby declare Messer Fino da Ferrara my best friend!'

A roaring applause and a loud stomping of feet on the floor wooden planks follow, pleasing a satisfied Mastro Filargiro who pensively raises his thumb and index finger to his chin.

'*Fino da Ferrara*. That is a good name. A good one indeed.'

The name 'Serafino' thus disappears from the school's vocabulary. Fino becomes worried for Filiberto though and before the end of the day enquires with him about the wisdom of the new liaison.

'Are you sure you are allowed to have me as a friend?'

'Best friend! No, but I will ask my old man. I am the heir, not much is denied to me.' He winks in conspiracy. 'If he forbids our friendship, we'll be wicked and will hide it.'

Aldighieri il Vecchio assents. He has visited the studio and Mastro Filargiro has shown him Fino's first finished drawing.

'The origins might be humble, yet the hand has divine inspiration.'

Aldighieri il Vecchio had admired the drawing in awe and looked inquisitively at Filargiro.

'Have you plans for the lad?'

'Yes.'

At the start, Fino has to endure a one hour walk to reach the gates of La Giovecca, but his ordeal doesn't last long.

After treading the semi-deserted trail for a few days, a few farmers and merchants with carts and donkeys start offering him a passage and he becomes so well known that he can actually choose his transport. They all seem eager to have the honour of carrying the young painter to the city and back. Some even share a bit of bread and prosciutto with him, chatting away, curious about his day in the company of the real *signorini*.

A few times he gets carried on the back of a big cart surrounded by a group of very friendly men on horseback. Fino likes them, they are funny and make him laugh. From time to time they lift the rough blanket covering the cart and give him a jar of olive oil and a hare or a rabbit for his parents.

He never quite understands why they have to drop him outside the gates though. When asked, they say in the most evasive way that they usually reach the city 'by other means'. He asks his now best friend and Filiberto throws a healthy laugh, slapping his hand on his forehead.

'Oh, Fino, my friend. Poachers and smugglers. Not to worry, they are no assassins, but don't get caught with them by the Duke's guards. They won't know you aren't one.'

Filiberto is a natural leader and has formed a mixed-rank gang. Although very conscious of his status, he finds the poor lads more fun and more adventurous in mischief. Between the occasional brawl and argument the little squad of half a dozen gets on like a house on fire.

Duke Alfonso's nephew has excluded himself, and, to Filiberto's annoyance, Fino has kept the habit of bowing at his arrival, something the young man seems to resent.

Around their afternoon *merenda,* Filiberto, now the de-facto leader, explains.

'Do not hate him. He's dying to join us. He cannot. He is a d'Este and also a prince. And his auntie now is a Borgia, god help him. In theory, even I should bow to him but he doesn't enjoy the deference. He sits alone while we go out to play and run in the mud. They wanted Filargiro to tutor him at the castle but he refused. He told the Duke that he thought his nephew was lonely enough as he was. Old Filargiro is not scared of the Duke.'

'He must be scared of Donna Lucrezia!', one of the boys laughs out.

'La "Duchessa" Lucrezia. You'll have your head chopped off if she hears you!'

That provokes a good deal of laughter, with another boy trying to strangle the offending lad. Filiberto opens his hands in resignation.

'The d'Este are too big. They are related to princes and kings in the Empire, and England too. He can't play with us. He can't tell you this. But I know.'

They have been sitting having their cakes on the floor - an endearing act of rebellion - while Ludovico remains at the table, seated upright, eating his cake in silence. From time to time Fino sees him looking over and quickly turning his gaze away.

One day, while Fino is intent on working on his first real painting in a separate room, the d'Este boy tentatively walks over and stops behind him, observing the first outlines of his work. He speaks in a very soft tone, almost afraid.

'I have seen your drawings. They are rather masterful.'

'Very kind, Your Highness.'

He huffs and turns his head in mild anger.

'Please, don't call me that. And stop bowing to me. It's ridiculous. I hate it.'

'But... I can't...'

'There is no one here. We are the same age.'

'I'm scared of getting into trouble, you're the Duke's nephew.'

'You are like the others. You don't want to be my friend.'

Fino walks closer and notices the boy's eyes starting to well up.

'I do. We all do. But... I'm a peasant. You are a prince.'

He takes Fino's hand in his and squeezes it.

'I'll come over for a few minutes every afternoon. Don't tell anyone.'

'I won't.'

Every day the Duke's nephew tiptoes to the loggia where Mastro Filargiro confines Fino to isolate him from the distracting banter of his fellow pupils. Hardly any of them is destined for a career in the visual arts and the period spent under his wings is merely viewed by their wealthy families as a rite of passage to refine their sometime unruly sons.

Every afternoon Ludovico d'Este peruses his secret new friend's progress with awe, comparing it with his own frankly disastrous rendering of the Nativity.

Fino is for the first time working in oil on canvas. His progress is constantly interrupted by a sneaky stream of nosy boys, in awe at details which they could not master if they stayed with Mastro Filargiro for a lifetime.

The tutor has to start discreetly sending them away, though his fears of them distracting Fino are unfounded. While having a quick chat - at times even a silly adolescent laugh - the young man carries on with short strokes of his brushes, swapping them over with more suitable ones, while listening and even joyfully participating in the banter. If anything, upon inspection, the presence of his fellow apprentices seems to inspire a new, more accurate brushstroke, a tiny correction to the light of the hay in the manger.

Every afternoon Ludovico discreetly holds Fino's hand in his, nervously checking over his shoulders. When he does that their eyes always meet and stall for a few minutes, their hearts pumping fast, neither of them reaching any meaningful explanation as to why it keeps happening.

Ludovico is very light-skinned, his eyes bluish-grey, his locks flaxen, the product of stubborn, recurring genes. His grandmother had been a princess hailing from the northern possessions of the Holy Roman Empire, duly dispatched to Ferrara to marry into the small but ludicrously wealthy House of d'Este.

They stay silent most of the time. The sensation brought about by their hands clasped together is too heavenly to be ruined by words.

One sunny afternoon that changes. Ludovico gently points at the left of the canvas.

'Your three wise men are very young.'

Fino stares in his friend's eyes.

'Are they supposed to be old?'

'I'm not sure. I think so. And with more garments on.'

Fino lowers his head with a hint of sadness.

'You don't like my kings.'

He feels a squeeze of his hand.

'Of course I do. And Mastro Filargiro?'

Fino smiles, reassured. For some reason he had felt sad at the idea of having disappointed his secret friend.

'He said the same. But he didn't ask me to change them.'

'Caspar looks familiar.'

'I hope I haven't offended you.'

'Nothing you do could in any guise offend me, Messer Fino. How did you manage to draw me without seeing me all day?'

'When you come over. I look at you. All the time.'

Ludovico smiles, happy.

'I look at you too. Some nights you are in my dreams.'

Ludovico looks over his shoulders and through each of the doors leading out of the loggia. Almost sure of their complete solitude he moves forward and kisses Fino on the cheek, their hands melting in one another.

They briefly smile at each other and the Duke's nephew leaves.

When Fino reaches his fifteenth birthday Mastro Filargiro orders his housekeeper, Donna Elvira, to serve torte alla crema and half a goblet of the best vino rosso diluted with water, the one in the barrel sent by Filiberto's father as a gift of appreciation for keeping his unruly cub out of trouble.

The boys adore Donna Elvira. In her early fifties, unmarried and with no children of her own, she has an oversupply of motherly affection and not afraid to bestow it on the young men with cakes, sweet drinks, hugs and ruffling of wispy hair.

She also arranges all the donations of clothing and shoes, knowing the boys who need them more urgently than others, remembering their sizes and even their tastes. She seems to be more affectionate with the sons of wealthy or aristocratic families. This is planned. She is acutely aware of the demands on them. Their mothers are probably similar to the Duchess and she regularly finds some of them in secluded corners of the house, hiding their sobbing. The poorer lads seem happier and less tortured in their destitution.

After the celebrations, everyone is swiftly ordered back to work. As he does every afternoon Ludovico appears behind Fino though this time he doesn't take his hand. He has a small blue leather box in his hand and holds his arm out in an offering pose.

'For you.'

Fino's brown eyes open wide, jolting Ludovico's heart to near explosion.

'For me?'

'Happy birthday.'

Almost shaking, Fino takes the box and slowly opens it. He holds the thin gold chain with a little square pendant in his hand, his jaw stuck open.

'I... I can't accept this, Ludovico.'

'I haven't stolen it. It is mine. I have a few. It has the image of San Contardo, the patron of our House. Our coat of arms is on the back.'

'It's beautiful. People will think I have stolen it. It's too much.'

'Hide it under your shirt. We shall be the only ones to know about this. I don't want you to ever take that off. It will remind you of me when far away.'

Life throws unforgettable moments at us. When we can no longer control the boiling cauldron of emotions that has been brewing over a fire of repressed feelings.

Ludovico performs his usual check and after some fretting hesitation meets Fino's lips with a spasmodic, almost unhinged thrust.

Fino slowly opens his mouth, their tongues merging, something in their chests close to a conflagration.

Ludovico takes his hand, leading him away.

'Come.'

He follows him down the staircase on the side, towards the back of the house, facing the ramparts of the walls. A small stream runs behind the house and this is where the apprentices go to discard used jars of paints into the river. It is very secluded though not entirely safe as any of the boys can arrive to perform such tasks at any moment.

When there, Ludovico gently pins Fino to the wall and the kissing become frenetic, unstoppable. Then their hands find their way into each other's hose and, as always happens on the first-ever fondling, they find themselves in the midst of a cataclysmic flood after only a few seconds. Heavily breathing, Fino lets his head fall on the shoulder of his secret friend, kissing his neck, oblivious to the almighty mess on their hands, some of it washing away in the stream.

Ludovico's hand is caressing his hair, panting.

'I think of you all the time, Fino. I can't even eat anymore. I don't understand what is happening to me.'

'I don't know either. All I know is that it is happening to me too.'

Ludovico slowly detaches himself and they haphazardly wash themselves up in the stream.

'We'd better get back. Someone might come.'

They hold their hands together until the top of the staircase, then Ludovico turns to Fino.

'I know we won't be together forever. You will be sent away, to some important artist's workshop. And I am at court. It's like a prison but that will be it. A choice will not be given to us. That is why I have given you the pendant. San Contardo will protect you and it will remind you of me. Don't forget me, Messer Fino.'

The following day young d'Aldighieri walks to the loggia with his usual endearing swagger and sits on the low marble bannister, peeling a pear. Fino turns and smiles at his best friend while noticing a sombre, reproachful stare.

'How's Filiberto's best friend today?'

Fino stalls his brush on the canvas, registering the sarcastic tone. Without turning he replies in a soft voice.

'I'm well, Filiberto, and yourself?'

'Splendid!'

The tone refuses to shed the sarcastic tinge. Fino drops the brush on the easel and walks over, placing his hands on the banister and looking out onto the street.

'Whatever I've done, I'm guilty. Are you going to have me hanged or sliced in two with your sword?

Filiberto shakes his small knife at him.

'You deserve both, my friend.'

'I deserve to be told what I have done.'

Filiberto jumps off the banister and places his hands on his hips.

'You are supposed to ask for my permission before kissing anyone, Messer Fino.'

Fino's heart jumps a little and his head lowers in shame. 'Oh.'

'I would have asked your permission before kissing a girl.'

'Will you forgive me?'

Filiberto gives a good shove to Fino's shoulder.

'Of course I do, you idiot. But I'm jealous.'

Fino frowns with a puzzled expression.

'But Ludovico is a boy.'

'Still jealous.'

'You're still my best friend. That is different.'

Filiberto cocks his head towards the back staircase.

'Sure as the Holy Trinity it is.'

'You followed us down there?'

'Quite a spectacle.' He bursts into a reassuring laugh. 'You are as crimson as a pomegranate, Messer Fino. You shouldn't worry too much. No one cares about that unless it is made public. At our age it's kind of expected anyway. You'll still have to marry and all that but lots of gentlemen have a young squire as a special friend. My uncle does. Perhaps my old man too, who knows?'

Filiberto throws the pear stalk into a small bin with skilled nonchalance.

'The backstairs of this dump are no place for romantic love. Leave it to me.'

He turns to leave. He stalls by the painting and turns back to Fino with a wink.

'Drawing Principe Ludovico d'Este as a semi-naked Caspar is neither a clever nor a wise move, my dearest friend. Your work will be seen by many.'

* * *

Messer Franceschino had just turned eighteen when dispatched by his guardians to the sumptuous palazzo of Filiberto's uncle. In need of another clerk, all Messer Galeazzo had needed to do was to 'spread the voice', the preferred and still used Italian method of recruitment.

A small room at the back of the courtyard was assigned to the young man and he had joined a sparse group of other young clerks, running Messer Galeazzo's wool and textiles business.

Franceschino hailed from the city of Brescia; he was very poor and probably an orphan, though that had never been clear to his guardians. As the lad had proven to be respectful, polite, and of few words, they had never bothered to research his origins and how he had ended up in the Duchy of Ferrara.

He mainly kept to himself and was content with his existence. He was the only clerk residing in the palace.

After a few weeks, Messer Galeazzo had spotted potential. He started to congratulate the lad on his work, careful to bestow such praise in the absence of his colleagues in order to avoid raising jealousies.

Filiberto's uncle was partial to male beauty and his breath had been often taken hostage when occasionally spotting the young man splashing his bare chest and face with cold water from the bucket outside his lodgings.

On one occasion, Franceschino had lifted his head to Messer Galeazzo's window and had seen him absorbed in contemplation, detecting desire.

Franceschino was aware of his sculpted, boyish handsomeness. He was often the target of young ladies' giggles of admiration in the streets of the city and everyone always seemed to want to stroke his long, black curls. The black eyes were piercing yet without menace; the embarrassed smile melted most hearts away.

On one of these moments, Franceschino had stalled for a few seconds with a towel in his hands, before bowing gently to a shaken Galeazzo who had then nodded with a tight-lipped smile.

Perhaps Franceschino had realised that maybe there were conditions attached to his employment in the business. On the other hand, Messer Galeazzo was still a handsome man of not yet forty. A wiry body in a sinuous frame, he kept his greying beard fastidiously trimmed to perfection. Unlike many gentlemen of that period, he also took great care of his hygiene and fitness, often walking miles and miles every day to stay in shape. He was, of course, married. More of a business transaction in reality. Donna Clotilde had endured copulation with her husband for the honourable reason of procreation. As far as she was concerned those three times were three times too many and she had no objections to her consort finding satisfaction elsewhere. The variety of the satisfaction hardly concerned her, maintaining decorum and discretion did. Their children, two boys and a girl, were growing up in a happy and rather liberal household, Donna Clotilde more than satisfied with the task of raising them as the scions of upper-class merchants.

Either way, one spring afternoon, summoned by Messer Galeazzo to his bedroom to deliver some papers, Franceschino rightly guessed that a gentleman of such collected deportment and restrained politeness might have never got round to ask, let alone try it on without the boy's permission.

Franceschino closed and locked the door behind him, noticed by a puzzled Galeazzo. He walked with silent steps to the windows and drew the heavy velvet drapes closed before tiptoeing back to the four-poster bed. Once there, he turned to his Master and smiled in amiable, reassuring fashion.

He then unbuttoned his shirt and took off his shoes and hose, revealing a Davidesque physique which made Galeazzo gulp. When bare, Franceschino climbed on the bed and hid himself under the blankets, waiting in silence.

Messer Galeazzo had not left his desk. Still in his armchair, he felt shaking with fear of the little god who had just climbed up in his bed.

'Messer Franceschino. You are under no obligation to please your Master.'

Franceschino did not move.

'I know I am not. This is my will, Master Galeazzo.'

He started to undress. When in bed he hugged Franceschino from behind. When the boy turned their lips met with vigour. After detaching himself he whispered in Galeazzo's ear.

'My first time. I trust you care.'

And Messer Galeazzo did. To his astonishment, young Franceschino demanded nothing for surrendering his youthful purity to his Master. No money, no clothes, no special treatment. When Galeazzo's infatuation got the best of him and caution was about to fail him, his young charge would discreetly slip away to avoid raising suspicions. He then berated his protector over the next blissful pillow talk, cuddled in his tender, manly embrace.

'Master, don't reveal what we have. I don't want to see you suffer. We are allowed to love in the secret of your apartments. No more. You know that. Don't buy me fine garments. Don't caress me in public. People might know but they don't want to see it.'

'But I want you to be happy. I want to make you happy.'

'You do.'

Nevertheless Franceschino had to keep turning down favours. He continued to have his meals in the servants' hall and when another embroidered silk blouse appeared on his bed, he put it away without wearing it.

Like all the well-to-do families of Ferrara, the d'Aldighieri attended mass in the sprawling cathedral. Franceschino walked with the rest of the servants to the small, inconspicuous church of San Francesco. One day Galeazzo persuaded him that it would be permissible for a clerk of the household to attend mass with the family. Franceschino wasn't convinced but he found it hard to say no to his Master.

He wore the best of the several embroidered blouses he had received and humbly bowed to Donna Clotilde when he entered the palace hallway to follow the family to mass. Donna Clotilde darted an inquisitive look at her husband without saying a word. Their children were present and too much was in danger to be revealed by a quarrel.

He sat composed in silent prayer behind the d'Aldighieri's pew. He knew people were looking and commenting. His beauty did not pass unobserved and his connection with such an important family was puzzling the members of the aristocratic and wealthy clans sitting around him.

On the way back, unheard by Franceschino, Donna Clotilde commented without animosity but in a firm tone.

'That was not wise.'

Galeazzo nodded. Both his wife and his young lover were right. Discretion was the only road to safety.

Once in the hallway, the young man bowed and made so as to walk to the servants' hall for Sunday lunch, Messer Galeazzo resigned to having his love for this extraordinary boy unrecognised by the wider world. Donna Clotilde called out with severity.

'Master Franceschino.'

He stalled, turned and bowed, ready to be chided for the effrontery; or even asked to leave the house. He wasn't sure how strong a hold his lover's wife might have had on their affairs. How powerful she might be.

'I believe this unfortunate idea was the brainchild of my dear husband.'

She briefly turned to him, noticing his dejected look, ready to be asked to send his boy away. Then she calmly addressed Franceschino again.

'You are a young man of exceptional discretion and very little need. It has been noted. I wish we could say the same of other members of the family.'

Galeazzo lowered his head.

'You will be joining our family for lunch. As our clerk. As for mass, I trust you remain fond of the parish of San Francesco?'

'I do, Donna Clotilde.'

'I thought as much. If only my consort had the same foresight. Families of our status do not share their affairs with the wider public. Our tolerance must remain confined between the walls of the palace. I trust you understand such endeavour?'

Franceschino nodded.

'I was in no doubt. Perhaps you would be so kind to convince my husband of the importance of such undertaking?' She offered her hand to Messer Galeazzo. 'Let us eat now.'

* * *

Young Filiberto is often seen at his uncle's abode. His father and his family are stricter and more serious than Messer Galeazzo's household. His cousins seem happier than his brothers and misdemeanours are more easily forgiven. Within their four walls they are also more liberal with conversation, sometimes skirting a few daring subjects, except when the Bishop is over for lunch or dinner.

Filiberto is a natural wheeler-dealer. He enjoys being one and he's rather shameless about it. Once he volunteered as a look-out for a friend's rendezvous with a young lady. Upon spotting her father walking up, he burst into the room finding the pair in full display. He just laughed while warning the lovers to get out fast.

Filiberto loves his uncle dearly, possibly more than his own father. Never one to miss a little indiscretion, he had quickly become fully aware of Franceschino's place in his heart.

With his usual swagger and swashbuckling attitude he shocks the young man while chatting away during a break.

'How good is my uncle in the bedchamber?'

They are sipping some wine which Filiberto has stolen from the palace cellars. Franceschino spits it out with his eyes on stalks.

'Messer Filiberto, please.'

Filiberto laughs.

'You must think me stupid, Messere.'

'One talks not of such affairs.'

Filiberto shrugs.

'I do. As a matter of fact, my best friend at Mastro Filargiro's workshop is desperately in love with a young nobleman. The pair needs a safe haven to part with their purity. One afternoon. After lessons.'

Needless to say, Franceschino's heart, being made of pure gold, agrees. He is concerned when Filiberto mentions that the young nobleman is a d'Este.

'He will get noticed.'

'This is a d'Aldighieri residence. There is nothing suspicious about a d'Este visiting, especially with me. Messer Fino will follow behind.'

When left alone in Franceschino's room Ludovico and Fino stare at each other for a while before Fino smiles while opening his arms in wonder.

'I... I don't know what to do.'

Ludovico laughs back.

'Me neither.'

But they do. In the end one always does.

Once all their garments hit the floor, they find their way into each other's soul. After a couple of hours they finally have to climb out of Franceschino's little bed and start putting their clothes back on.

'Take me to court. As a page. A stable boy. Anything. Please.'

'No. I could do that, yes, my uncle hardly notices courtiers coming and going, but I would never do that. You are not my servant. We are lovers.'

'They will separate us.'

A tearful hug.

'They will.'

It will be his sixteenth birthday soon. After breakfast he starts the usual stroll to the city gates. After some two hundred yards a cart approaches and he jumps on at the front, the son of the farmer driving with his arm around Fino's shoulders.

The two years at Mastro Filargiro's workshop have also

taught him to read and write in the vernacular *Volgare,* the mastering of Latin reserved to the scions of wealthy merchants and aristocratic dynasties.

When he enters Mastro Filargiro's house, he greets Donna Elvira with the usual happy smile which melts her heart every morning without fail. When he walks into the loggia he finds his tutor looking at his painting with his arms folded.

'Good morning, sir.'

'And good morning to you, Master Fino.'

They stand side by side, contemplating his work.

'Is it finished?'

'I don't know.'

'An artist should know when his work is finished.'

'I think it is.'

'So do I. Joseph is such a handsome young man, Fino. And almost naked.'

'Is he supposed to be ugly?'

'No, not really. Though... they were poor people, scruffy, dirty. Everyone in your painting is, how can I put it, sumptuous?'

Fino apologetically lowers his head.

'You are not happy with my work, Maestro.'

'On the contrary. It is the most sensational work I have seen in decades. It almost scares me. The perfection.'

'It isn't perfect.'

'For the artist nothing ever is, above all his own work.'

Mastro Filargiro takes a black pouch out of his cape. He then grabs Fino's hand, holding it with the palm open, and deposits the small bag in it.

'Although this is no longer your work.'

Fino holds the pouch in front of him, it's rather heavy.

'I don't understand.'

'Messer d'Aldighieri is your first client, Fino. Ten ducats. The painting is now his.'

Fino's jaw drops.

'Ten ducats?'

'Yes. Undervalued, I must concur.'

'I... I don't know what to do with that kind of money. There must be some mistake.'

'There isn't. D'Aldighieri has secretly followed your progress. He was adamant he wanted the painting.'

Fino walks to the bannister and stays silent for a while, distractedly observing the noisy morning rush of carts, merchants and beggars bellowing in the dusty road below.

'It was meant for someone else. Not as a sale. As a gift.'

Mastro Filargiro walks to his side and gently wraps his arm around Fino's bony shoulders.

'His Highness? Young Ludovico?'

Fino's head turns and nods, his face crimson.

'Not much ever escapes my scrutiny, young man. Besides, your Caspar. Only love can paint such perfection. But it is a love which is not meant to be. And it won't. No matter how painful. You surely understand that.'

Fino nods.

'You need to sign your work.'

He turns and walks to the easel. Having dipped a small pointed brush into a pot of black paint he nervously scribbles at the bottom right corner of the canvas: *Fino da Ferrara*.

'There is more, Fino. Your time at my workshop has come to an end, my dear boy. You ought to master fresco techniques and we cannot do that here. Your work in oil hardly needs any improvement. I have found you a placement with Jacopo da Cremona. I believe he is achieving some recognition as *Il Formaggiaro*. I think his parents sell cheese or something of the sort. He is working on a series of frescoes in the cloister of San Procopio lungo il Canale, near the city of Chioggia. He has agreed to take you on as an apprentice. You will be assigned sections of the frescoes to master all on your own. He will guide you through the technique and the exact way to proceed. He will be impressed, I am sure. Food and lodgings will be provided by the parish. They received funds from Rome to pay for it.'

'But it is three days' ride from home. I won't be able to see my family.'

'No. You won't. But your future is elsewhere.'

'I'll lose all the friends I have made here. I don't want to. I'd rather scrub floors than leave.'

'That would be an affront to your art.'

The farewells are heart-breaking. Filiberto's swagger and endearing adolescent insolence evaporates in unashamed tears and in sulky, resentful stares at Mastro Filargiro for sending his best friend away. He encircles Fino's neck with his arm and kisses his hair.

'Who's going to defend and protect you now?'

Fino hugs him back.

'I'll just take the beatings.'

He's looking at his completed work for the last time. His first painting. Sold for ten ducats. He has never even held one ducat in his hand.

Mastro Filargiro walks into the loggia with Ludovico at his side.

'I thought you two should bid farewell to each other with a quiet moment.'

He walks away, leaving the two young men staring at each other. In pain.

'It was meant for you. As a present. Sorry.'

'I knew you wanted to give it to me. Do not worry, it is in my heart. It will never leave. And neither will you.'

They hug tight, a little stream of tears gracing their rosy cheeks.

'You know where I am. And who I am. One day I might be a powerful man. If you need help, do not hesitate to send for it. I will send an army if you are in any danger.'

'I would have gladly spent the rest of my days at your feet. At your command.'

Ludovico opens Fino's shirt and holds the gold chain with his fingers. Then, without checking whether they are alone or not, their lips meet for a long time. Not long enough.

He drops the black pouch on the kitchen table with a thump. His parents, brothers and sister flabbergasted at the ducats disgorging onto the dirty wooden surface.

Donna Ippolita hugs him tight. Not to thank him for the money. They have been informed of his new assignment and know that they won't see him for a long time. And if more far away engagements come forward, perhaps forever.

His father takes one ducat and drops it in Fino's pocket. He hears no protest.

'Keep at least one. You might need it.'

III. ...are alike

He picks up the card the following morning.

Dear Parker,

I might have mentioned that I am a good friend of the curator of the Velasquez exhibition currently running at the National Gallery. After a chat and a coffee she has kindly arranged a free pass for you to visit the museum between eight and ten in the morning and draw one or more of the paintings. After ten you may stay if you wish but it will be open to visitors and you might find it difficult to work.

I hope you'll take up the offer, there are some fantastic exhibits. I look forward to seeing your work (and marking it) when you return to school.

Happy Birthday

Miss Moore

'What kind of birthday gift is that?'

No one expects Tommy to understand, above all Parker who never belittles his brother's innate philistinism. Olivia shrugs while his mum is more than pleased.

'I'll bike over tomorrow morning, Mom.'

Elizabeth startles.

'Parker, I don't feel completely comfortable in letting you cycle over on your own to the National.'

'They have built a lot of bike lanes.'

'Yes, with lots of dangerous junctions in between them.'

Tommy solves his brother's problem straight away. He loves solving his little bro's problems. Even better when it involves exercise.

'I'll go with him,' then he turns to Parker, 'I won't stay, too boring. But I can come and pick you up. It's only twenty minutes. We can race, bro.'

Elizabeth takes Parker to an art shop and splashes out on the best quality paper and crayons, together with a pricey rectangular rucksack which allows him to stow all the materials without bending the albums.

At seven-thirty they are ready to set off. Elizabeth has prepared a slice of cake and a fruit juice as provisions.

'Boys, don't take your helmets off. I know you do when you ride to school, but you're going through the city.'

This time Parker convinces Tommy to leave the helmets where they should be. They have a good ride. Sun is blazing hot, the roads not that busy.

They arrange a pick-up time and Tommy sets off to meet his pals. Parker is ushered in to meet the curator, a fifty-something lady with elegantly coiffured grey hair. She guides him through the doors of the exhibition.

'How much do you know about Velasquez?'

'A little.'

'Well, what I recommend is that you choose a painting you want to draw first and then maybe acquaint yourself with the artist later, during opening times. You won't be able to work during those, I'm afraid, the exhibition is a great success.'

'Will do, thanks.'

'There are a few other students doing the same. We offer this to a few schools.'

Parker starts ambling wearily along the rooms. He sees a couple of girls and another boy already setting to work and greets them with a smile. They smile back in silence.

When walking into the third room, he stops. He has found it. He knows. The Forge of Vulcan is the one. He feels it. He's not quite sure why but he does.

He opens up the stool the lady has kindly provided him with and starts setting up his little stall. He takes a sip of the fruit juice and a small bite of the cake, nervously checking that he's not dropping any crumbs on the floor.

He has decided to use colours. He was prepared for both black and white and colour drawing. But the ochre hue of Apollo's tunic proves irresistible, though he will have to nag his mom for another trip to the art shop as that colour doesn't seem to be in the box.

After an hour, he has mastered the perspective and the outlines. A boy walks over and stands behind him in silence. Parker doesn't turn and waits for him to talk.

'Stunning work.' He bends over to peek at the drawing. 'In colour? Man, that takes guts. Why did you choose it? The bodies?'

Parker reddens. He's still not quite sure why but that is the truth. That is why he chose it.

'Yes.'

'Apollo is rather flaccid, I find that weird. Vulcan and his four workers not so. Who's your favourite?'

'I don't have one.'

'You will at some point. Imagine yourself in the scene. Right in the middle, between them.'

Parker isn't pleased with the interventions of the boy and the sudden, unwelcome stirring in his pants at the thought of being right in the middle. Between them.

He doesn't turn or acknowledge him.

'I'm trying to work.'

The boy leaves, though his insolent hints stay behind, as insolent hints do. Parker stops frequently to ogle the forge worker with the ruffled, curly hair, his tender expression of astonishment, his light beginning of a beard. That beard will be fiendishly difficult to draw despite Parker's eyes being transfixed on him, on his dumbfounded eyes.

And the man enters his mind and heart. He starts picturing the forger at his side. In his bed. Holding him. Caressing him. Pressing his dirty thumb on his lips. He feels himself being kissed and he shivers in fear, as if his thoughts could be seen.

The second day the curator approaches while he's at work. He doesn't turn but, unlike the boy, the lady has struck him as friendly and sympathetic.

'You have started with the smith in the middle. Aren't you worried about losing the perspective?'

'A little.'

She puts her spectacles on and leans over to peruse the drawing more closely.

'We shouldn't have to worry about that. The emotion in your drawing. Miss Moore was right.'

'Right?'

'Yes, about your heart.'

'Do you think I chose the right one?'

'You chose the one you love the most. That is the only thing that counts.'

She leaves silently, not before gently stroking Parker's hair.

He doesn't show the drawing to anyone. He promises to everyone that he will one day but he's not so sure. Tommy though is never one to be discouraged from a little investigation into his brother's soul and on the fourth day, while Parker is in the bathroom, he lifts the corner of the canvas cover and takes a peek. He smiles and, hearing Parker's steps on the landing, shuts it back in a hurry.

After the first week, the drawing is nearly finished. The annoying boy has stopped his unwelcome visits, possibly discouraged by envy. After a few days, he had started to notice the mastery of Velasquez gently transferring onto Parker's canvas without much effort. A few corrections here and there, the colouring near to perfection. He had then even stopped to smile at Parker, almost snapping his brush in two when he saw him entering the room. They had both stayed over beyond ten and a small crowd had gathered around Parker, discreetly whispering their appreciation, pointing at some of the details, marvelling at the precision of the execution. The other boy had a few passing visitors taking a glance at his rendering of one of the few self-portraits. They had left promptly, indifferent to the subject - a genius indeed but with rather boring features - and dubious about the boy's skills. Or, in some cases, more than sure about them.

The curator has made Parker promise to let her know Miss Moore's markings after his return to school while offering to let Parker in for the whole duration of the exhibition.

'I'd love to see you working on another painting.'

'Thank you, very kind. We're off for our vacation. We're driving to Nantucket next week to stay with my grandparents.'

'Take your canvasses with you. There will be some delightful landscapes to draw. Get up early and try dawn. How much do you know about Turner?'

'Not a lot.'

The curator looks at her watch.

'I have a minute or two. Come with me.'

Parker collects all his materials and follows the curator through the halls of the museum. When they reach the Turner room, she points at the works on the walls.

'Take a good look. Draw inspiration. The light of the sea will be very different but it is up to you to create your own work. To have your own voice.'

The Range Rover and the Ford Explorer are packed to capacity. Thankfully Larry's parents have purchased bikes for everyone and theirs need not be loaded. Parker is a bit disappointed at leaving his new flashy new toy behind but he comforts himself with the thought that it might get damaged in the car journey.

Parker, Tommy and Olivia are driving Larry and Elizabeth insane by doing what most children do when excited at the prospect of a holiday: running around without getting ready.

They are on their way, Larry with the boys, Elizabeth right behind with Olivia. The drive is just about over ten hours but there is the ferry ride at the end and they have decided on a motel stop mid-way. These stops are usually fun and a priceless chance for the males of the house (all three) to pick a earthy food outlet for a family dinner, somewhere where ribs, oversized burgers with buckets of French Fries and other coronary-inducing delicacies feature heavily on the plasticised menus. In any case, risotto and other European nonsense are nowhere to be seen at any of the eateries dotting Highway 95.

Parker has brought the Velasquez drawing along. He still hasn't shown it to anyone, more because of the subject rather than fear of criticism. He's still not sure what game he fears of giving away though he's pretty sure there is one.

They always enjoy the ferry ride. It's only forty-five minutes but rather scenic. Thomas and Barbara are on the porch waiting. Parker, Tommy and Olivia are the first to run to them. Kissing and hugging take a good ten minutes to be done with before they are all ushered in and let loose to their bedrooms, Larry and Elizabeth reminding them to help with the luggage.

Larry's parents' house is very spacious, a seven to eight bedroom mansion on two floors, majestically overlooking the white sandy beach in restful seclusion. The heated pool lies between the rear of the house and the sea. The style is rigorously New England, as if the island authorities had dispatched a permanent surveyor during its construction; one white wooden plank out of place or a light blue window fixing of the wrong hue would have probably warranted immediate deportation to Puerto Rico.

Although the interior didn't have to follow strict planning regulations, Thomas and Barbara have stuck to the same rigorous style: soft armchairs of the kind you would expect Angela Lansbury to perch on while solving another murder mystery in the not-so-distant Cape Cod.

Olivia misses Jack and worries about him cheating on her but Tommy and Parker love coming here. Their grandparents spoil them rotten and they can feel how genuinely welcomed they always are. Snowball, the Siberian Husky, always recognises them right away and jumps up their legs or rolls on the floor with them like they had never been away for months.

No need to settle down. The holiday gets off in full swing. Larry is up at six and enjoys a solid hour of backstrokes while a rising sun gradually blesses his sinuously floating limbs. Barbara, Elizabeth and the maid have breakfast on the porch ready at eight though, unlike back in Washington, the boys are up and running around at seven sharp. Getting up for school is one thing, waking up for swimming, cycling, kite-surfing and more of the same is another.

The first three days flow away in joyful merriment, noisy dinners and both Thomas and Barbara hugging and cuddling Parker no end, well aware of Tommy's aversion to touchy exchanges and Olivia now not-so-tender age. Parker loves it. For him affection must involve contact; he struggles to understand why it shouldn't be so.

Dinner is on the light side tonight. Soup and cod mornay as a main course. Barbara volunteers an affectionate rebuke.

'You boys always overdo it a bit in the first few days. Too many hamburgers and fried food.'

Larry has started to fill Tommy's glass half way with some of the remarkable reds his father keeps stored in the cellar and the young man has started to join the conversation over vintages and 'full-bodied' tastes. While pouring, Larry turns to his father.

'Dad, Jeff and Steven are coming over tomorrow, on their way to Provincetown. I have taken the liberty to invite them to stay for a couple of nights, if it's ok with you.'

Thomas nods.

'Of course it is. Barbara, we'll have to have Bertha over for dinner, you and Elizabeth cannot manage so many people. It's not fair.'

'Oh, they don't want to impose. They have offered to take all of us out for dinner to thank you for the hospitality.'

Tommy takes a sip of his wine.

'Man, I like Jeff and Steven, they are cool. Steven always beats me at basketball, he's a pro.'

Thomas smiles and turns back to his son.

'I like them too. Though I've never forgiven Jeff for snatching you and Elizabeth away from Boston.'

'I couldn't ask for a better boss, Dad, you know that. He keeps throwing promotions at me.'

'That's because you're good at your job; Jeff is no pushover. Is he coming over to talk shop with you? Provincetown is another ferry ride from here. Quite a detour in fact.'

Parker's curiosity ignites.

'Dad, why do they always go to Provincetown?'

A short embarrassed silence descends on the table. No one knows whether to go first. Elizabeth breaks the ice.

'They have a house there, Parker, quite a lovely one

actually, right on the waterfront. And friends.'

'Yes, but why Provincetown? Why not here? We are their friends too.'

Elizabeth glances anxiously at her husband. They just don't want to say the word. They are unsure of how much Parker knows or understand and they know he belongs to the same tribe. They are afraid of pushing the subject. It is too early for his closet to be opened.

'Well, other friends. Like you, Tommy and Olivia have friends in common and other friends. That is how society works in general.'

Parker lowers his gaze.

'I like them though. I wish they had a house here.'

The Lincoln MKX can be seen trundling the dusty path up to the house. The Hendersons - all of them - are scattered in front of the porch. Tommy is already in his shorts and vest, the basketball yo-yoing between his hand and the wooden planks. Steven made it almost to pro in the game and he won't be able to get out of a good game with Tommy.

Olivia is furiously texting Jack. He hasn't replied for one hour. One hour! 'He must be out with another girl', she almost screams at Elizabeth who can only raise her eyes and hugs her shoulders.

Jeff and Steven alight amid a chattering ocean of hugging, hand-shaking, cheek-kissing and high-fiving with Tommy who has already thrown the ball in Steven's direction. After catching it and running around Tommy with it, he holds the young man's neck with his strong biceps.

'Man, give me the time to change.'

Then the back door opens and Olivia lets out a piercing scream.

'Jack! Oh. My. God.'

Jack, in shorts and t-shirt, lightly waves his hand with a half-smile before being submerged by Olivia's hugs.

'Your Mom spoke to my Mom. And here I am. Can stay three days.'

The boys high-five Jack, as pleased as Olivia to have him over for games, swims and runs. Olivia, now on an emotional trip to planet Mars, runs to hug her mother.

'I thought it would be nice to have Jack here for a while. Now, his parents are a bit more conservative than us. I had to swear that Jack will shack up with Tommy and Parker. And no sneaking at night.'

That makes Tommy and Parker even happier than Olivia. Stupid talks, cosmic bedroom chaos and computer games before being shouted into sleep by Larry and Elizabeth or their grandparents. What beats that? Parker and Tommy have already retrieved Jack's rucksack from the trunk and are taking him upstairs to show their lair to their mate. Olivia never resents how well her brothers get on with her boyfriend; better having him sequestered for whole afternoons for games and general stupidity than setting eyes on other girls.

Larry slowly strolls inside with Jeff and Steven.

'Thanks for shipping young Jack here safe and sound, guys. Much appreciated.'

Jeff waves his hand in gentle dismissal.

'Pleasure. Really quiet dude. Slept most of the trip on the back seat.'

Steven smiles while thinking of the trip.

'Also very chilled these youngsters nowadays. We booked two rooms at the motel on the highway. You know, to be mindful. At reception he said it was stupid that we did that and he asked to change into a family room.'

They leave the guys to settle down in their room. Steven opens the window to take in the blinding light of the Atlantic and throws a sweeping look at the pool area. Tommy and Jack have already changed and are gyrating around the basket pole in a sweat. Jeff joins him and hugs him from behind while frowning unseen.

'I thought he was sent up here to be with Olivia?'

Steven pats his forearm.

'Straight boys. Come on, you must have worked that out by now. The company of other men always comes first. The only difference is that they don't have sex with each other.'

'Sweeping statement.'

'The sex or the company?'

'Hard to tell.'

'Do you ever find anything "easy to tell" in Foggy Bottom?'

'Seldom. We are intensely proud of our lack of clarity at the State Department.'

Tommy spots them on the balcony and promptly shouts.

'Hey, we need a pro here!'

Jeff pats him on the shoulder.

'You're not gonna get out of this one.'

'Oh, I knew that. They're good players though.' He shouts back. 'Where's Parker?'

'Changing, he always takes longer. Come on, dude, get down here!'

74

Steven whispers before shouting back.

'Bet he does. Down in a sec!'

Jeff shoves Steven's hip with a punch.

'Leave my godson alone, he's a smashing kid.'

Jeff and Steven were already a couple when the former lured Larry down to DC before the birth of the two boys. They became close friends with the Hendersons and were duly rewarded by being chosen as godfathers of Tommy and Parker. When they married, Steven's family found an excuse for not travelling from Nebraska to attend the wedding, something like snowy roads in July, or lack of a passport.

Larry was swiftly asked to be Steven's best man, something of which he was very proud. His parents were a bit slower to warm to their shiny new friends. Thomas and Barbara were unrepentant east coast liberals and staunch Democrats but from a different generation. The wheels of tolerance and acceptance took a little longer to grind on.

All the same, after a 'Guess who's coming for dinner' moment at their house in Nantucket, they warmed to the pair and Thomas hadn't even needed to make the Spencer Tracy redeeming speech before supper. Larry's father and Jeff were already deep in political debate well ahead of the first helping of risotto alla marinara hitting the table.

It hadn't been difficult to like Jeff and Steven. Jeff already high up at the State Department, Steven a successful dentist, they were and remain the archetypal "good" pair of gays.

Not yet in their forties, good-looking, fit and healthy, they are a sort of Ralph Lauren-Tommy Hilfiger walking commercial. Their preppy looks allow no derailments; once Larry took a picture of them on the sandy dunes of Nantucket and seriously thought of sending it to one of the two fashion houses, dead sure that it would make it to Vogue or GQ.

Larry and Elizabeth are also reassured that their children will be in good hands if anything were to happen to them.

On the second day, Tommy, Jack and Steven are off wind-surfing, Olivia happy to lie on the sandy dunes watching her beloved kept away from other girls by her brother's thundering camaraderie. Olivia remains stubbornly unaware that Jack is hardly a Casanova despite being rather easy on the eye. He's in love with Olivia but it's a quiet love. Devoid of drama. He struggles to understand her jealousy as it has never crossed his mind to cheat on her.

Jeff is not as sporty as his companion and he stays behind. Besides, Thomas was right and he did indeed stop over to talk shop with Larry. They set off for a long walk into Nantucket and stop for a working lunch.

Elizabeth, Barbara and Bertha set off for grocery shopping. They have turned down Jeff's generous invitation to a restaurant dinner and stated that it would be much better for such a big crowd to eat in the spacious dining room overlooking the ocean. Jeff had agreed but had volunteered to help with the preparations in the afternoon.

Windsurfing is not Parker's thing either and he happily stays behind to work on his drawing. The Forge could not be shipped to Nantucket so he follows a picture on the big computer screen in his grandad's study with Snowball sneaking a nap at the foot of his chair; it is almost finished anyway.

Larry and Jeff are back in the early hours of the afternoon.

Jeff catches Parker in the kitchen helping himself to a glass of milk.

'Good afternoon, young man.'

'Uncle Jeff.'

They call them 'uncles' even if they are not. It happens in families when no other title would fit.

Jeff gets a hug as he always does when alone with Parker.

'What have you been up to?'

'Drawing.'

'Yes, I've heard of the gift from Miss Moore.'

Parker takes a sip of the milk.

'Do you want to see it?'

'I understand I will be the first.'

'And maybe the only one.'

He follows Parker in the study. He picks up the drawing and takes it near the window to peruse it in the soft afternoon reflection of the ocean. He stays silent for a little while.

'Amazing work, Parker. You are very talented. I love it.'

'I'm still putting the final touches. What do you think of the subject?'

'The Forge is a masterpiece, excellent choice.'

'They are beautiful, aren't they? The men.'

Jeff sits on the sofa while still looking at the drawing. He gazes affectionately at Parker.

'Yes, Parker. They are.'

He sits by Jeff and snuggles up under his arm.

'An annoying boy at the museum said that I should be imagining myself in there. In between them.'

Jeff gulps.

'And have you?'

He feels Parker's arm squeezing his chest.

'Yes.' The pause feels a little painful. 'I'm not sure it's a good thing.'

'When it happens, love is always a good thing.'

'I'm not sure I should show it to anyone.'

'Why not?'

'I don't know.'

Jeff detects a knot in the throat in the middle of that sentence. He shakes Parker gently.

'You know all of your family loves you, no matter what.'

He kisses Parker's hair letting him settle in his embrace. He knows that it is comforting to him and it would be cruel to try to end it. Some old lyrics of a Dom McLean song spring to Jeff's mind.

'I can't save you from your trouble and pain, Parker. At some point you'll have to tackle a few things by yourself in life. It's the way it goes.'

'It's ok to be a little scared?'

'Absolutely.'

Jeff looks out of the window.

'It's a beautiful afternoon, Parker. What do you say we take a long walk on the beach? We can take Snowball for a good run, I think he's gagging for it.'

They are already barefoot. They leave the study via the French windows and start walking, Snowball jumping with canine excitement. Parker feels the elation we all feel when in the company of unthreatening, loving human beings, those who understands our fears, our problems, our insecurities.

They gape at the silvery line at the end of the ocean, in silence. Their reassuring little silence.

From time to time he turns to Jeff who smiles in return, enough to reassure him that he's there. Parker picks up a pebble and throws it skimming on the placid surface of the sea. He pauses and turns, half-smiling.

'I love you, uncle Jeff.'

They are back in time for Jeff to keep to his promise and help with the table and some of the cooking. A crowded and happy dinner. Jeff and Thomas dig with passion into the politics of the new President while the elder boys talk sport with Steven. Parker dutifully helps the ladies to shuttle crockery and glasses between the kitchen and dining room, receiving either a kiss or a caress from his grandmother every time he returns to the kitchen. The young things well know that their grandparents are rather fond of their cacophony at the dinner table, an overcompensation for the months going by without seeing them at all.

Larry seems a bit pensive. Thomas and Elizabeth notice that among all the merriment though they put it down to maybe some work-related issue discussed with Jeff in the afternoon.

At around ten, the young things have finally exhausted all the energy young things possess and head for bed. In peace and quiet the adults tie up the evening with some grown-up nightcap conversation about, well, everything.

Eventually, Jeff and Steven bail out. Steven's fitness is on the side of extraordinary but a whole day of windsurfing followed by a round of basketball has taken its toll. He is after all twenty years older than Tommy and Jack.

They walk up the stairs and open the door of their room.

They always leave the smallest of the table lamps on before they go out, wherever they are, hotels or friends' houses.

Once inside they stop. Then look at each other in silence. Steven tightens his lips with a frown. Jeff gently raises his hand to suggest he's going to do the talking. The bump on the bed is completely covered by the duvet though a socked foot sticks out at the end of the mattress.

Jeff walks softly towards the chair by the window then turns and throws a fake cough.

'Parker. That's our bed.'

'Mmm...'

Jeff looks up to Steven who opens his hands holding their water bottles.

'And may I ask you what you are doing in it?'

'Hiding.'

'From what?'

'There's a storm coming. I'm scared of lightening and thunder.'

'You got Tommy and Jack in your room.'

'Tommy is fast asleep and Jack has sneaked into Olivia's room.'

'Ok, I will pretend I didn't hear that.'

'When there's a thunderstorm I sleep with Mom and Dad.'

'Aren't you too old for that?'

'No?'

Jeff picks an item of clothing from the chair. Steven can't quite see what he's holding up with one finger.

'Do you take your underpants off when snuggling up with Mom and Dad?'

The thought of his uncle holding his underpants in his

hand together with the constant brushing against the soft mattress almost causes a burst. His adolescent crush lives suspended between Jeff's appearances. When he comes to visit the 'crush-o-meter' tends to reach Chernobyl levels of Roentgen readings: the handsomeness, the impromptu hugs and the hair ruffling. Every movement spellbinds Parker away in a hazy fairy tale, where uncle Jeff invariably rides in on his white horse, picking his godson up with a theatrical sweep of his muscular arm.

This afternoon he didn't bother to hide his visible excitement when snuggling up in his uncle's arms. Jeff could swear that he felt Parker's lips furtively kissing his chest. That is why he proposed the beach stroll: to clear Parker's overexcited mind.

He worked for the afternoon but when Parker walked by their bedroom on the way to his, he surrendered to a sudden impulse and went in, taking the pillow on Jeff's side and inhaling the manly waft.

He now imagines Jeff sending Steven back to the kitchen with an excuse. Then he will slowly slide under the duvet. His strong biceps will hold him down, their fingers interlocked, his lips pecking and biting his small ears, his thin, pale neck. Then he will gently do away with his innocence. It will hurt but he won't have anyone else but him doing it. It will be a flood and he will feel the manly tide inside him.

But uncle Jeff is a good man and deep down Parker knows that none of it will happen.

He won't send Steven away and he will not take advantage of his throbbing wet purity. He knows how disrespectful to Steven his infatuation is. He has tried to push it away but the intensity of it always overwhelms him.

Steven shakes his head with a smile. Another uncertain moan resonates from under the duvet.

'Come on, pal.'

'I've got my socks on.'

Jeff throws Parker's underpants back onto the chair, sighing.

'Well, that makes it alright then.'

'It does?'

'No, Parker, not really. Now, here is the deal. Steven and I happen to have forgotten our water bottles downstairs. We are going to pop to the kitchen to get them. In the meantime young Parker is gonna put his pants on and sneak into his parents room before the thunderstorm gets here. How does that sound?'

'Mmm...'

'I'll take that as a disappointed yes. Parker, dude, it will happen soon. He will be a beautiful boy, perhaps someone you meet at school. And it will be a wonderful day, I promise you that. But this is not the way it happens and it is not the way it's going to. You understand that, don't you?'

'Mmm...'

'Good man.'

They walk across the landing after softly closing the door behind them. Steven shakes his head with a somehow sardonic smile. He lifts the water bottles up in front of him.

'And you wonder why I love you so much.'

'I never wonder about that, Steven, I know it.'

'Man, never expected that. That was a hell of a Monopoly move.'

'A what?'

'Go straight to "Threesome" without passing through "Loss of Virginity". Collect one-hundred extra "Sleaze points".'

'Don't start flattering yourself stupid into thinking we are the next Tom Cruise and Brad Pitt. Hormones play funny games at that age; he clearly had no idea of what he was proposing, he was just horny as fuck and no one to go to. And it might be my fault. He was in dire need of tender loving care this afternoon and he might have misunderstood my affection. I overplayed the message perhaps.'

'Played beautifully old man. You care a lot about Parker, don't you?'

Jeff nods and gazes inquisitively into Steven's eyes, searching a reproach, yet meeting with blazing pride.

On their way back they stall by Olivia's room. Steven turns to his husband.

'Have they put something in the water tonight?'

Jeff raises his eyes to the ceiling and silently turns the knob of the door. The heavy breathing and moaning noises abruptly stop.

He doesn't want to look inside but he realises that the two young lovers must be scared to death realising that they have been caught. He then inserts his head between the door and the wall, spotting Jack's naked back, Olivia under his body.

'Relax. It's Jeff. Would you two keep it down? They can hear you in fricking Boston.'

Jack's head turns, his face crimson.

'Sorry.'

He closes the door behind him and starts walking back

with Steven. When in front of the room, he half-frowns, half-smile.

'Hell of a nice ass.'

Dinner was fraught. Their three guests well on their way to the beaches of Provincetown and back to DC, the extended family had gathered around the long dining table for what it was meant to be a return to the everyday holiday routine.

But Larry had dropped a bomb. A good bomb, if there ever was one, but it still detonated between a serving of Elizabeth's truffle risotto and the anticipation of the t-bone steak sizzling in the kitchen.

While everyone was wondering where the hell she had found Italian truffle shavings anywhere on the eastern seaboard, Larry had decided it was the best moment to let it out.

And in some quarters the proverbial lead balloon had thumped on the table, spraying specks of truffle all over the startled faces, some with spoons still half-way (it had always been an impossible task to force Tommy to eat risotto with a fork).

The glass of neat JD feels warm in Larry's hand, helping him to gather his thoughts while taking in the blazing sunset. The deck is deserted. Perhaps he has been deserted by his family, he wonders.

Thomas tiptoes to his side and joins him in the sunset-gazing in pensive silence, perhaps reproachful. Larry slightly turns and sees the tumbler in his father's hand. He frowns.

'Your mother thought I could do with one tonight.'

Larry nods in agreement.

'I don't expect you to be happy about it, Dad, or approve.'

'You are not a little boy anymore. Not for me to approve.' He takes a sip. 'That tastes awesome. Goddam blood pressure. Better enjoy it while I can.'

'I am sorry about the timing, I was struggling to find the right moment to announce it. Has anyone said anything before heading to bed?'

'Your children are very predictable, son. Not much will change for Olivia, just a longer flight across the pond on her Princeton breaks. Parker is on cloud nine and Tommy... well, Tommy hasn't taken it well. Not well at all. You will need to have a good talk.'

Larry nods.

'I expected that.'

'Tommy is as American as a cheese burger, perhaps even more. He's made of stars and stripes. He will suffer.'

'I know.'

'You must remember that your mother and I went to Italy for our retirement trip.'

'You both loved it, didn't you?'

'We did. But we were on holiday. Even the scraggiest part of the world looks beautiful on holiday. It is a beautiful country but it is very different from how we live and from how we want to live our lives. Their perspectives seemed different. I found their lifestyle sophisticated, perhaps too much. And they are very dismissive of other civilisations. They barely consider ours to be one. Theirs seems to be the only one that ever existed. Tommy is a good kid but Florence and the Florentines will be like Mars and a bunch of aliens to him. He won't mix.'

Larry sighs.

'Parker?'

Thomas guffaws with a hint of pride.

'He's likely already browsing language courses and Florence's High Schools. The only part of your announcement he seemed to dislike was your promise to send them to the International School.'

'Jeff seems to think that the posting as a Consul General will be brief, he's already circulating my name for the ambassadorship. Rome is a very important embassy, Dad, I didn't feel I could turn it down. Jeff has been real good to me.'

'He's probably already mentioned you to the President. I'm starting to tire of Jeff taking my family farther and farther away from me.'

Larry grabs the bottle of bourbon on the table and refills both their glasses.

'You and Elizabeth are not running away, are you?'

Larry turns and the glance is long, deep, vaguely suspicious.

'No. Why would you say that?'

There is no answer.

'You wouldn't consider leaving Tommy here? With us, I mean. There are some good high schools around in Rhode Island. I know the dean of the MIT, the boy seems to be technical.'

'No, Dad. Florence might not be the best place in the world for Tommy but he's too young to be separated from me and Elizabeth. He's a tough kid, he'll make it.'

'He will. For you.'

Elizabeth is brushing her hair with long, slow strokes. She was made part of the news the day before so the shock has worn off. In any case she has always been an unrepentant north-eastern seaboard swallow. Quite a lot of people up there freely flow between their European roots and American ones. Like their accents, they feel positively mid-atlantic and the thought of Florence as the wife of the Consul General generated good vibes. The food, the lifestyle, the weather. She had immediately worried for Tommy, well aware that, if it weren't for this, he would have never even applied for a passport in his life. But she was over the moon for young Parker who for her was still not an adult. Not even a child as a matter of fact, her baby more like.

And she is lovingly and patiently listening to an avalanche of plans coming from him, slumped on his front on the big bed in his polar bear pyjamas, lower legs up and restless, a laptop in front of him.

Larry walks in and jumps on him, tickling his sides, both bursting into hysterical laughter.

'There is no storm coming.'

Parker lifts himself up and crosses his legs, holding the laptop on them.

'Tommy is in the middle of a huge sulk.' He points at the screen. 'I found an awesome Italian online course, Dad. And a teacher in DC who's within the budget Jeff gave you for language tutoring. And there are workshops at the Uffizi. Maybe Miss Moore can put in a good word for me. She said once that the Smithsonian are always in cultural exchanges with the most important museums in the world, and...'

Elizabeth turns from the table with the brush in her hand.

'He has been like this for the last half an hour. I haven't been able to get a word in.'

Larry smiles.

'Ok, draw breath. Glad to hear you are taking it so well. All good for me but we must all support your brother, Parker. He doesn't share your enthusiasm for Florence, I'm afraid.'

'How can he not? Boy, it's going to be awesome. Always wanted to go to Italy.'

'Always? You are fifteen.'

'Well, that is what you adults always say.'

He's tapping furiously on the keyboard, Larry and Elizabeth desperately trying not to cry at the thought that this wonderful little thing is really their son.

'I've been thinking, Dad...'

'Yes?'

'Do I need to go to the International School? The Italians have these High Schools for the arts, they are called *Licei Artistici*. I found one not far from the consulate. It's a state one so it won't even cost any money.'

'Laiceo Artis...?'

'No Licei if it's plural, Dad. Their plurals end mostly with 'i' and 'e'.'

'You've started studying Italian? When?'

'Only had a look.'

'No objections in principle. Well, two actually. First, will your Italian be good enough? You don't want to sit in a class without understanding a word of what is being taught. The second one, well, I was hoping that you would be in the same school with Tommy. You know, just to be near him.'

Parker lowers his head, disappointed but understanding. 'Ok.'

Elizabeth jumps on the bed and hugs him tight.

'Let's think it over another time. We don't have to decide everything now.'

They all slide under the soft duvet, Parker in the middle, hugging his mother from behind.

'I know I'm too old for this. Last night, I promise.'

Larry kisses his hair feeling a pang of sadness.

'We wish for it never to end but, yes, it is true. You are too old for this.'

IV. Lungo il Canale

The cart is almost ready. He has parked it carefully in front of Mastro Filargiro's house and he's now sheltering in the shade of the portico, the summer heat already unbearable in the early hours of the morning.

He has found a good horse. He hadn't been sure whether Mastro Filargiro's funds would stretch to it and he had started to ask around for a decent donkey but Messer d'Aldighieri had chipped in to help. He has wrapped the wooden frame with the cleanest of cow hides he could find and a couple of threadbare cushions have been placed at the end of the uneven wooden floor.

There are no provisions as Mastro Filargiro has calculated all the costs for two nights at some reasonably priced inns and a spot of unpretentious fare for him and Fino.

Tonio is wiping his forehead with a dirty rag, beads of sweat dribbling along his temple, wetting the rim of his straw hat. He walks back to the cart to double-check its joints and the axle underneath; the way to Chioggia is all flat and relatively easy to negotiate, but if a summer storm gets in the way the mud and the stones can become a bit uneven and less than robust carriages have been known to overturn.

When he lifts himself upright a slim yet wiry forearm locks his neck in a strong hold while he feels the cold blade of a knife against his unshaved, ragged neck.

'I swear I will kill your wife and children one by one if anything happens to Messer Fino.'

Filiberto whispers in the poor man's ear trying his best to make up a manly, threatening voice, the kind he imagines a rogue bandit would emit in such a situation.

Tonio doesn't move.

'Messer d'Aldighieri, if you let go of my throat I might be able to reply to such a warning.'

Filiberto stands back while keeping his knife pointed at the peasant's chest: a present from his uncle, a handcrafted half-sword with the handle of mother-of-pearl, the clean beauty of it making it rather unthreatening without blood marks. Young Filiberto has yet to murder anyone and the likelihood is that he never will. Tonio could probably knock the lad to the ground without much effort but he's wiser than that.

'Messere, your own father and Mastro Filargiro are rewarding my services with a reasonably handsome sum. Why, in the name of god, would I want to hurt your friend? And, yes, my family is here, my young children doing errands and small jobs for your own uncle, and I would want very much to return to them in safety. Your protégé will reach San Procopio unharmed.'

With a sharp, quick twist of his strong hand he disarms Filiberto and a much more seasoned weapon appears in his callused palm. Filiberto could swear that the sharp edge of the blade still shows some red marks, the product of years of fighting for his life while growing up in the more deprived recesses of the Estense capital.

He picks up the young man's weapon from the floor and dusts it off before handing it back to him, guffawing at the lad's embarrassment.

'It slashed a boy's chest when I was barely twelve, Master Filiberto. He survived and so did I. Messer Fino is safe with me. More that he would be with you, I'm guessing.'

He has no need to knock at the door of the Osteria della Lepre. The entire family saw the cart a long way off, a dot slowly getting bigger against the deserted, dusty trail.

They hug him one by one, tears flowing, his mother smothering him against her bosom while checking the he has everything he needs for the long journey: a water bag, the light trunk packed with young noblemen's cast-offs, some bread, hard cheese and a couple of ducats hidden in his shoes.

Tonio greets him with a nod and he jumps onto the cart, sitting down on the cushions with an awkward movement.

The hide cover has been lifted to facilitate air circulation, allowing Fino to continue waving at them until he's no more that a little spot far away, indistinguishable from the cypresses and a few other carts now starting to slowly populate the trail.

The first day is the worst. In his short existence of sixteen years he has never left Ferrara and never slept away from his home or without his brothers.

They cover a good distance and they reach the small village of Copparo in the early hours of the evening. Tonio enquires about inns and taverns and they end up at a decent one, the hosts rather welcoming.

Despite Tonio's encouragement, Fino touches no food, a heavy weight hanging on his stomach, looking at Tonio's in silence.

Once upstairs, Tonio proceeds to re-arrange the wooden beds. He blocks the door with his, places his knife by his pillow and gives his metal mug with some water in it to the boy. He then closes the shutters, wedges a wooden bar to lock them tight and moves Fino's bed by the wall.

Fino follows all these preparations with a mixture of surprise and apprehension, without understanding the reason for them. Tonio notices his puzzlement.

'Anyone trying to get in will wake me up. If you hear any noise, throw the water on my face and wake me up in haste. Shout if you have to.'

Fino opens his round brown eyes to maximum capacity.

'Who would want to come in?'

'One never knows, that's the problem.'

They reach the crossing of the Po river at Crispino. While Tonio barters the fee with the old man in charge of the semi-derelict flat ferry, Fino gets off the cart and walks to the river bank. He splashes his face and sweaty locks with the cold water and returns to the cart. He hasn't had much of a conversation with Tonio who has only been told that Fino is a painter travelling to Chioggia for an apprenticeship, something artists do, though the purpose of such endeavour remains mysterious and inexplicable to him.

'He won't leave for another two hours. He says he's just returned and wants more customers than a cart and two men. Stubborn old fool.'

'Well, I wonder if I could walk down the river and have a wash by a deserted spot, Messer Tonio.'

'You are the master young man. But I am in charge of your safety and I won't leave the cart here with this scoundrel of a ferry captain. Just walk down to where I can still see you. If you see anyone suspicious, shout.'

Fino is still highly puzzled by all these precautions. He opens his arms in a pleading gesture.

'But it's just me and I haven't got any money.'

'All the same.'

'There are people about, I don't want them to see me swimming. I mean... without clothes on.'

Tonio bursts in a thundering laugh, Fino is crimson.

'The lad is bit of a prude, I see. As if anyone would swim with theirs on.'

He follows the path along the river and stops when Tonio shouts not to go any further.

The low temperature of the water hits him with a sudden, welcome pleasure, the heat and sweat of the day vaporising, his mind slowly clearing. He splashes and swims about without worrying about the time. He finally reaches the shore and starts to put his clothes on when Tonio shouts that the old man has decided to cross.

He feels much better and the mood prompts a polite thanking.

'Thank you Messer Tonio, I'm very grateful.'

'You are very respectful for a little peasant.'

He's not offended. He feels some sort of affinity with Tonio. His talent hasn't wiped out his roots yet.

They reach Adria at the onset of the second night. As they get nearer and nearer to the swampy Po delta, the mosquitos seem to become a permanent feature, aided in their quest to ravage Fino's legs by the heavy, fetid air and the malodorous streams of muddy waters. When not dozing off on the cushions, he dreamily observes the landscape, wondering why everyone seems to always and only paint Christs and Madonnas, Last Suppers, Suppers at Emmau, weddings and yet more Suppers at Canaan. These people either give birth to Messiahs, eat or marry, he thinks; they never seem to do anything else.

At the tavern a friendly and chatty wench takes pity of the scratching young man and hands him an unspecified ointment which proves surprisingly efficacious. He can't help sporting a sceptical expression when Tonio repeats his routine of barricading the small room assigned to them for the night.

'We look and are dirt poor, Master Tonio. The poorest in fact.'

'Scoundrels are not just after ducats, young man.'

Fino opens his hands in puzzlement.

'What else?'

Tonio gently holds the boy's narrow, beardless chin with two fingers and his thumb.

'Skin smoother than a young, pure maid. Some men hardly care about the difference. And I daresay there isn't much of it.'

Fino instinctively retreats to the end of the bed, closing his shirt with both hands, holding the edges tight. Tonio bursts into loud laughter.

'Messer Serafino, no fear. I am a ladies' man and my roving eye exclusively falls on young, pure maids; much to the ire of my dear wife, I must add. Sleep safe, I can indeed tell the difference.'

On the third day, after a fraught crossing of the river Brenta in the middle of a raging summer thunderstorm, they reach the flat and sizzling peninsula of Isola Bacucco, still scorching despite the late dusk.

Tonio pulls the bridle with a grunting noise and jumps off the cart. At speed he retrieves Fino's trunk and unceremoniously dumps it in front of the rickety wooden door. Amid the deafening silence and the presence of no human being, Fino jumps off too and stands by the trunk with a dismayed expression.

'Well, there it is, Messer Fino, San Procopio lungo il Canale.' He waves his mocking hand in the building's direction. 'In all its splendour.'

Fino turns his head and distractedly peruses the crumbling bell tower and the dirty facade of the church at the end of the courtyard.

'You are not staying the night?'

'Ah! The city of Chioggia is all but half of one hour ride to the north. The Serenissima it ain't, but still, can't be short of a few willing young ladies either.'

'But... I'm not sure there is actually anyone here. I can't hear any voices.'

'Hardly my problem. I have delivered you to San Procopio. That was what I was paid for. You're well and safe. Farewell, lad.'

He jumps onto the cart and shakes the bridle with another grunt. Sooner than Fino would like Tonio is all but a hazy dot a long way down the dusty trail.

He walks to the door of the house and tentatively knocks. Then he remembers it is Vespers time and walks across the courtyard to the entrance of the church. When close he finally hears the sound of singing filtering through the big entrance door.

He resolves to walk back and patiently wait, sat on the trunk. The sun slowly disappears behind the bell tower.

When the door finally opens with a screeching sound, he has dozed off on his luggage, exhausted by three gruelling days of travel. A hand shakes his arm a few times before his eyes blink open. He rubs them with his fists before opening them with an air of disorientation.

'You must be Serafino. Fino da Ferrara as mentioned by Mastro Filargiro in his correspondence.'

He stands up and tries to compose himself by dusting his trousers off and buttoning up his sweat-drenched shirt.

'I'm Father Gaudenzio. Come inside. There is a bucket of clean, cold water to refresh yourself with at the back of the house. Donna Giovanna has dinner almost ready.'

Fino thanks him with a bow and follows him inside while observing him close. Father Gaudenzio must be in his early fifties, the frame of medium size under threadbare but neat clerical attire. Fino notices his habit of obsessively adjusting his spectacles while talking.

Once inside, he sees a big wooden table laid out for dinner. He instinctively counts five plates and five chairs.

As there is no one else to be introduced to, he leaves

his trunk in a corner and walks to the backyard where he splashes himself with generous ladlefuls of water, before drying himself and returning to the dining room.

A man of possibly thirty is standing by the table, reasonably well dressed, with long and rebellious black, wavy locks. He doesn't acknowledge Fino until Father Gaudenzio introduces them to each other.

'This is your tutor, Fino, Mastro Jacopo da Ferrara. He has kindly agreed to complete the frescoes along the cloister behind the church. I'm sure he will be delighted to have your services as his apprentice. Mastro Filargiro had nothing but praise for your nascent talent.'

Fino bows to a rather unfriendly, almost acidly menacing pose. Messer Jacopo does not return the bow, though Fino puts it down to his position as master. He doesn't proffer a single word while he takes his seat at the table. Fino respectfully waits until invited to sit by Father Gaudenzio, still to be addressed by his future tutor.

The door squeaks open and a lad of more or less Fino's age strolls in, barefoot and with his hands in his pockets. He sits by Fino and turns to face him.

'Hey. You must be the scribbler; Fino, right? I'm Lionello, Head Boy of the orphanage next door. That's why I eat the shit served here rather than the one served in the refectory.'

Donna Giovanna has entered and, hearing Lionello's language, she smacks the back of his head before positioning her arms on her hips in reproachful pose.

'Perhaps you shouldn't be "Head" of anything with such profane language. Apologise to Father Gaudenzio now. Unless you fancy sleeping with no dinner in your stomach.'

He smiles and winks to Fino before opening his mouth. The first and only person in the household to actually smile to him.

'Sorry, Father.'

The room is bare though rather spacious. There is an uneven sort of closet in one corner and a desk with a jug of water. It is tidy and clean. Donna Giovanna, the *Perpetua,* struck him as an avuncular dictator, running the house with dedicated determination.

He undresses and rolls into a foetal position under the single crisp sheet. He closes his hands in two fists before laying them on his face to soften the sound of the sobs. Mastro Jacopo had not addressed him at all during a silent supper. Donna Giovanna was busy shuttling in and out of the kitchen while Father Gaudenzio seemed absorbed in what seemed to be a constant prayer, though he had addressed young Lionello from time to time with questions about the orphanage. After what had seemed to him a friendly wink, Lionello had largely ignored him throughout the evening.

And that was it. There was no one else. And he is alone in this big room, the walls bare and grey; the first time in his life sleeping without his brothers, without even Tonio and his knife guarding the door. Only unfriendly strangers on the other side of the door, the stony, dark silence of the swampy countryside surrounding the parish interrupted only by the sound of the cicadas and the mosquitos circling with a menacing buzz, ready to feast on tender meat.

And, exhausted, he cries himself to sleep.

Donna Giovanna shakes him at thirty minutes past six. Not that he had much sleep. Half of an hour is just enough to wash himself and trot to the church for morning mass. At eight he's back and respectfully sits at the table for what turns out to be a decent fare for breakfast. Donna Giovanna is a hardworking lady.

Mastro Jacopo still hasn't spoken to him and Lionello obviously has his breakfast with the other boys of the orphanage. He feels like bursting into tears but rightly guesses that he cannot show himself to be too needy.

Father Gaudenzio distractedly peruses his breviary. Fino suddenly feels Donna Giovanna's hand on his shoulder. He's somewhat reassured by what seems to be a friendly touch.

'You don't look too happy, young man.'

He lowers his gaze without replying.

'What is that is eating you?'

He hesitates before almost whispering his reply.

'I... I have never slept all alone, Madam. It's very dark. I am... well, a bit frightened. Sorry.'

Mastro Jacopo's snort while getting up confirms his qualms about revealing such weakness to unfriendly hosts. His eyes are welling up. Donna Giovanna squeezes his shoulder while Mastro Jacopo leaves, her sharp stare in Father Gaudenzio's direction redolent of intention.

'We'll see what we can do.'

He changes into his working gown and tentatively walks to the cloister, already terrified of the obvious unfriendliness of his tutor and afraid he will be beaten. He's shaking when he approaches the portico. Mastro Jacopo is busy working on the third panel, the second almost completed. Noticing

Fino's presence, he cleans his hands with a dirty rag and walks towards him. Fino bows.

'I was in no need of an apprentice. I did not ask for one. Try not to be too much of a hindrance.'

'Yes, sir.'

'Come here. I left the first panel for you. I have finished the drawings though.'

'I... I have only worked with oil on canvas, sir. I have never worked on frescoes. I... I don't know how it's done.'

Mastro Jacopo sighs and turns in a rather pompous and theatrical way.

'Mastro Filargiro could have shown you something! He's expecting me to waste days teaching you! Just because of some extra funding from Rome! Bah!'

The dismissing enmity of his tutor cuts through his heart. In Mastro Filargiro's workshop he had been repeatedly told that art is from the heart, that it was the toil of good men. This is a rude awakening.

'I... I learn fast. You will only need to tell me once, Mastro Jacopo.'

His tutor shakes his head in arrogant resignation.

'Very well then.'

With surprising patience he starts explaining the use of dry powder pigments, the way they merge with the plaster, how to follow the sketching and even the correct posture to maximise the perspective. Fino follows everything in silence before being told to stand in front of the panel and take it in.

He moves around the panel, cocking his head, looking at it from both sides before returning to Mastro Jacopo who has gone back to his panel.

Assigning the first panel to his apprentice was a stroke of unparalleled callousness on behalf of Mastro Jacopo. Jesus is condemned to death and that involves a crowd of Roman dignitaries and Pontius Pilate deliberating in sumptuous surroundings. The sketches look complicated, the choice of colours and hues fiendishly challenging. It is indeed the deep end.

Fino stands silent behind his master.

'Sir...'

'Yes?'

'May I... may I corr... modify the sketches?'

Mastro Jacopo's stare appears so angered, Fino steps back, afraid to be hit.

'Change my sketches?'

He must lie.

'They... they are too difficult for me. I'm only an apprentice.'

The suspicious look worries Fino that his lie has not passed muster.

'Mmm... go ahead then.'

At lunchtime Donna Giovanna brings a straw basket with cheese and cold meats. Fino lets his master choose the best bits before retreating under the shade of one of the chestnut trees gracing the square of the cloister. He's finally hungry. He has been concentrating hard on his tutor's instructions and has started to correct the sketches, trying hard not to redraw the whole panel. Messer da Cremona had noticed how furiously Fino had been switching charcoals and strenuously applying himself to the panel.

Dismayed, Fino had found it difficult to know where

to start. Pontius Pilate was looking the wrong way, Jesus had neither a humble or dignified pose as he almost looked dismembered. He couldn't tell whether the dignitaries and the guards were deliberately ugly and swarthy or if that was Mastro Jacopo's taste. The hand of one of the judges was disappearing behind the head of one of the guards, making it hard for Fino to decide whether he was arguing his version of the case, waving or even slapping the guard's head.

Seated under the tree while laying the cheese slices on the fragrant and crunchy bread, he keeps looking at the panel from a distance: *what a mess*.

He breaks out of his thoughts and realises that Lionello has perched himself by him, eating the gruel from the orphanage.

'Hey, scribbler, you wouldn't share any of that, would you? They poison us boys.'

Fino lays a piece of ham and one of cheese on a slice of bread and hands it over to Lionello.

'Good stock, you are. Knew it as soon I saw you.'

Fino smiles. At an age where friends and family are more important than all the gold on the face of the earth, he has been separated from all of his. Lionello seems a sort of rough diamond. Very rough, but still a diamond.

'How's Mastro Arrogante treating you, my friend?'

'As coldly as he can, I guess.'

Lionello throws an earthy laugh.

'I'm no master of your trade but I have walked by his work a couple of times.'

'And?'

'It's a pile of shit.'

Fino smiles. He's learnt that the hard way. Despite his corrections, Jesus is still looking like he will never recover from a bout of polio. He had to add a beard to one of the guards as his jaw was almost disjointed. He had been told that Romans were almost always clean-shaven but he had run out of options, the perspective was almost offensive.

'How...?'

'Son of the richest merchant of Cremona. Fancies himself a Sanzio or the new Mantegna. Nearly everyone laughs when they see his work. I think that is the reason he was sent in the middle of this swamp to paint frescoes no one will ever notice.'

Fino laughs while covering his mouth with his hand.

'I can't be disrespectful. He's my tutor.'

'He's a pompous idiot.'

Lionello finishes his fare and turns to Fino.

'My scraggy camp bed is being moved to your room as we speak. Donna Giovanna has seen to that, you bloody wuss.' He shoves Fino's shoulder. But it is a friendly one, he feels it.

'Sorry. I'm not a bloody wuss. I've just never been away from my family.'

'That makes you a bloody wuss. Not to worry. The dormitory is hell. Cockroaches everywhere and my fellow orphans need a thrashing or two, the way they wreak hell on earth. Glad to share, mate.'

Fino proffers his hand. Lionello's shake is ponderous and rough, his callused palm holding Fino's with force.

'A word of warning, scribbler: I sin myself stupid every night. Till Kingdom Come. Well, till I come. Don't mind if you do.'

No shock on Fino's face.

'Myself and my brothers were at it almost every night too. Though sometimes we were just too tired, even for that. Do you tell Father Gaudenzio when you go to confession on Sundays?'

'Nah, don't be stupid. Just tell him you have stolen an apple.'

'An apple?'

'Yes. All the boys say the same. Father Gaudenzio is a trusting soul. He probably wonders how come there are still so many apples around if all the orphans are stealing them.'

He's had a good sleep. A short silly chat with his new room-mate before the vigorous theft of an apple skimmed off excessive testosterone and delivered them into the arms of Morpheus before the bell tower struck eight.

He finds Mastro Jacopo pensively perusing his corrected sketches of the first scene. He's nervously scratching his head. Fino approaches cautiously but he receives neither a rebuke nor an order to change it back to what it was. Messer da Cremona leaves abruptly and returns to his third panel. The day before Fino had managed to sneak a peek of his tutor's work and the falling Jesus was already on the floor. Or at least that was what the painfully incompetent perspective was showing. He was afraid to even take a passing look at the completed second scene.

Pontius Pilate is now visibly happy, strangely handsome in his anguished hauteur. The guards' muscles resurface from under their armoured breast plates: milky white, wiry and sinuous. Jesus' expression is already showing the onset of a calm and dignified response to the accusations, his soon-to-be cerulean pupils inquisitive, arguing for justice. All this before any pigments have even been mixed with water or plaster, let alone applied; it makes Mastro Jacopo's blood turn to lead.

Lionello is a friendly roommate but he's still Head Boy at the adjacent orphanage and Fino only sees him at the dinner table and before falling asleep, while they sin themselves stupid. Lionello likes relaying his fantasies about young ladies to his new friend who wisely does not relay his back.

After a few days of furiously correcting the drawing - he is now becoming excited about his panel - he stands in front of the long wooden table, laid with jars, powders, brushes and solvents.

He shakes in fear when he realises that he has forgotten Mastro Jacopo's instructions as he dreads asking him again.

He tries hard to remember the sequences and how to use the dry powder. He starts moving jars about while scratching his long black, wavy locks. No use. He has, indeed, forgotten everything.

He is too afraid of his tutor to go up and ask him, but there is no point for Messer da Cremona to keep an apprentice who has no idea how to work on a fresco. Besides, the extra funds from Rome were sent for Fino, his blood boils every time he remembers that.

He stand behind him with his hands on his hips and the usual envious anger.

'You have forgotten everything, haven't you?'

Fino lowers his head.

'I am so very sorry, sir. I have been concentrating on the sketches.'

Mastro Jacopo turns to the panel with a snort. There is no longer any trace of his unfortunate drawing.

The bile has been rising. He has dreamt of Fino's new sketches at night. They appeared in his hazy reveries mixed with the ones by Raffaello da Urbino. He had woken up with a scream when they appeared to be even better than Mastro Sanzio's.

He goes through the techniques with his apprentice again with a warning that he would not repeat all this again. Fino listens with nervous attention.

Two Sundays later the pigments are starting to drape the tunic of Pilate, the eyes of Christ have already turned a serene sky blue, almost half-grey, mesmerising. Mastro Jacopo is at a loss to comprehend how Fino could mix the powders and the paint so skilfully, creating hues which would stop a crowd. He sees him working almost in a trance, correcting some brushstrokes with his small fingers, getting covered in paints and powders, oblivious to anything around him.

And the results do, indeed, stop a crowd. After mass, the few wealthy landowners and noblemen of Isola Bacucco - very few indeed, no nobleman from the Venetian Republic or even Chioggia would ever venture to this forgotten swamp - gather in front of the first panel amid startled confabulating.

Jacopo da Cremona stands by, now a nervous wreck. A tall man of somewhat regal appearance turns to address him, his hand stretched towards the panel.

'Mastro Jacopo! I am at loss for words. I was fortunate enough to travel to the Republic to view some of Mastro

Vecellio's works, but this... well, this has taken my breath away.' He turns to his fellow peers with a sweep of his red velvet mantle. 'I say, *Signori*, happy to stand corrected, but this work is far better than any by Messer Sanzio or Vecellio.'

Hums of approval while perusing closely the details, no one is remotely interested in the second and third scene. Mastro Jacopo is close to fainting with rage but he understands that it is no use to lie. The other panels stand there, unharmed by talent.

He bows his head.

'My apprentice. Serafino. Fino da Ferrara.'

More stirs and frowns. They turn to each other, puzzled. 'Who?'

'A boy of sixteen. From the Estense city.'

The landowner with a red velvet mantle extends his arms in wonder.

'Sixteen? A boy of such age has done this? Are you making fun of us, sir?' Jacopo shakes his head. No. He is not. 'Where is this boy?'

'He's gone to lunch, sir. And if you excuse me, they are expecting me at the very same table.'

He leaves on the verge of tears, green with bile.

The winter is hard. The winds blowing from the Adriatic are sharp and relentless. The snow keeps everyone inside their abodes except for Sunday mass. There is no heating anywhere in the house except for a fire in the dining hall and it only flickers into life during lunch and dinner. Fino and Lionello wrap themselves in so many layers they almost struggle to turn in their beds. One night, when the temperature outside dips well below zero, Lionello jumps into Fino's bed and hugs him tight, before falling asleep. When he explains, a whiff of steam materialises by Fino's head.

'If we don't warm each other, we might be dead by tomorrow. This cold is the work of the devil.'

He has been assigned the fourth panel but not much work gets done over the winter months. The first stands finished and regularly admired by the mass goers.

The parish is hopelessly poor. The funds from Rome were sent for Fino's apprenticeship; Donna Giovanna and Father Gaudenzio are obliged to use the money to purchase material for the frescoes. The pantry has been stocked for the winter though and no one ever goes hungry, not even the orphans who - in the words of Lionello - continue to be poisoned with gruel.

At the onset of spring, life seems to come back with a vengeance. Maids are seen strolling by the parish again, the boys from the orphanage - fewer in number as Old Father Winter always takes the weakest away - flood the cloister again chasing ragged balls and breaking into fights. Fino and Mastro Jacopo are back to their panels.

Messer Jacopo by now wonders if fame will ever touch him while positively wanting to murder his apprentice every time he spots him applying a masterful stroke with maddening ease.

There are no free days. Everyone seems to toil all the time. After Sunday mass there is usually a good lunch and a long siesta but that is about it.

One Saturday, Lionello is in chirpy mood at the dinner table.

'It's the eleventh of June tomorrow, San Felice e Fortunato.'

Father Gaudenzio speaks without lifting his head from the plate.

'It is indeed. Chioggia's patron.'

'Can Fino and I go to the fair? Please, Father.'

Fino hasn't been consulted about this plan, but the idea of getting out of this dump for even a day elates him.

Donna Giovanna intervenes, while ruffling and stroking Lionello's hair.

'I can't see why not. There will be guards at the border though and it is a good hour walk.'

'We are not smugglers and we never walk anywhere here. We'll leave early. Please.'

Donna Giovanna turns to Father Gaudenzio and Mastro Jacopo with her usual earned authority. The household would crumble without her.

'Fino needs permission from his tutor and you both will need a few scudi to get about.'

Messer da Cremona is all too happy to get rid of his charge for a day and Father Gaudenzio's only condition is that they must leave early and reach the Adriatic town by eleven, to attend mass.

Lionello eagerly promises though he has no intention of wasting one hour of their wild day in Chioggia attending mass, let alone confession.

June is proving to be warmer than usual and the boys sets off in earnest at dawn. After a couple of miles a farmer sweeps them up at the back of his cart and regales them with an apple each. A real one, that is.

Fino enjoys the day immensely. He likes Lionello. They haven't exactly become the best of friends, but there are no alternatives and they have quietly entered an alliance of lonely souls.

They stroll between fire-eaters, sweet stands and a cacophonous array of more or less legal activities while chatting about stupid things, away from the dread of the orphanage and the - admittedly now exciting - fresco panels.

On the way back no good farmer picks them up but they don't mind the walk along the web of canals. The dusk is fresh, the scent of the blooming flowers lining the path soul-lifting.

The silence is broken by Lionello, hands in his pockets, a stem of grass between his lips, straw hat cocked cheekily on one side, gaze fixed ahead.

'Who's Ludovico?'

Fino stops, red in the face. Lionello keeps powering ahead.

'You've been reading my diary. That is dishonest.'

'Nah. You talk in your sleep.'

They are back side by side.

'A prince. The nephew of the Duke of Ferrara.'

'Wow. You don't fuck with us peasants, do you?'

'He is my best friend.'

'And I am the Doge of the Republic.'

'I don't want to talk about it.'

Lionello is unperturbed.

'Personally, I don't care. And you haven't tried it on with me in any case. You think about him when we steal an apple, do you?'

Fino nods his head in shame.

'Thought so.' He shoves his shoulder. 'Cheer up, I had a great day, mate.'

'So did I, thanks for taking me with you.' He pauses to reflect. 'I do miss him very much.'

'Yeah. I thought you had left a loved one behind. The brooding, the sad eyes. Mind you, there isn't much to be happy about round here, San Procopio is a dump and Messer da Cremona a right old cunt.'

Fino smiles.

'Lionello. The language.'

'Still a bloody wuss, you are.'

After a long pause Lionello is at it again.

'You're not the only one with a secret.'

Fino doesn't reply.

'Messer Serafino, as a painter, and a bloody good one as far as my ignorance can take in, you must constantly observe people, don't you?'

'I suppose I do.'

'Then I dare to say that you know.'

'It is none of my business, Lionello. It is bad manners to nose into people's private affairs.'

'You know then.'

A reluctant nod.

'I caught you a few times watching me and Donna Giovanna. When she stands behind me with her hands over my shoulders, when she ruffles my hair, when she worries about me catching a cold.'

Fino stays silent. Yes, he has.

'And your painter's eyes switching between Father Gaudenzio and myself, slowly studying our features. We only have one mirror in the orphanage but I have used it. Over and over. They were so happy when you gave them an excuse to let me sleep in the house. I was never allowed that. Because of the rumours.'

'Lionello, you can count on my complete discretion.'

'Oh, I know I can. You are good stock. You keep your mouth shut.'

Another pause before the long-repressed need to tell him overwhelms him.

'When it happened, they didn't have many options. Mother travelled to a convent near Vicenza and stayed for nine months. Luckily her sister is a nun there. Normally I would have been packed off to any orphanage of the Republic or in the Duchy and never seen again, but somehow mother's pleas got a hearing from the Mother Superior. Perhaps my aunt helped, who knows.

'To save appearances I was dispatched to the San Procopio orphanage a few months later. When I was old enough, they made me Head Boy. That gave them the excuse to have me over for dinner, though sleeping in the house was still too risky.

When they were younger they were rather handsome and people gossiped all the time about the likelihood of sinful activities. The Bishop of Chioggia once came to visit and asked to be guided by me around the orphanage. His eyes kept bouncing back and forth between myself and my parents. We were nervous wrecks.

'They told me the truth about a year ago. I was happy with it. The thought of having parents, even if they will never be able to recognise me as their son. But I know they love me and that's enough.'

He keeps staring ahead while sliding his hand into Fino's softer, more boyish one; the hand of a bloody wuss. Lionello is a boy for the ladies, and one who does not entertain an adolescent diversion. In any case Fino has never found him remotely attractive. Clasped together, their hands are bereft of any sexual intention, thus releasing a comforting feeling of mutual affection, the love which dares indeed to speak its name.

It would have served the ragged parish of San Procopio better to have been built anywhere else but *'Lungo il Canale'*. It is rather a malodorous waterway, its slow flow pulling along fetid, strange creatures, sometimes alive, more often dead and rotting away.

Isola Bacucco used to be the southern furthermost outpost of the serene Republic before becoming part of the d'Este possessions. It keeps being passed around like a used toy between the two, a pawn in their tug-of-war, disdainfully ignored by both. It is presently under the Duchy but that could change at any moment. Even the border is not regularly manned: Lionello and Fino were waved through by a visibly bored guard, keen to retire for a deserved nap after letting through the only two travellers to sleepy Chioggia.

Perhaps no unfortunate soul should inhabit this flat and far too vast piece of land. Any kind of agricultural enterprise is hindered by the quality of the soil, the mosquitoes and the unforgiving microclimate. The winters are harsh, the parish battered by bellowing winds from the Adriatic and sudden, heavy snowfalls. The summers are hot and humid beyond survival, with not even a clean river to splash in for a good, refreshing swim. The canal would see you dead with typhoid in a matter of days if you were so careless as to jump into it.

The boys of the orphanage are humbly resigned to a fierce Darwinian selection. In winter the weakest ones succumb to consumption or other seasonal ailments. In the summer months, malaria carries a considerable number of them to the common grave. Either way the undertaker's cart is a regular feature. Fino's throat ties itself in a knot every time he sees it parked across the cloister, outside the church's big iron door.

Donna Giovanna and Father Gaudenzio struggle to maintain anything remotely close to a decent nutrition as the numbers never seem to go down.

Every other day a basket with a screaming toddler is left on the steps of the church. Catching the young lady who is abandoning the fruit of her sin would be of no use. The poverty would very likely kill them both. From time to time, boys of any age turn up at the door. They don't ask for anything, sometimes they have no strength left to talk and they fall lifeless on the steps of the church. The Sacristan, a kind, worn-out old man, regularly finds some of the youths collapsed along the canal, their mouths not even able to open for a spoonful of soup.

They take them all in, though not many survive beyond their twelfth or thirteenth birthday.

The days flow away in the hazy backwater, each one hotter and hotter as the season progresses. Towards the end of June, both painters work shirtless as the cloister's ceiling provides little to no shelter from the blazing rays.

Da Cremona continues to seethe with bilious anger as the fourth scene progresses, possibly even more outstanding than the first, if that were even possible.

As he sees no more local squires or strangers from far away lands stopping by the frescoes, he is nurturing hopes that the works will remain forgotten as their location obviously warrants.

But not for long.

On a sweltering day in early July, Fino walks to the dining room to retrieve his lunch basket to share with Lionello, now the steady companion of his midday breaks. Donna Giovanna is aware of Fino's generosity towards her son and she regularly sneaks extra food in the basket.

After visiting the privy and diligently washing the paint away from his hands, he enters the house to find Mastro Jacopo at the table. He does retreat to the house for lunch, mostly to get away from Fino.

'Mastro Fino, your presence is requested at the cloister.'

'By whom? I've just left to wash my hands.'

'Two gentlemen are on site.'

'Who are they?'

'Just scram, you insufferable pest!'

He lands a fist on the table without apologising to his hosts. Neither Father Gaudenzio nor Donna Giovanna have taken to Messer Da Cremona. They barely countenance his arrogant hauteur. When they had realised that their son and Fino had struck a meaningful friendship, they had started to take umbrage to the daily mistreatment of his apprentice.

The gate of the cloister is open. A white and gold carriage stands in front of it, the type of carriage a place like San

Procopio has never seen in its long history. Quite a few boys from the orphanage are circling it, some asking for a coin or two, the driver shooing them away, visibly annoyed.

He walks towards the cloister and spots Lionello perched on their usual lunch spot, under the chestnut tree by the well.

He glances at him, perhaps asking for a hint. Lionello lifts his finger without moving his hand, calmly pointing at two elegantly attired gentlemen confabulating by the first scene. Fino approaches without stepping on the pavement. He stands still with his arms flush along his hips.

The older gentleman, wrapped in a richly embroidered silk mantle, turns and notices him. He lifts his stick, grabbing the ivory head at the top of it. He then points it at Fino.

'Young man. Do you happen to be Messer Serafino? Fino da Ferrara, as I believe you are now known?'

The younger gentleman hasn't turned. He's stooping lower, holding a magnifying glass in front of his face. Fino bows.

'Yes, Your Excellency, that is me.'

'I'm no Excellency and no need for the bow either. Messer Rucellai. Filippo Rucellai, Master of the Collection of His Excellency Piero de' Medici, ruler of Florence.' He absently changes into a sneering expression. 'If only by the will of the King of France, that is.'

Fino bows again anyway.

'And this gentleman is, of course, Mastro Sanzio.'

The young man is even more finely attired, his mantle cream white and embroidered in gold swirls. He turns, looks at the dishevelled Fino and returns to his magnifying glass. Fino is starting to shake.

'Sa... Sanzio? As Mastro Raffaello?'

'Da Urbino, indeed. You are correct.'

Fino kneels down.

'Young man, that is ridiculous. Stand up, please. Now, I believe that you are the author of the first and the fourth panel. Am I right in thinking so?'

'I... I mean. Yes. I'm Mastro Jacopo's apprentice. I can go and call him for you, sir.'

The laugh is subtle but sardonic, the following snort much more vicious.

'Please, my boy, leave that vainglorious fool where he is. We dispatched him there as we have no use for him.' He turns disdainfully to the second scene. 'And neither do these unfortunate panels.'

'Sir. He's my Master.'

'Messer da Cremona is master of nothing but offensive waste of precious paints. Have you re-drawn the whole scene?'

Fino lowers his head.

'Yes, sir. Sorry. It was... I mean...'

'The work of a cheese-seller?'

He doesn't reply. As much as he detests his tutor, he finds the two gentlemen far too aggressive in their condescension.

Mastro Sanzio lifts himself up and sweeps his mantle behind his back with a rather theatrical gesture, before frowning with a hint of suspicion.

'Mastro Fino, who taught you?'

Fino hesitates. Has Raffaello Sanzio da Urbino just addressed him as 'Mastro'?

'Mastro Filargiro da Ferrara, sir. I am very grateful to him, he did a lot for me.'

'Yes, Messer Filargiro is a generous soul. Although I guess it wasn't generosity which drove him in this case.'

Fino has no idea of what that might mean so he resolves to stay silent. He still doesn't understand what these two gentlemen are doing here, one of them the undisputed master of the time.

Raffaello points at the powders and brushes table.

'Pilate's tunic. How did you...? I mean, how did you arrive at such a tone? How did you mix it?'

'I felt it, sir.'

Mastro Rucellai frowns in wonder.

'Felt it? You mean in your heart?'

'Yes, sir. That is what I feel when I paint.' He smiles cheekily. 'But it's also good fun.'

Four eyes on stalks. The horror.

'Fun?'

Fino retreats.

'Well, it is of no harm to anyone, sir. I would love to be able to paint other subjects though. Landscapes... or... beautiful people. Why does it have to be Christs and Madonnas all the time?'

They laugh at the boyish sincerity. Mastro Rucellai points at the fourth scene.

'Show us.'

Fino picks up the brushes left on the table and after a quick preparation he starts applying brushstrokes to the panel. His movements are carefree and unplanned. From time to time his thumb gently corrects an infinitesimal detail, seemingly without any thinking process. Naturally.

'I'm working on Mary. Everyone seems to go for the pink

and blue cape, but I have decided on an off-ochre. Almost gold. I mixed four powders to get what I wanted.'

Mastro Sanzio puts a closed fist to his mouth, almost driven to tears. He has noticed the face of Mary, the unsettling perfection of the contours of her face. He moves back with a sharp turn.

'Messer Rucellai, I think we have seen enough. Thank you, young man, your work is exquisite. Farewell.'

Mastro Rucellai pats Fino on the shoulder.

'He means it. Farewell, and keep up the good work.'

Hearing that sentence, Raffaello darts a ferocious look at his companion while storming through the begging boys towards the carriage.

Once inside, he wipes his forehead with a handkerchief, the heat having the best of him, his travel companion now at his side, the carriage still stationary.

He frets in his seat, his face red, turning left and right in nervous anguish.

'Keep up the good work! Have you gone insane?'

He hits the door of the carriage with his fist, causing a loud thump. The driver shakes the bridle and starts cantering away.

'That panel. Not a single mistake. The colours, the hues, the shades. How does he do it? I have never seen anything like it, and that includes my work. That's God's work.'

'Mastro Sanzio, you ought to calm yourself. It might not be God's work but there is undoubtedly a divine inspiration. Excellence in art is either easy or impossible. For that boy it appears to be the easiest of tasks.'

'If this boy gets anywhere near Florence or Rome, we are

all finished, including Messer Buonarroti and his ridiculous attempt at painting.'

'Well, Messer Bramante and Mastro Ghirlandaio turned down the chapel to set Buonarroti up to fail. Which he will. He's always been more of a sculptor really, the lack of craftsmanship will show. That is what they want. But you, Mastro Sanzio, even the King has nothing but praise. No one is threatening your position in Florence.'

He hits the door again with a mighty thump. The carriage stops. He lowers the window and shouts at the driver.

'Do not stop, you fool! I was just banging the door!' He closes the window and covers his nose with the handkerchief. The driver shrugs and shakes the bridle again. 'Wretched canal. What do they keep in there? Dead bodies? Let us travel to Chioggia in haste, this place reeks.'

He's quiet for a short while then he bursts out again, furiously waving his hands.

'The perspective. I felt I was standing on the soil of Palestine. He's sixteen. Sixteen! If he decides to paint the Supper at Emmaus, the brats from the orphanage will be queuing up for the bread to be broken by Christ.'

'He is, I must admit, rather realistic in his work.'

His fist is about to hit the door again. Mastro Rucellai takes hold of it, lowering the hand down.

'Mastro Sanzio, please stop this. We'll never get to Chioggia if we keep ordering the driver to stop.'

'The boy must never be allowed out of this dump. He must never leave. Never. No one must know of his work.'

'Well, it might be already a bit late for that, I'm afraid. How do you think I got hold of the news? I believe word has already reached the Holy See. You know how fond of art the current Pontiff is. Among other things. Uncouth as the local squires might be, they can anyway spot a genius. And they are not that good at keeping their mouths shut. In any case, why should they? To please you and Mastro Buonarroti?'

'At least keep him away from me. From Florence.'

'I'll do my best. Mastro Sanzio, the peninsula, if not the known world, is awash with princes and dukes fighting over talented artists. There is space for everyone I dare say. Messer da Vinci was informed of the boy while at the Sforza court in Milan. Apparently he just shrugged.'

'You don't understand. He will cause everyone else to be forgotten.'

Fino returns to Lionello who has retrieved the lunch basket during the conversation. While slicing the bread he sees his friend a little stunned.

'Who were they?'

'Important people. Very important. One of them was Mastro Sanzio.'

Lionello's eyes open wide.

'Raffaello Sanzio?'

Fino nods.

'What did they want from you?'

'I'm not sure. They seemed interested in my painting. Not sure even if they liked it. They seemed angry. And arrogant. They kept insulting Mastro Jacopo.'

Lionello laughs.

'Bet they did.'

'He's trying his best, Lionello. Don't laugh at him.'

'You'll always be a bloody wuss.'

Donna Giovanna is at the well by the canal. She always smells and tastes the water before taking the wooden bucket back to the house. The well is indeed too close to the filthy waterway. She has just put the ladle to her mouth when she spots them. Dots along the cypress-lined path on the other side of the canal, slowly getting bigger and bigger, the standard-bearers at the side. She puts a hand to her forehead to try to discern the colours but they are still too far away, perhaps another two hours, and there is the canal to cross; the old bridge is narrow and rickety, possibly allowing only two horses or four men at any one time.

In any case there is no need to wait to know what power-that-be the long black and grey dots might belong to. She knows what armies do. Of any colour.

She drops the bucket and runs to the orphanage, hurrying the Sacristan to lock all the boys in their dormitories. Then she gathers the two painters, Lionello and Father Gaudenzio in the house. There is no point in locking up any door. It is an army.

They discuss various scenarios. Are the Republic and the Duchy back at war? No news ever reach this god-forsaken neck of the woods. Are they imperial soldiers from the north? The ones from across the Alps are the most feared. Their empire and emperors might be holy, their behaviour anything but.

They keep peeking between the curtains of the small windows. Eventually the stream of men reaches the canal, allowing them to see the standards. There is a common sigh of relief. They are all white and yellow and the coat of arms in between the two is unmistakable: Rome.

The Sacristan is ordered to open up the orphanage and gather the boys in the cloister. When the first clattering of horses' hooves is heard, they are standing in line in front of the orphans, Donna Giovanna holding Lionello by his arms, occasionally caressing his hair.

The Sacristan opens the gate and bows as what appears to be the Commander canters inside the cloister with four horse-mounted guards behind him.

He halts the small convoy by lifting his right hand and peruses the cloister and the church before even looking at the impromptu and bedraggled welcome committee parading respectfully along the dusty courtyard.

He dismounts, leaving the bridle in the hands of what appears to be his page. He then takes his gloves off and slowly walks towards Father Gaudenzio.

'A very good morning to you, Father.'

Father Gaudenzio lightly bows.

'Peace and joy to you, sir.'

'Thank you. Is everyone residing in your parish present?'

'Yes, sir. It is just us and the orphans.'

The gentleman takes a sweeping look of all presents before speaking again.

'Father, and all of you good people of the parish of San Procopio. We are the soldiers of His Holiness, Julius II. The Republic is threatening to again invade our ally, the Duchy of Ferrara. We are on our way to meet them with all the force of our army. I am in command of this regiment.' He bows with the utmost elegance. 'Farnese. Ferdinando Maria Farnese, Prince of the Church. Humble servant of the Holy Father. At your service.'

Everyone is down on one knee, bowing their heads. Father Gaudenzio speaks first.

'Your Highness, we are so honoured.'

'Please, good men, ladies and boys, stand up. Your faith and loyalty is rather evident. You have nothing to fear.'

He moves around, almost as to make sure everyone will hear him.

'We will establish our base here. For how long we do not yet know. Diplomacy is still working for a solution. The Venetian ambassadors are locked in talks in Rome, Ferrara and who knows where else. They tend to be everywhere these days. We expect neither foraging nor billeting. We have tents, provisions, and some good hunters. If anything, we will be generous when the trophies exceed the men's needs.' He moves towards the scrawny boys lined up in the background. 'These young men could do with a roasted snipe or two, I say.'

He walks back to Father Gaudenzio.

'We will be putting up camp along the stretch of land between your parish and the frontiers of the Republic. If talks break down, we might be the last to know. The Venetians are not to be trusted.'

He makes back for his horse but then turns, like he had forgotten something. He approaches Father Gaudenzio and whispers in his ear.

'Who is Fino da Ferrara?'

Mastro Jacopo, who's standing next to Father Gaudenzio, hears the question. He lowers his gaze and closes his eyes in anger. Not again. Not him. That insufferable pest.

Father Gaudenzio, once over the surprise at the interest

expressed, points his finger in Fino's direction.

He sees the Prince turning, favouring him with a look redolent of intention, the eyes searching, slightly frowning. He doesn't understand and he starts shaking in fear. What has he done? Ferdinando Maria Farnese knows his name. He sheepishly stares back at the handsome, rugged face, the dusty beard, the hollow and wiry cheeks, the wavy chestnut hair; and the eyes, as dark as a winter night. Yes. St. John the Baptist. Him.

Almost overnight the camp is up. These are soldiers by trade. The ranks are interspersed with mercenaries from all over the papal possessions, some barely understanding each other.

In any case they seem to be on their best behaviour. Travelling to Chioggia for willing young ladies is out of the question - the Venetians hold the city - but quite a few maids do the travelling themselves. The news about young, handsome soldiers and the silver ducats which go with them spread fast. Prince Farnese asks for Father Gaudenzio's understanding and forgiveness for the extra-military activities of his men with the promise that he will force them into confessing their sins. Despite his efforts, the poor priest's Sunday mornings are still tediously spent hearing the orphans stealing an extraordinary amount of apples.

Their sexual proclivity aside, after a few days some of the soldiers start dropping unexpectedly in both Donna Giovanna's and the orphanage's kitchens carrying hares, rabbits, partridges and all sorts of game.

They are good hunters and there is enough to go around. Some of the boys stare at their plates before even attempting to eat food they have never seen. Donna Giovanna beams with gratitude every time the hunters drop by.

The orphans have started to show fewer bones and more muscles on their tiny limbs.

Prince Farnese attends Sunday mass with his Lieutenant General, everyone else has to make do with Father Gaudenzio trotting across the camp, blessing the holy army. The local noblemen and landowners now attend the service in vast numbers: there is a Farnese in the front pews.

He's polite and gentlemanly though he keeps very much to himself and rarely smiles. They have yet to invite him for dinner as they are afraid to offend him. Besides, they have never met a prince before and are at a loss about what the etiquette would dictate.

The boys of the orphanage love trotting to the camp. They spend the afternoons playing with helmets, body armour and other military paraphernalia, the soldiers carefully hiding the most dangerous weapons away from over-enthusiastic young men.

Both the Commander and his Lieutenant encourage the mixing. Not just for the good morale of the troops but for a very good reason: recruitment. Quite a few of the inmates are almost of military age and captains and privates alike occasionally throw the idea around: 'You seem to like playing with that sword, young man. Have you given any thought to enlisting?'

Father Gaudenzio and Donna Giovanna do not mind in the least. Once they reach eighteen the boys have to leave and their prospects are always invariably worse than being a soldier of the papal army: petty theft for the strongest, starvation and abuse of any kind for the weakest.

Lionello is now almost always at the camp. As he's now sixteen, some soldiers are teaching him to ride and Fino has spotted him learning to fence, after trying on some body armour.

Two brothers of roughly six or seven years of age, Cosimo and Marsilio, regularly visit the Commander's tent. The soldiers are surprised to see the Prince smile and play about with them. He carries the laughing young things on his shoulders and, in his spare time, sits with them at his desk, teaching the brothers to read and write.

Days of summer haze away, brightened by the merry presence of the troops, full stomachs and, ultimately, the disappearance of loneliness.

The soldiers occasionally stroll by the frescoes. They understand very little about them, but at least they don't seem to tell the two artists' works apart, which pleases Mastro Jacopo no end.

Prince Farnese is playing with Cosimo and Marsilio when his Lieutenant General comes in the tent unannounced.

'Ferdinando, allow me a word in private, if you could.'

Agnolo Aldobrandini is himself a Prince of the Church and Ferdinando's brother-in-law.

He spots the corrugated forehead of his deputy and, after leaving the two boys in the hands of his page, he follows him out for a slow walk by the canal.

Agnolo stares ahead in an absorbed pose, hands behind his back.

'You seem to be very fond of Cosimo and Marsilio.'

He nods. As no more words are added, Agnolo presses further.

'Care to tell me why?'

Farnese lowers his head, hands behind his back too.

'You do know.'

'I'd prefer to hear it from you, to be sure that I'm not under some sort of misunderstanding.'

Farnese sighs.

'Very well. I suspect Cosimo and Marsilio to be the product of some unfortunate coupling between one of our peers and possibly a peasant maid or something of the sort. The names they have been given are of nobility. I find that strange. They also already have good manners and have refused to learn swear words from their fellow orphans. Their poise and behaviour reveal...'

Prince Aldobrandini turns with a sharp move, facing his brother-in-law, his glare unforgiving.

'It won't do, Ferdinando. It won't do.'

* * *

Princess Beatrice, Ferdinando's beloved consort is barren. Or so is what has been decided, as it always is. These are times where all the world's ills and faults fall on the ladies. Never mind the truth. A thuggish, unpleasant monarch of dubious dynastic legitimacy on the English throne regularly blames his Aragonese wife for not giving him a male heir. This world.

Beatrice bears the humiliation with stoic dignity and no complaints. Her father is always apologetic to the Farnese for having bestowed his infertile daughter on the most important member of the most important family of Rome.

It is no small issue. His sons would be destined to become

cardinals, Commanders, special envoys and, of course, Popes. The daughters would be dispatched to convents or married to the grandest families across the never-ending constellation of European aristocracy.

But there are none.

Farnese defends his beloved wife as much as he can from his family's contempt and, inexplicably to him, hers.

He knows, above all, that he's the barren one. If anything, the absence of a pregnancy demonstrates his wife's loyalty.

When still a young and handsome squire, Ferdinando proceeded to have sizeable quantities of carefree fun. Like any noble young gentleman of means, the trysts encompassed the full universe of Roman peasantry and nobility.

The rules of the game haven't changed. When the seduction of a young aristocrat lands a noblewoman in troubled waters, she usually disappears into a convent for a year, before resurfacing with some formal excuses. As formal and as unconvincing as they could possibly be, but that's hardly the point. The fruit of her sin is then swiftly dispatched to places like the San Procopio orphanage and never seen again.

In the case of peasant maids and other sorts of lower provenance, a decent sum of silver ducats resolves the issue and years later the little foundlings can be seen roaming the streets of the holy city, blissfully unaware of the cerulean blood flowing in their veins. As Prince Farnese rightly suspects, Cosimo and Marsilio might belong to such roaming stock.

While his peers had to regularly enlist their fathers or lawyers to arrange for a discreet obliteration of their impending offspring, Ferdinando's father had remained largely unbothered and not for lack of trying on behalf of his son.

Farnese had been as carefree - and careless - in his gallivanting as his fellow princes and counts, but no lady of any rank had ever come back carrying the fruit of their sins. As a reckless youth, he hadn't made much of it, but when the princely couple had entered their third year of marriage without any sign of procreation, all the pieces of the jigsaw had started to fall into place.

* * *

'I was going to write to your sister.'

'You will not do such thing, Ferdinando. She will refuse. And rightly so. How do you propose to introduce them to our respective families? They will be cast aside in horror. They are not blood. They are bastards, hailing from an orphanage of bastards. My father and I myself have already apologised profusely to you and the Farnese for giving you my infertile sister in marriage. We can do no more. But this is not the way.'

Ferdinando's blood boils at hearing Agnolo referring to Cosimo and Marsilio as 'bastards'; his affection had already started to grow beyond the point of no return.

He grabs his brother-in-law's arm with force.

'And, pray tell, what way do you propose? You very well know that it has nothing to do with your sister. I misbehaved as badly as you in my youth. I understand you have a few brats of your own running around the streets of Rome. Perhaps stealing or starving. No illegitimate blood of mine is anywhere to be seen.'

Agnolo shakes the hand off his bicep in anger.

'By convention it is the lady. Always the lady.'

His tone is almost one of fear. Men's fear of being lame. Ferdinando shakes his head in sorrow.

'And you are wrong about Beatrice. She won't refuse. I was planning to ask that young painter to draw the boys so I could show them to her. You are wrong, Agnolo, she would love them as much as I do.'

Agnolo turns away. In sadness more than anger. Perhaps, if it were down to him, he would rejoice at the idea. But it isn't.

'All the same, I beg you to abandon such plan. Neither the Aldobrandini nor the Farnese will countenance such effrontery. Blood is blood. It's not me, Ferdinando. You'll have everyone against you.'

He nods. Agnolo is sadly right. He won't ask Fino to draw Cosimo and Marsilio. He will not send any letter. There will be no heirs.

Quite a few of the older boys are now soldiers of the papal army. They have transferred to the camp, been given a few silver ducats as a joining bonus and provided with armoury and the rank of privates. Some of them have been spotted as visibly brighter than the serving men and soon they might be in for a little advancement. Fino and Lionello see them training with older soldiers, fencing and learning to ride. Lionello is invariably silent and brooding at such sights. He wants to join, that much is clear. But the other boys have no one and no future. He is the only one with a family.

On yet another hazy and lazy day - no sight of news or Venetian troops on the horizon - Prince Farnese hauls the battalion's secretary from his desk and orders him to take a ledger, a pot of ink and a quill with him.

When he enters the cloister, Fino and Lionello are having their lunch under the customary chestnut tree in the middle of the courtyard. Lionello elbows a day-dreaming Fino when the Commander walks in with the secretary in tow.

They walk to the frescoes and the secretary lays the small pot of ink on the marble bannister while holding the ledger and the quill. He then follows the Prince in his steps.

Farnese outright ignores da Cremona's frescoes and stands in front of the first panel. After observing it with slow and methodical care, he whispers in the ear of his secretary who almost immediately starts writing on the ledger.

They move on to the fourth panel, unaware of the two boys perched under the tree.

Fino suddenly gets up, handing his bread and cheese over to Lionello who in turn grabs his arm.

'No, Fino. No.'

But he walks over and stands to attention behind the Prince. When he turns, he bows with respect, receiving a light nod from the nobleman.

'Your Highness. May I know the reason for your interest in my frescoes? Your secretary seems to be intent in writing notes about them.'

Farnese turns back to the wall and with an expression which is neither unfriendly nor menacing, replies with an absent tone.

'You may not.'

Fino is incandescent. At the end of his teether. He stamps his foot on the floor, his voice louder than it should be in the presence of aristocracy.

'Then I won't paint anymore! That is it, sir!'

His first rebellion, and one he immediately regrets by sheepishly retreating with his hands clasped behind his back. At the shouting Lionello stands up, letting his lunch rolling away on the dusty gravel. The secretary, behind the Prince and therefore out of his sight, stares at Fino in shock while shaking his head in a friendly warning.

'Messer Fino, you are forgetting yourself. His Highness...'

Farnese waves away his secretary's friendly rebuke. He walks towards Fino and with his big, rough hand caresses his chin.

'Nothing to worry about, young man. Do not stop painting. Under any circumstances, do not stop. By the way, St. John the Baptist? Me?'

'My apologies, sir. I have no models here.'

'Honoured.'

'You are?'

Fino sits on the wall and let his head fall in between his hands. On the verge of tears.

'Forgive my insolence, sir. I always do as I am told. But what is it that you all want from me?'

Farnese's hand lands on his head, softly stroking the long locks.

'I'm amazed you don't already know.'

September brings much needed relief from the oppressive heat. The thick humidity slowly starts to dissipate, between gentle gusts of eastern breeze.

No Venetian troops of any description are anywhere to be seen, the guards busying themselves searching annoyed farmers and hunters for smuggling and other misdemeanours.

But these are soldiers trained for war and war is what they live for. Brawls are starting to break out here and there. Over the girls, cheating at a game of cards, rations of wine. Farnese has to rein in his brother-in-law who would like to make examples of the restless transgressors with some hangings for deterrent effect.

One day a well-dressed young gentleman escorted by four guards appears on the road from the Republic's direction. They are immediately surrounded by edgy sentinels, the tips of their spears nipping the necks of the unknown soldiers. The young man calmly raises his hand.

'I'm the envoy of His Holiness' Legate Consul. I am on my way to Rome with dispatches for the Pontiff. I understand your commander to be Prince Farnese.'

He receives due hospitality but the dispatches are clear: negotiations are continuing and his troops must remain stationed on Isola Bacucco.

Farnese adds a letter for the Pope, highlighting the restlessness of the troops after such a long encampment in a rather insalubrious location. The envoy will report but the order will stay the same.

The heat has returned as it always does in the first two weeks of September. Fino and da Cremona are back working shirtless, sweating and inhaling the fumes of the powders and paints.

His fourth panel is almost finished, Jacopo still working on the second, trying hard to learn from his apprentice's astonishing technique.

We covet what we see. Every day.

He feels the presence behind him and a whiff of breath reeking of wine. Fino doesn't turn when he sees the man behind his master placing his arm around his neck while stroking his chest. The speech is slurred.

'Captain Almerini, you must be the chief scribbler.'

Da Cremona drops his brush and tries to lift the captain's arm off his body but he's a strong, battle-worn man and he's a scrawny young painter.

'Please, Captain, let go of me.'

But the hold tightens, his nose now smelling his long locks, the tongue lasciviously licking his neck.

'Captan, you're drunk and…'

He can't finish his sentence. The soldier's hand is holding his neck, the sudden cold feel of a blade against his throat makes him tremble.

'I've had an eye on you for sometime, scribbler. I've resolved to have you as my rightful wife. One shout and you'll be a dead one.'

He turns to Fino with a bloodshot, murderous glare.

'And that applies to you, child.'

Fino looks on aghast and in horror while the captain grabs Jacopo by his hair and pulls him along the portico like a sack of coal, towards the back of the church, where no one ever goes. Where he can take him as his wife in safe hiding.

Da Cremona tries with both hands to free himself from the tight and painful grip but it's no use. Fino takes a decision in a split second. He runs across the courtyard to parade himself in front of the drunken soldier. Once the captain has stopped in shocked horror at his daring, he kneels and puts his hands together in a begging prayer.

'Messere, please leave my Master alone. Please'.

'Away with your whining! Your Master will please me as much and as long as I care to wish.'

Fino extends his arms wide, like a crucified Christ, opening the palms of his hands wide. He remembers Tonio's words.

'I am younger, whiter, and pure. My skin is softer than any young maid you might have ever come across. Take me.'

The captain startles. His grip on Jacopo's hair holds firm, though his arm is lowered, leaving the painter almost laid across the floor, now crying. Fino pledges with his arms forward.

'I come willingly.'

The soldier throws da Cremona against the wall. He knocks his head against it and almost falls unconscious. Fino turns and starts walking in soft steps towards the back of the church. The old, discarded paint table will do. He bends over it and in a matter of seconds he feels the dirty big hands caressing his hips. When they hit his hose, they pull them down with force, ripping them away. His callused hands are now grabbing his buttocks. He hears him gasping with deranged lust when the big thumb enters, causing Fino to moan and grab the edges of the table.

He's shaking with fear and for a good reason. He has no idea of how painful it will be.

In the end Ludovico had not been able to bring himself to go through with it. Despite his young age, the Prince's manhood had well and truly reached maturity and, noting his beloved's grimaces of pain when fondled, he had refused to deflower him. He had taken him in his arms and kissed his neck while whispering in his ear: 'I can't hurt you.' Besides, there was so much other fun to be had anyway.

He hears the sound of the captain's hands rustling open his trousers and he squeezes his eyes closed, fearing he will die of this. He feels the thumbs easing his cheeks apart and groans in fear.

The thud is abrupt and sharp, like something dropping on the floor. Some drops fly over his face and he feels the viscous texture of them slowly leaking along his left cheek and on the ground. Perhaps, in the excitement, he has spent himself and will now be harmless. He's still afraid to look but nothing happens and the grip of the thumbs has loosened.

He finally resolves to open his eyes and the wall is splattered with crimson streaks, his hand, still holding the edge of the table, dark red.

He remains still until he hears Farnese's imperious voice flying over his head.

'This swine will no longer importune you, Mastro Fino. You are now safe.'

He slowly turns and the captain is still standing behind him, Farnese's sword through his chest, blood still spurting in all directions.

Farnese withdraws his sword and the captain falls on the ground with a loud thump, while the Prince stands back holding his blood-dripping weapon.

'Lionello. Go in haste and fetch some clothing for the dignity of Mastro da Ferrara.'

'Yes, sir.'

'And remember: discretion.'

Lionello bows and runs away without further words. Yes, Farnese thinks: a lad of few words, that is what a Commander always needs.

Preceded by the Prince, Lionello walks a shaken Fino along the portico, holding him up with his arm. Jacopo is still sitting on the floor by the wall, trembling, staring ahead. He sees Farnese walking by and perhaps understands his thoughts behind the severe look he pierces him with: *If only you were a man.*

At the sight of their Commander holding his bloodied sword, the troops interrupt their everyday activities in shock.

'Soldiers. Captain Almerini has tried to commit a heinous act of which I do not intend to make you part. Only the prompt reporting of young Lionello and my sword have prevented him for carrying out his sinful quest.

'He deserves no burial on the sacred land of the parish. Agnolo, take four men and dispose of his body downstream in that fetid canal. May he rot in hell.'

After a couple of days and nights in bed, shivering and shaking, Fino is somehow back to his old self, well looked after by Donna Giovanna. He can't stop thanking Lionello, who had to shake Mastro Jacopo from his feverish shock to find out what was happening and, rightly guessing that he was no match for an army captain, had decided to run to the camp and alert Farnese. His strategic decision, discretion and loyalty have not gone unnoticed.

When Fino returns to work on his panel, Mastro Jacopo avoids any acknowledgment and keeps his head bent in either shame or anger. He doesn't thank him either for saving him from ravishment.

After a few days of thick, resentful silence, Fino parades himself in front of da Cremona.

'Master. I'm not expecting you to be anyway thankful, but I fail to understand your anger. If that is what is driving you to ignoring me.'

Da Cremona snorts in contempt before turning his face away from Fino.

'"I come willingly?"'

The second half of September brings along more rainfall and mud together with the arrival of another envoy from the Holy City.

The fourth panel is now finished and Fino awaits for Jacopo to instruct him on his next assignment, but da Cremona now barely speaks to him, unable even to peek at Fino's work without snapping brushes in two or kicking easels away.

One evening Fino finds a whole soldiering paraphernalia in his room: shields, swords et al.

When Lionello enters, he meets Fino's reproachful glare and sits on his bed staring at the floor.

'You are going to break their hearts.'

Lionello huffs, visibly annoyed at the scolding.

'Yes. But what am I going to do here for the rest of my life? There isn't even a maid to marry. And marry for what? To be dirt poor and have children dying one after the other at birth? What do you want me to do? The Prince likes me. Because I follow orders and keep my mouth shut. I can't become an officer, my rank is too low, but powerful Commanders always need loyal and discreet soldiers at their side. He will look after me.'

Fino stays silent. He knows Lionello is right. Deep down

he's sad at losing the only shred of a friend he had here. The thought of being left behind in San Procopio, at the whims of Jacopo's sheer hatred and with no one to even talk to, has him on the verge of tears.

'Worry not, Fino. I'm an ignorant peasant but I have a pair of eyes like everyone else. You will be taken somewhere else. Perhaps Florence or Venice.'

'I don't know anymore. Everyone orders me about.'

The following day Farnese knocks at the door of the house and he is let in by a bowing Donna Giovanna. Lionello is behind him, in full uniform, standing proudly to attention. Father Gaudenzio and the two painters stand up and bow.

'May I ask your forgiveness for interrupting your lunch. The envoy from the capital is staying at the camp. The papal Legates have reached an agreement with the representatives of the Republic. We are at peace. We are no longer needed here. As we speak, my men are dismantling the camp. We will be leaving no later than the second dawn from today.'

He walks towards Father Gaudenzio and drops a black pouch in his hands.

'This is for the parish. My personal token to thank you for assisting us in good spirit.'

Father Gaudenzio bows.

'Too generous, Your Highness. The Lord be with you.'

Farnese turns to Fino, himself standing to attention.

'Mastro Fino, you are ordered to Rome. You'll be travelling with us in complete safety. Can you ride?'

Fino is shocked but he feels a certain happiness at not being left behind in this forgotten hamlet.

'I cannot, Your Highness.'

'Never mind, we have carts.'

His hollow eyes meet Lionello's proud gaze before walking over to Donna Giovanna.

Farnese's intelligence was never to be insulted by subterfuge. A few days after his arrival, his searching eyes had landed first on Father Gaudenzio, then on Donna Giovanna, before finally matching their faces with Lionello's traits.

But he is a gentleman of the world who understands the consequences of temptation and the value of discretion. He is also known to be reluctant to swift condemnation.

'Donna Giovanna. We will make a fine soldier of young Lionello, perhaps something more.' He lands a quick look on Father Gaudenzio. 'You should be proud of him. I know I will be.'

They know they cannot hug him. They just look in his direction and detect the eager happiness at having some kind of a future, but also an immense gratitude for letting him leave.

Among the shouts of the troops getting ready to march, Fino walks to the camp after bidding farewell to his hosts.

Jacopo da Cremona sits alone on his stool in front of the panels, hypnotised by the haunting beauty of St. John the Baptist, enraged by the mastery of the execution.

Perhaps he will throw solvent on them, or - even better, he resolves - claim them as his own. *If only he were a man.*

Farnese is on his white horse, cantering around the now barren camp, giving the last orders, the dark clouds menacing rain.

With Agnolo at his side, he gallops along the wall of the parish until they reach the gates of the courtyard, intent on giving more orders to some unruly soldiers.

He sees them by the gates, Cosimo, the elder, holding Marsilio's hand, standing against the wall.

They both stop, Agnolo carefully observing his brother-in-law's reaction. Their eyes meet and Agnolo's still carry the same stern disapproval without even the need to shake his head. Farnese stares at the boys with a knot in his throat.

At such age and among such deprivation, they had never even really comprehended what a prince was, or how rich and powerful Farnese could be. They had dreamed neither of sumptuous palaces nor of unlimited riches. Perhaps their hope was just to be taken away. By him. Or someone else. Anyone. To belong.

Agnolo approaches Ferdinando's horse as the first drops of rain start to fall on the dusty trail.

'You ought to give the order, Commander. Time.'

Farnese takes his stare away from the brothers who stand still, asking for nothing, perhaps understanding that it is not going to happen. Amid the rain now falling fast, he raises his gloved right hand and looks at his soldiers.

'To Rome.'

Wrapped up in his cape, unsure of what awaits him, Fino peeks through the covers of the cart. Between the raindrops, and for the last time, he takes in the crumbling walls of the orphanage and the semi-ruined bell tower of San Procopio Lungo il Canale.

To Rome.

V. Painting Telegonus

By perching over the window sill he can take in the whole of Ponte Vecchio. The September afternoon light is sharp, ideal for the drawing he has been working on for days.

Tommy lies on his stomach on his bed, tapping furiously on his smartphone. Despite the size of the four-storey house rented by the State Department as the official residence of their Consul General, they are still sharing their room. This time Larry and Elizabeth were pleased. Tommy goes in and out of depression, finding everything and everyone 'weird'. The roads are too narrow, the cars too small, the mopeds everywhere, and the food... well, the food is cooked by aliens from another planet. He had found a McDonalds after the day they arrived and on the first family outing to a local trattoria he had perused the menu in horror, annoyed by Parker demanding to have every single dish explained to him. Larry and Elizabeth know that Tommy will struggle to fit in, at least until he start at the International School, so they hope that his brother will be of some company.

But Parker is hovering over his new adopted city like an infatuated helicopter, his enthusiasm and eagerness to fit in driving his brother crazy.

As he has another week before the year starts at the Liceo Artistico Leon Battista Alberti, he's using it to immerse himself in Florentine life. They have been here a week and he kind of feels Italian already, which is, of course, nonsense.

The whole family had attended the welcome reception at the consulate, just a short walk across the Arno. Parker had noted how elegantly dressed the delegation of local dignitaries and their consorts were. Tommy had stood in awkward silence, bored and embarrassed, while his brother had launched himself into conversations in Italian like a kamikaze pilot. He had been brimming with pride when the wife of the mayor had remarked how good his Italian was. As the wife of a politician, she was adept at shameless lying, especially to the son of the American Consul General.

By the second week he had already become a member of the Gallerie degli Uffizi and learned his way around the city. He had already walked to his new school, even if it was still closed, just to master the route in a dry run.

Tommy had kept laughing - at least he had made him laugh - and had remarked on several occasions that there was no rush for all that: 'We live here now, bro'.

To the relief of Larry, Elizabeth doesn't seem to miss DC at all. Always with a European predisposition, she is getting to grip with all things local, albeit at a slower pace than her younger son's furious one.

Larry's position and its perks help. The house is a Renaissance palazzo on Lungarno Guicciardini with a loggia in brick and wood on the top floor overlooking the river and the imposing cupola of the Duomo. It has a small garden at the back, but it isn't used much as the spacious terrace offers a much better view for a quiet espresso, lunches and dinners.

But it is decided that it will be Parker's studio for the

summer months. That decision sends him off on an excited tangent and after a few days an easel appears, together with paints, brushes and other paraphernalia.

The rooms leading to the loggia are panelled in oak, the long corridors separating them lined with floor-to-ceiling shelves filled to capacity with old tomes, folders and ancient volumes with hard threadbare covers.

The walls are dotted with landscapes, portraits and *Nature Morte*. Some are signed by minor artists, others are anonymous or damaged by the passing of several centuries. Heaven knows how many more have been stolen, sold or smuggled out of the country.

The three-times-a-week cleaning ladies and gardeners are from Peru, the maid a calm and obliging fifty-something Italian lady, herself mother of three children.

Parker and Tommy slowly - and happily - get fully to grips with the inexplicable hold boys have on Italian mothers and, being polite, respectful and well-behaved, they are more or less treated like two little princes, not even allowed to pour a glass of water for themselves. When Elizabeth, whose Italian is improving by the day, goes all-American and tries to explain to Signora Elvira that her sons need to start doing some chores and back-breaking tasks like emptying the dishwasher or tiding up their room, she is met with a puzzled and genuinely horrified expression of disapproval.

'But... they are boys, Signora Henderson. Boys don't do those things. Signorini Parker and Tommaso have to study.'

Welcome to Italy, Elizabeth.

He puts the black and white drawing in his rucksack, thinking that maybe some teacher might want to see it.

He's up at six. Unnecessarily that is, as the walk to the Liceo is no more that twenty minutes. After a light breakfast - they have no say in that, Signora Elvira prepares it and here breakfasts are never heavy - he's nervously checking he has everything that he has been told to bring for his first day.

Slicing through the hordes of tourists, he has some time to take it all in one more time. When he fends off a group of American visitors in a narrow street, he extends his forearms forward and shakes his fists in joy: *I live here. I really do.*

He stops in awe in front of the fifteenth-century facade of the school before walking up to the Headmaster's office. Larry and Elizabeth had volunteered to accompany him on his first day but he turned down the offer. He's unsure how being taken to school by one's parents at fifteen is seen here. He's vaguely afraid of being taken for a weakling at the very start of his four years of Liceo.

He introduces himself to the Headmaster's secretary with the best Italian he can muster, now finally afraid of not being fluent enough. The welcoming smile comes as a relief together with the realisation that the middle age lady has actually understood what he was trying to say as she opens the door and explains that the American pupil they were expecting has arrived.

He stands respectfully to attention in front of the huge desk, taking in the vaulted and frescoed walls behind it, not an Italian flag in sight. In Georgetown High there would have been several with the usual picture of the current President hanging on the wall.

The Headmaster, a fifty-something gentleman in an elegant suit welcomes him at an evidently slow pace, unsure of Parker's level of fluency.

'I will introduce you to your class. Of course we don't do this for everyone but I think it's best to highlight the fact that you might need some support with the language, although I notice that it has improved considerably since we last tested you when you applied. Also you missed the first year so your classmates all know each other by now.'

'Thank you, sir.'

He leaves and sits on a bench in the courtyard, waiting to be picked up and taken to the classroom. He's nervous but relieved at having understood at least seventy per cent of what the Headmaster had said, his calculation perhaps a bit optimistic.

Over the past few weeks, he had engaged his painter's searching eyes and carefully screened boys and girls of his age, perched on the riverside walls by Ponte Vecchio or strolling around the narrow streets of the city.

Elizabeth had then taken him on a shopping trip as he was determined to look like a local come what may.

'The shoes, Mom. Their shoes are always clean. All the time. I can't wear my grubby trainers. That won't do.'

Elizabeth had patiently consented to the attempted transformation, needless to say mocked by Tommy, whose trainers and jeans are worn up to the moment of their disintegration.

While sitting on the bench, he checks his canvas shoes and panics when he sees the first scuff on the white sole. He buttons up his new green Lacoste and just wishes he had a put a mirror in his rucksack.

A small group of chattering girls and boys walks by the bench. They whisper to each other and smile to him before walking up the stairs.

The Headmaster appears and they walk together towards his new future. Once he opens the door, a class of perhaps twenty or twenty-five raises to attention, the teacher at the desk greeting her boss. He softly grabs his arm and presents him to the curious crowd.

'Good morning everyone, please sit down. This young man is Parker Henderson, from Washington. He is the son of the Consul General and he enthusiastically applied to study at our Liceo.'

Parker doesn't know where to look, the stares are not unfriendly but over-inquisitive.

'Henderson has only been in Florence for two weeks, but we tested his Italian and we judged that with some efforts he will be able to follow the lessons. He is taking private lessons and he is improving. I'm sure he can count on your help to fit in.'

He points to an empty desk in the front row. He knew it was going to be the front row. Maybe they hope a bit of lip-reading will help.

When seated, he is greeted by the teacher. She seems friendly enough though he still doesn't know what subject she is teaching. He slightly turns to meet the eyes of the boy on the left who favours him with a friendly nod.

He returns it and when everyone takes a book out of their rucksack, he tries to sneak a look at the covers to get hold of the right one but everyone has theirs already open on the desk. The boy on his left sees him rustling papers and books in his rucksack and taps him on the shoulder while showing him the right cover. He nods in a thanking gesture and lays the book on the desk.

After ten or fifteen minutes, his heart, his formerly beaming, happy heart sinks into a well of despair. He struggles to follow and he hasn't even managed to understand what subject she is teaching. His hands start to shake.

When she orders the class to open a specific page, the boy again lifts his book and points at the page number, absently noticing that he might be on the verge of tears. Parker sees him raising his hand.

'Professoressa, can I join my desk with Henderson?' His hands open in pleading fashion.

'Yes, I think it is a good idea.'

When adjacent, his classmate closes Parker's book and places his in the middle, his index finger carefully travelling along the paragraphs the teacher is talking about. Parker turns.

'Thank you.'

On the first break, the boy pats his shoulder.

'Don't panic. It's philosophy, not that easy for us too. Must be a nightmare for you.'

'We don't even have this subject in High School.'

'Ah, that came out ok. Takes a few days. Just chat with everyone. We love chatting. My name is Marini.'

'Marino?'

'No. Marini. Cesare Marini. We address each other by surnames in schools. No idea why, but we do. Isn't Parker a surname?'

'In America it can be both. I know, weird.'

He sits on the low wall of the courtyard eating his panino in silence, vaguely afraid of being mocked by passing classmates. Apart from the boy no one has spoken to him yet, but he has just arrived after all.

The lesson in Pittura goes much better. There is less talking and more working with drawing and painting.

The teacher, a forty-something rather eccentric man, asks around if anyone has any drawings to show from their holiday. Parker understands that and carefully takes his drawing of Ponte Vecchio out of his folder. He ventures to impress the teacher after carefully building up the phrase in his mind with the best grammar he can muster.

'It isn't a holiday drawing really, I just sat on the windowsill of my bedroom over the last few weeks.'

Marini lifts his head and puts his thumb up with a wink, making Parker smile with justified pride.

The teacher takes the drawing in his hand and rebukes him without looking up.

'"*Finestra*" is feminine, Henderson. Feminine.'

He lowers his head.

'Sorry.'

But the teacher is now perusing the drawing in earnest, lifting it closer to his glasses. After a good examination he frowns at Parker.

'Have you done this?'

'Yes. It's only a sketch. Sorry.'

'We don't apologise every other word, Henderson. It's rather unnecessary. I'll keep this for the moment.'

He thinks the affronted hauteur rather pompous and

152

verging on the ridiculous. When he spots Marini mocking the teacher with funny faces behind his back, he knows he's not the only one with that thought. When the teacher leaves the boy swirls his index finger at his temple while raising his eyes to the ceiling, making Parker laugh.

On the second and third day he feels more relaxed. The private tutor goes through all the words and grammar he struggles to catch in class and Marini proves a willing help. He notices that small cliques have started to form though no informal invitation has come his or his deskmate's way and Marini seems to be a bit of an eccentric loner.

At the end of the week he can understand the Storia dell'Arte teacher when she orders them to open a specific book.

While shuffling the pages in search of the right one he sees a note.

Ciao Henderson, Patrizia, my WhatsApp is 3135785755. Kiss.

He turns to his mate while holding the note in his hand.

'The slutty hens. They've wasted no time. You got yourself a snog booked up.'

'Who's Patrizia?'

'Fuck knows, girls avoid me like the plague. Some stuck-up bitch. Face it mate, you're hot. And exotic for us; you're bound to pull like mad.'

'Not interested for the moment.'

Marini lowers his gaze on the open book on their joint desk.

'No. I didn't think you would be.'

At the bell, Marini stops him before he makes for the door.

'Henderson, the history Prof is going to get you on Monday, you know, for the *Interrogazione,* not sure you have that kind of thing in America.'

'Possibly. Sounds like the Holy Inquisition.'

'Much worse. They go down the register and pick one at random, but he'll pick you.'

'Why me?'

'He's an old Communist fanatic. He hates you because you're American. He made some nasty references to your country in the last lesson but you didn't pick them up. He made sure to use words you couldn't understand, the fucking coward. The class just winced. What a twat.'

'I'm dead meat.'

'More or less. But I'll help you. He's only done two chapters and it's the founding of Rome, easy stuff. He can't ask you anything he hasn't gone through in class.'

'My place or yours?'

'Better at yours.'

They walk to his house and are greeted by Elizabeth who makes Marini very welcome, relieved that Parker has made at least one friend at school.

They climb the stairs to his room, Marini flipping his head left and right in admiration of the frescoes on the walls.

'Wow, that's how the other half lives.'

'It's not our house. It's for the consul and his family. We don't own it.'

'Still, better than the Case Popolari where I live. Crammed and in the crappiest part of town.'

Despite the language barrier, Parker is learning to detect

facial expressions and the one on Marini's face is unmistakably one of mild resentment.

For the first time he also notices that Marini's clothes, despite being tidy and clean like everyone else's, evidently hail from shopping trips to cheap outlets.

They study hard and Marini coaches Parker the best he can on how to phrase all the possible answers. Mid-afternoon, Signora Elvira walks in with a well-deserved *merenda*, Marini's face now ostensibly resentful: a maid?

Parker, squatting cross-legged on the floor, understands and flattens himself against the wall, dropping his shoulders in exasperation.

'I can't help being the Consul General's son, can I?'

On Monday morning the history teacher pretends to flick his finger over the register on his desk, until he convinces himself that everyone is taken in by his pantomime.

'Henderson.'

Among a sigh of disapproval of the entire class at such a callous choice, Marini turns to him with the palms of his hands wide open.

'What did I say?'

He then raises his hand with confidence.

'Professore, the Headmaster has said that Henderson should be tested with someone else. You know, the language thing...'

'Well, you come out then.'

'With pleasure, sir.'

They smash it. The teacher simmers with undisguised anger at each of Parker's well rehearsed answers and his now more confident use of the language.

'Eight for Marini, but seven for Henderson. Because of the grammar.'

Among the howls of angry protests, a lonely voice echoes from nowhere at the back of the class.

'How good is your English grammar, Professore?'

The howls of disgust turn into roaring laughter which the vicious professor, now red in the face, struggles to stop. Marini winks at Parker. A wink of victory.

For the first time he realises that he might be popular, even if no one has yet spoken to him, though he is on his third note from a girl. They might not be talking but they clearly want to snog him.

Marini had warned him at the sight of another WhatsApp number landing on his desk.

'You better kiss at least one of them. They can become a little vicious if spurned.'

Once back at his desk he confidently turns to look at the rest of the class. For the first time, that is. Until now he had remained petrified in his chair, looking down at the book, writing notes, afraid of being mocked for, well, he's never been sure what for.

And when he turns right he spots them, between moving faces and laughing lips. Two glistening specks of coal, between bodies and flying paper balls. Enthralled.

He's about to bite his focaccia, sitting on the wall in the courtyard, his usual lunch spot.

He stops when he sees the jeans and the white Adidas Stan Smiths taking position next to him. He turns and the glistening specks of coal are still transfixed, searching. They belong to an angular face, contoured by longish, black, rebellious locks, the complexion smooth and bleach white, on top of a scrawny body, the chest disappearing inside an extra small dark blue Lacoste. By now Parker knows how to spot the *de-rigueur* uniform of upper-middle-class Italian boys: not a designer label in sight, only carefully selected brands. Very carefully selected and always impeccably ironed. We wear clothes. The rest of the world merely puts them on.

'Ciao.'

'Ciao.'

'Crivelli. Giuseppe Crivelli. But everyone calls me Beppe. No relation to the painter by the way.'

'The Annunciation?'

'That's the one.'

'Parker Henderson. But you already know that.'

'Isn't Parker a surname?'

'Also.'

'Your Italian is getting better and better.'

'Thanks. I'm trying.'

The conversation flows on to the contents of their sandwiches and other nonsensical small talk before the bell interrupts it.

'Marini did a good job with you. We can study together too if you want.'

Every time Parker looks at Beppe's eyes, he gets lost in wandering, delaying his answers. He seems to make Beppe smile. The reply is eager, very eager.

'Yes.'

The first afternoon is spent at Beppe's apartment in the area of Poggio Imperiale.

When out in the street, Beppe leads him to his flaming new Vespa Primavera. He extracts his helmet from the rucksack, offering the spare one in the small compartment of the moped to him.

'I've never ridden one of these.'

'I'm doing the driving, you just hold on to my sides. Don't worry, I can't drive like we do here. This was my birthday present and mother has made it clear that it will be taken away if I have an accident.'

He dons the helmet and hops on to the back of the scooter. Beppe starts the engine and Parker feels so Italian, he really does. And he feels Beppe's ribs, his hands gently against the bony torso, touching him for the first time while negotiating the narrow streets of the city. The sweet smell of his skin hits his nostrils, only an inch away from his neck. And almost immediately he has to shift backward, terrified, looking down at the unwanted reaction. He can't see Beppe. Smiling Beppe.

His mother is a doctor and both the area and the house reveal a comfortable status. Beppe doesn't mention a father or any other siblings and Parker refrains from enquiring. His upbringing causes a much more indifferent reaction than Marini's when Beppe comes over to the Renaissance palazzo.

When he takes him up to the loggia, he's much more interested in the painting on the easel than the breathtaking views of his city.

'What's the subject?'

'The leaving of Telegonus, for Ithaca.'

'Unusual. I forgot the history behind it.'

'Well, more mythology, I think. He was Ulysses' son with Circe. He left her island to find him.'

Beppe peruses the drawing as the painting hasn't yet started.

'Wow, a bit of a talent there, mate.'

Parker reddens.

'Let's go and study.'

They start to be the embarrassed targets of friendly banter: 'You two are like glued together!' Their pairing up doesn't deter the girls of the class who now propose double dates with them.

Parker, submerged by notes who now actually land on his desk in ball shape during lessons, seeks advice as he's convinced he's at the receiving end of angry looks by girls whose snogging quests are repeatedly ignored.

'You Americans have mirrors in your houses?'

'Eh?'

Beppe turns Parker around to face the mirror of his bedroom.

'We are hot. There's not much going around it. But you lot are not very vain, so you still haven't noticed it.'

'Do you want to go out with them?' - *No. Please. Say no* -

'Not really, but let's do it once. For fun. They don't want any sex. Most are just curious and want to snog an American.'

After a couple of weeks, his parents and Tommy enquire about his new friend at the dinner table. They regret their curiosity as hurricane Beppe sweeps in, leaving a trail of destruction in its wake: Beppe says this, Beppe says that, Beppe is always right, Beppe is wearing this, Beppe won't wear that. Now, Beppe would never do that. Beppe has this amazing Vespa. Beppe's mother is a doctor. Beppe wants to be an architect. Beppe here. Beppe there.

When he draws breath, Tommy guffaws.

'Does Beppe wear a Superman outfit under his clothes?'

'Haha, very funny.'

Elizabeth smiles, happy at her son's blasting integration into his school.

Unsurprisingly Tommy finds the International School 'weird' but he has landed himself a Swedish girlfriend, perhaps the daughter of some big shot at Ikea. His initial depression has turned into some kind of benevolent indifference which is, everyone agrees, better than perennial sulking.

'Let's invite this Beppe for Sunday lunch then.'

Next time Beppe is over, he brings his easel and the painting he's working on. Looking at Telegonus on the shore of Circe's island, now taking shape on the canvas, he turns to Parker with a frown.

'That looks familiar.'

'Hope it doesn't upset you. I thought you would be perfect as Telegonus.'

He goes over to the bannister, suddenly veiled with a surreptitious sadness, staring at the cupola of the Duomo.

'I am. More than I would like to be.'

He turns and winks, jolting out of a pensive trance.

'Let's go swimming.'

'But I thought we'd paint...'

'Never mind, let's go swimming.'

Say no to Beppe? Not in Parker's world.

Parker lends a pair of trunks to Beppe and they are off to the public pool on the Vespa. Without asking Parker, he walks with him in the same changing booth and start hanging his clothes on the hooks. As he notices his friend's near paralysis, he turns with a disarming look.

'No point in using two booths, no? We're mates.'

'N-no. S-sure.'

They see each other naked for the first time, if only for a brief moment before the trunks go up. Parker goes full red while adjusting the trunks around his excitement.

'I..I am so sorry. Being nervous makes me, well... oh no...'

Beppe smiles. That confident, reassuring little smile. Every time they part, his lips dissolve Parker's heart into molten lead.

'Hard?'

He lowers his head and nods in shame.

'Big deal. Leave you for a minute to come down. See you at the pool.'

He exits and walks through the showers. Smiling.

On the way back Parker's arms slowly encircle Beppe's torso, his palms sensing his flat, almost bony stomach, the smell of chlorine from the pool water wafting from his neck towards his exploding senses.

Taking that selfie was a mistake. Just out of the pool, Beppe's locks were dripping wet. His smooth chest was covered in sparkling crystal drops, his grin simultaneously cheeky and loving.

And he can't go to sleep whithout staring at it for far too long. Tommy shouts at him to turn the phone off, knowing that Beppe's picture is behind that silver light flashing up from his brother's bed.

Elizabeth and Larry fall for Beppe's genteel charm too, attempting to make lunch an Italian-only conversation. This proves difficult as Tommy and their father's mastering of the language is a way off, despite the private tutoring. Beppe's English, like that of many local kids, is ropey at best.

One morning he finds the desk next to him empty and he stalls in front of it before sitting down. He turns and sees Marini at Beppe's desk, furiously writing on a notepad.

Before he even attempts to stand up and walk over to ask for an explanation, Beppe throws his rucksack on the floor between the desks and takes his seat next to him. Parker turns to him, eyes on stalks.

'What the...?'

Beppe shrugs.

'He's asked me to switch. The Prof of Italian agreed. She's the one who decides who sits where. He seemed a bit angry, but then he always is.'

'But...'

He's hit on the head by a ball of paper from Marini's direction. After darting a worried look at Beppe, he unwraps the crumpled missive.

'Didn't take long to dump us plebs for your new rich friend. YOU'RE A FUCKING STUCK-UP CUNT.'

He turns white while fixing his big brown eyes on Beppe's. He turns the paper over to him.

'It says...'

'I understand what it says!'

He regrets the angry snap but he's too upset at having made his first enemy, and one who had helped him to settle in. He turns back again towards Marini, but he's still furiously writing on his notepad, perhaps another angry note to be rolled up in a ball and hit him on the head with.

His shoulders fall in dismay.

'I'll go and say sorry.'

'Waste of time, mate. When it comes to grudges we work in centuries. Pisa and Genoa still detest each other as the Maritime Republics they once were. Five-hundred years ago. Most of us talk of the Romans like their empire ended yesterday. Our memory isn't just long. It has no end. He will never talk to you again. And I mean, never.

'Besides, he's a little too angry for anyone's liking. I'm not saying that he helped and befriended you out of interest, but he has no other friends. He's a bit too intense on the class war thing. We get it, he lives with his big family in a council house and I'm sure it's a big deal, but this is a *Liceo Statale*. It's free, and almost everyone here is left-wing. We're not exactly billionaires. My mother is a doctor, not an heiress. There are a couple of pretentious and obnoxious little shits, of course, the two girls from Milan, for example. But they are from Milan, what does he expect? He needs to chill.'

'He helped me when I thought I wouldn't make it through. I feel awful.'

'Yep. Course you do. It's all that gold you have in there.'

He points at Parker's heart with his finger while winking in support.

His official dumping by the black sheep of the class seems to unblock an avalanche of sudden new friendships. Beppe is popular and his official new best and surgically attached friend is now welcomed into ever-expanding - and at times contracting - groups of friends. Most no longer even bother to refer to them as two separate entities: 'Ask Crivelli and Henderson if they are up for an ice cream at Piazzale Michelangelo.'

Between senseless chats and laughter, Parker's eyes occasionally catch seething glances from Marini, intentionally walking past another shining new clique. It will take a long time to get rid of the nagging remorse. Beppe is right, all that gold in his heart.

The core group of sporty boys - there is always a core group of sporty boys, America or not - is next to parade in front of Parker and Beppe with a menacing or friendly look, at that age one never knows.

The boy who seems to be some sort of leader holds a basketball firmly in his hands.

'Crivelli, the American boy you're glued up with. He plays basket?'

Parker turns to his friend in wonder.

'Basket?'

'Basketball, that how we call it here. Sure he does.'

The throw is quick, sharp and direct. The ball lands safely in Parker's hands. He starts bouncing it around the supposed leader who enters the game in earnest to test him. The ball gets snatched from their hands in no time.

'No playing basket in the corridors, how many times...'

'Sorry, Mr. Wilson.'

'I'll return this later, you bunch of idiots, Headmaster is around the corner.'

They thank him for the heads up and before dispersing, the leader of the pack turns back to them.

'Cool play. We need two new players in the team. You're in.'

After a series of 'high-fives' they follow the group to the basketball court, Parker lithely surfing a silvery wave of deserved popularity. He's in. Definitely in.

Autumn starts to wrap the splendour of the city with misty mornings, ghostly layers of fog slowly flowing over the placid waters of the Arno. The temperature becomes much cooler, sparking a very Italian rush to puffy jackets, elegant scarves, gloves and woolly hats. When Parker sees Beppe for the first time all wrapped up warm in his Moncler jacket, he opens his still short-sleeved arms in disbelief: 'It's twenty degrees!'

Beppe laughs while doing some explaining: 'Our fear of catching a "chill" is only marginally less terrifying than the worry of "not looking good".'

One morning he finds his classmates assembled in front of his easel before the painting class is about to begin. Beppe turns and summons him.

He fends through the small crowd and sees his drawing on the easel. He picks it up to read the red mark on the post-it attached.

'10 con lode'

Beppe wraps his arm around Parker's neck.

'Well done, mate.'

Parker reddens while everyone pats him on the shoulders in congratulations.

'He went to the Academia Delle Belle Arti to check you hadn't stolen it or someone else had done it for you.'

'What? Why would I do that?'

'Well, we do cheat here too, we aren't saints. The technique and the details are above the average. Way above. He became suspicious.'

'It's only a sketch.'

'To you, perhaps.'

* * *

After graduating from Cambridge, Mr. Wilson had briefly returned to live with his parents before embarking on the gap year he had missed between High School and university. As in most backpacking tours of the continent, Florence had featured as one of the destinations. A fateful choice in a way, as the travelling abruptly stopped when he was told by a friend already living in the city that a *Concorso* for the post of Professor of English at Liceo Leon Battista Alberti had opened up.

He was very confused at first, as he explained to the clerk that he wasn't a 'Professor'; however it was explained to him that it was the way secondary school teachers were called here. A copy of his degree was posted by his parents, he excelled at the tests and, before he could phone them to relay the news, he was behind a desk, facing a couple of dozen of unruly teenagers, his Italian still not enough to order a beer (not really true, that was actually the first phrase he learnt).

After the best part of five years and now almost thirty, he's still in love with both the job and his new adopted city. And he is by far the most popular teacher in the school. Still looking like he has never passed the age of twelve is of immense help. Visually, he is automatically considered "one of them" by all pupils, girls and boys alike. He holds informal lessons in the courtyard, puzzling colleagues and pupils with his propensity for pastoral care, a concept widely unknown in a country where family troubles stay in the family, at least until the police find a body under the floorboards.

His thin blond hair, angelic looks, freckly cheeks and round glasses bestow a gentle air of vulnerability which even the most disruptive of all bullies would find hard to counteract. His lessons are the quietest, possibly because everyone would feel guilty at wrecking them.

At the beginning he had tried to establish an all-English hour, but he had soon had to give in to the mind-bogglingly useless curriculum which involved a disproportionate amount of translation and didn't force anyone to actively learn the language from scratch.

* * *

His decision to appoint Parker as his assistant is a cunning masterstroke. Being diligent and now popular, he has formed a line of communication with the most unruly pupils, except, of course, Marini, who still turns his face away in anger every time he comes across him. There is a small drawback in the scheme as Parker uses American words and expressions which, to Mr. Wilson's annoyance, seem to appeal more to the class.

Mr. Wilson is the only teacher who walks around the class when distributing essays and tests, sometimes commenting in person about the grades, praising the good ones and lashing out in humour at the most disastrous efforts. But this is Italy and the humour invariably falls flat in either language.

Today though he is determined to have a bit of fun and leaves two essays right at the end, when he parades in front of Parker and Beppe's desk, favouring them with a severe look.

He lays the papers on their desks, while holding another two in his hand.

'Boys and girls, it would appear from his essay that Mr. Crivelli has suddenly mastered such knowledge of my native tongue to put William Shakespeare to shame.'

Beppe and Parker giggle as the game is up. Not that it unduly worries them. They know they are both Mr. Wilson's pets.

Mr. Wilson lays the other papers on their desks.

'And Professoressa Boiocchi had the pleasure to discover that Mr. Henderson's Italian grammar has now reached the sophistication of Alessandro Manzoni's; the subjunctive seems to have ceased to be a mystery to him, at least in the written form.'

He stoops near their giggling faces.

'She's not impressed.'

Beppe's smile is cheeky, the words even cheekier.

'We were bored, Mr. Wilson, and wanted to go swimming. And we thought we were supposed to help each other.'

'Nice try, Crivelli, but that's cheating.' He can't help a little laugh. 'How on earth did you think you could get away with it?'

Parker shrugs.

'Yeah. That was stupid. Are we getting detention?'

Among the laughter, Mr. Wilson explains that there is no detention in Italian schools and that they will shred the papers to avoid a trip to the Headmaster. The bad news is that Professoressa Boiocchi is going to have a massive go at them.

The paper ball hits Parker's head with the customary precision. They are used to them. They regularly fly in from Marini's direction, though they have stopped turning around to try to catch him. What's the use anyway?

Parker unwraps it and shows it to Beppe.

'Mr. Wilson's puppy dogs. Do you suck his cock together?'

Beppe shrugs.

'Now, there's a thought...'

'Beppe!'

In the meantime Marini's deskmate has hit him on the head with a ruler, tired of his relentless bellicosity and petty resentment.

'Get a grip, you asshole. Leave them alone.'

In bilious retaliation Marini tries to punch him in the face, starting a vicious fight which Mr. Wilson has to break up by expelling both from the class, to the dismay of Beppe and Parker who see no end to Marini's hatred.

He had tried to make amends. One day he had decided

to confront him in a deserted corridor, flanked by Beppe who was determined to keep his mouth shut, resigned to the futility of Parker's endeavour.

'Can you stop throwing those stupid balls at us? I've tried to say sorry so many times. Why can't you just accept my apology and become our friend? You're making a fool of yourself.'

Marini had stormed off, leaving Parker red in the face with despondence, Beppe patting him on the shoulder.

'Man, your Italian is almost perfect when you're angry. We're a stubborn breed. That includes me, by the way.'

Their little prank goes on the pile of the increasing amount of tiny moments which every day cement their now almost unbreakable connection. Except for dinner and night-time, they are never seen more than a metre away from each other.

The afternoons are Parker's favourite. He has Beppe all for himself. They lie on the rug of his room, revising. Sometimes, bored to distraction, they mock-fight or go for a ride on the Vespa, though the harbinger of winter and the occasional rainy day is making the forays to Piazzale Michelangelo less frequent.

Beppe's room is spacious and comfortable, his single bed tucked in the corner, his desk adjacent to the large window.

Parker goes through these afternoons fighting the usual reaction down south, while taking in Beppe's angular features; for the painting of Telegonus, as he explains when caught staring at him dreamlike.

But one afternoon the dam suddenly breaks. He is too close for comfort and in a lapse of judgment, while smelling his sweet breath, his lips quickly land on Beppe's, withdrawing almost immediately.

He stands back covering his face with both hands.

'Please don't hit me. I just... I don't know... I am so sorry... ok, hit me.'

Beppe slowly grabs his hands and lift them off his face, his eyes still closed, fearfully expecting retribution for his dare.

'Can we stay friends after you beat me up?'

But Beppe's thumbs are now caressing his sweaty, trembling palms and before he can reopen his watery eyes he feels Beppe's lips pressed against his own, his soft tongue making its way inside, all the way to his thumping heart.

His head lies sideways on Beppe's chest, his lips kissing his smooth skin from time to time, his thumb caressing his nipple. Beppe's hand is through his hair, his finger softly tickling the nape of his neck. The early winter dusk has started to wrap up this extraordinary afternoon, one that Parker will never forget.

'It wasn't your first time, wasn't it?'

'No. Does it trouble you?'

'No. I'm so happy mine was with you.'

'What was that nonsense about beating you up? I could never do that. Are you nuts?'

'I was afraid that I'd got it all wrong.'

Beppe laughs while flexing his lithe biceps in mocking fashion.

'That's because I'm so macho.'

'Sorry for the bursts.'

'You're kidding? Loved all three of them. Where do you keep all that stuff?'

Parker's turn to laugh.

'Don't know. Well, first time, got a bit excited.'

'Hope it didn't hurt.'

'That's how I understood it wasn't your first time. You knew what to do. But I would let you hurt me anyway. I would let you do anything to me.'

Beppe laughs again, as he has suddenly thought something funny.

'Why... I mean... why do they cut your willies?'

Parker joins in with the laughter.

'They don't "cut" our willies, they circumcise us.'

'Well... why? No one in Europe does that.'

'Hygiene, I think. Does it bother you?'

'No. As long as you still feel, well, me.'

'I burst three times?'

'True. Man, what a flood. Where do you keep all that stuff?'

'Stop asking me that!'

Their mouths meet again, the tongues on manoeuvres, ready for another tumble. The embrace is warm, soft. Parker buries his face in Beppe's neck, kissing it with renewed passion. He feels his lips kissing his hair.

'I'm so happy I feel like bursting.'

'Again? Where...'

'Not in that way, you idiot.'

The pause is blissful, the silence allowing them to hear each other's heartbeats, their soft breathing.

'Beppe, I need to ask you a favour.'

'Anything, mate.'

'Not that he ever will, but if Tommy asks you... well... I mean...'

172

'If I fuck you?'

'Yes, that. Can you lie?'

'Anything, I said.'

'Thanks. I don't think he has a problem with me, I mean, us being, well, whatever we are. But I know he would freak out at that. Something to do with protecting his little bro. Or wanting me to be the man. Maybe it's a straight men thing. I don't know.'

'I read somewhere that the Romans were a bit like that. They were ok with the ones doing it, not so much with the ones being done. And the Greeks. Man and boy was kind of good, two adult men, not so hot. Funny world.'

'Do you think we're gay?'

'Maybe.'

'I want to be with you all the time, Beppe.'

'Nah. Not enough for me. What about forever? Until we are so old we can't stand each other anymore?'

The laughs hide the tears of happiness at the start of a tickling wrestle. They slide under the duvet, holding each other tight. And the world goes a beautiful dark.

Late spring and they're almost at the end of the year. Parker has cracked it. His grades are good and he now speaks in English only with his Dad and Tommy, who are sadly still struggling.

Tommy has distractedly gone through some sort of United Nations of girlfriends at the International School, his fear of commitment only second to that of excessive physical contact.

Olivia is on her way to Florence without her boyfriend,

after a successful first year at Princeton. Jack still hasn't cheated on her though he patiently endures her long rants about all the affairs he never had with beautiful girls he never met. *Man, if only.*

When she finally draws breath and he manages to wedge a word in, he just says that he loves her, wants to marry her and that he's hungry, so, what about a burger?

He's spending the summer break in his native Montana, where, according to Olivia, beach parties with semi-naked, pole-dancing strippers are definitely a thing.

Jack frowned at that; he grew up in the land-locked, semi-deserted state, helping his dad as a farmhand between attending school. Beach parties?

Parker's 'Telegonus leaving for Ithaca' receives the now customary *10 con lode*, while raising a few eyebrows at the striking similarity between Beppe and the brooding Greek boy. But everyone is now used to the pair being literally a single item. Rumours emerge here and there but this is Italy, as Beppe explains to his inseparable companion: 'As long as nothing comes out, it's all well and good. They won't question. We are best mates and that's all. They like us as we are but they don't want to know what we do.'

And they do it. Furiously and tenderly, as often as homework allow, the wall by Beppe's single bed now needing a change of wallpaper. Parker can't help it. When Beppe holds him from behind with his arms around his chest, biting his neck between the vigorous thrusts, his fingers inside his mouth, he's unable to hold out for long and ruins the wallpaper just a little bit more, sometimes without having even touched himself. Beppe loves to annoy him with the now tired remark.

'I still don't understand where you keep all that stuff.'

Not being a couple makes monogamy irrelevant though at now almost sixteen, they still have no real opportunity to explore alternatives, though Beppe points out that Parker should one day try perhaps a slightly older boy.

As expected by Jeff, Larry is proving a diligent and conscientious Consul General, running a smooth operation at the Consulate. He loves his post and glows at seeing his family in a happy place, despite Tommy still missing America. But then, he resolves, he always will, no matter what.

The owner of the local *baretto* around the corner from the Consulate now greets him with a sunny 'Buongiorno Signor Console!' every morning, though he had pulled a funny face when he made the mistake of ordering a cappuccino after a quick lunch.

'A cappuccino is for breakfast, Dad.' Parker had beamed. 'Any other time of the day and they think it's dead weird.'

They are all genuinely fond of Parker's now inseparable companion. He is invited to family outings and they finally get to meet his mother at a parents' evening. She is charming and with a much better level of English than her son, ushering a few evenings together at some good restaurants, steering well clear of ordering cappuccinos after dinner.

They are becoming impatient at Parker's reticence at announcing the obvious but they agree in secret to hold back. It has to be the day of his choosing.

But it will never happen.

One afternoon, immersed in his homework at the kitchen table, unusually without Beppe and already suffering withdrawal symptoms, he lifts his head and looks at the back of Elizabeth, intent on cleaning and tiding up the kitchen cupboards.

'Mom...'

'Yes, Parker.'

'You know... Beppe...'

'Yes, I do know Beppe.'

'I mean... Beppe and I... we...'

She halts her cleaning tasks, holding the rag in her hands, standing still, staring at the Arno. She has built up a huge reserve of tender loving care for this moment and she's not afraid to use it.

'You guys need the big speech? I mean... the one they do in the movies? When they gather the family in the living room and all that?'

She turns and looks at him. Those round brown eyes, releasing what he still fears might be a shameful secret.

'No. There is no need for that.'

Parker stands up, petrified at having revealed something he never suspected they all knew. He stares at the floor. Still afraid.

'And I can stay? You're not sending me away? I'll understand if you and Dad don't want me anymore.'

She brings the rag to her mouth, sobbing. The thought that Parker had remotely contemplated that they could send him away hurts. She almost runs up to him and holds him so tight he can hardly breathe.

Winter is one of lazy afternoons, cocooned by the warmth of Beppe's room, his sometime smelly duvet, napping on the fluffy rug between scattered homework papers, hands clasped together, Parker's nose buried into his friend's soft jumpers.

On colder days, when frost or even the occasional flurry of snow paint the postcard views of the city with a light grey brushstroke, they walk to a narrow street near Santa Maria Novella, where Beppe knows a place serving the best hot chocolate in the whole of Florence. Scrap that: Tuscany actually. Well, the world. When we like something, we tend to go off a tangent of superlatives. When we don't, the object of our scorn is toast. When it comes to food and clothes, don't ever challenge us, we don't take prisoners.

Beppe is in possession of a rather awesome hi-fi system, crowned by a state-of-the-art turntable and a remarkable collection of vinyls, featuring left-wing song-writers from the roaring (and shockingly violent) 70s.

He also plays their songs on his guitar, mostly out of tune. Parker loves listening to him anyway. In his universe, between the four walls of that little heaven the bedroom has transformed itself into, Beppe is his superhero. Never mind a few (quite a few) wrong notes blithely murdering De Gregori, Guccini and De Andrè, local icons Parker is getting acquainted with.

Novelty has not worn off. And all that time spent indoors had brought on a wealth of quirky discoveries. All of them in a very organic and spontaneous way.

One afternoon, about to doze off after finishing an essay, Parker had found himself with his face very close to Beppe's foot. Without any thinking behind it, he had inserted his fingers in the hem of the sock and had gently pulled it off. Beppe's soft moan had heightened his curiosity and he had tentatively started to suck his toes, while uncovering the other foot with the other hand.

The moans and the heavy breathing were the loudest he had ever heard coming from Beppe and he had looked up in wonder. Beppe had been clutching his cushion with tight fists, his face buried in it, biting the cover, sweaty and flaming red.

Parker had caught his watery eyes with a cheeky smile.

'Boy, I caught a little spot there, have I?'

Beppe had gasped, unable to hold out.

'Mate, that sends me off totally crazy. I'm done.'

Parker had winked.

'Awesome. Because I like doing it.'

From time to time they had used his mother's bathroom as it featured a walk-in shower, thus plenty of space for fun games involving her ludicrously expensive Guerlain shower gel. Once, when about to step in together, Parker had made to turn back.

'One minute, I need to take a pee.'

Beppe had grabbed his forearm, dragging him into the cubicle with a mischievous wink.

'So do I.'

Parker's eyes had widened in willing disbelief. He wasn't sure he'd like it but he was unable to say no to anything Beppe would ask.

Beppe hadn't turned the tap on but had wrapped Parker's bony torso with his arms, kissing his neck, an almost boiling stream wetting their legs, Parker moaning in delirious ecstasy. He let Beppe push him down on his knees, the stream then flushing furiously over his hair and face. When up again and after a very wet kiss, he had reproached his idol in jest.

'You're a wicked sex maniac.'

Beppe had burst in a loud laugh.

'We are.'

'Telegonus leaving for Ithaca' had gone up in the corridors of the Liceo. Parker had been a little embarrassed, not by his success, but rather by the evidence of his adoration for Beppe exposed to every student in the building.

Beppe had spent an inordinate amount of time at Parker's house, now so loved and welcomed by the Hendersons that a functionary of the consulate had once mistaken him for Larry's son. Parker couldn't help notice that the misapprehension had somehow pleased his mate.

The basketball team had done well in tournaments between local schools and, hilariously, the two of them had one day been enrolled in the *'Bored Boys Club'*, a core of the sporty boys staying behind in the changing rooms after a match or a training session.

When Parker had asked what a *'Bored Boys Club'* was, Beppe only had had to shake his fist a little to make his friend's jaw drop.

'It'll be fun. No touching, it isn't sex.'

It had been fun. They were kept apart, perhaps intentionally, and Parker's knee got brushed by a muscular teammate from time to time, the 'no-touching' rule occasionally overlooked.

Parker had looked up to Beppe with a worried frown when the very same 'knee-brushing' teammate had stood up, without interrupting his activity, and had noisily dragged a bench in the middle of the room.

'Henderson is the bucket today.'

Beppe had just shrugged. Part of the fun.

Parker had obediently laid flat on his back until his initiation had come to an end, Beppe being the last to baptise him before he had released his customary flood, to the astonishment of some of their teammates and the envy of the ones with less biblical plumbing.

After a few seconds to recover from the exhaustion, he had sat up while bursting into a laugh, Beppe now in stitches.

'I can't see.'

His eyelids literally glued together and his eyes now stinging, he had felt a towel landing in his lap and started to clean himself up, elated at hearing another confirmation of his acceptance: '*L'Americano* is a good sport.'

Between dinners and receptions at the consulate, Larry and Elizabeth occasionally attend opera performances at the Maggio Musicale Fiorentino. The tickets are of course always free, part of the package of being the American Consul General. One night they take Beppe and Parker along - Tommy and opera are completely incompatible - and the boys make an endearing effort to look their best, bow ties and all, making Larry and Elizabeth glow with pride. At the interval, Beppe can't help whispering in Parker's ear.

'Boy, you're so beautiful it almost hurts.'

A few weeks to the end of the year and they are dreading it. Holidays will be spent separately and they can't do separation. Parker can't help but exaggerate things out of proportions. Together with the syntax, he's unwittingly acquiring a certain penchant for theatrical melodrama.

'I think we will die.'

'Yeah, not sure I can breathe if you aren't around me. What are we going to do?'

'A suicide pact?'

Beppe guffaws while shaking his head.

'Listen to us. What a pair of cretins. We'll talk on the phone every day.'

'Every day?

'I mean... every hour.'

Parker lowers his head in a well of sadness.

'Ok, ten minutes.'

'Five.'

'Done.'

But they laugh, knowing full well how stupid they are being. 'Dicks', Beppe says.

A few weeks before the end of term they enter the class and see Marini's desk empty. Another day of sickness like any other, they guess. They had a few themselves with various ailments and Parker sprained his ankle during a hard-fought basketball game.

But Mr. Wilson doesn't mention his name in the roll call. Parker and Beppe look at each other in puzzlement and then at the rest of the class, some opening their hands in wonder. No idea.

No gossip filters through and, perhaps saddled with residual guilt, they tackle Mr. Wilson in the corridor.

'Marini will not attend this school in the future.'

'But, why? What happened? Where is he?'

'Boys, I can't...'

Parker feels trembling.

'Is he... is he well? I mean nothing has happened to him?'

'He isn't dead. No.'

'Why has he left? Ok, he wasn't popular but I've seen worse bullying in America, come on.'

'Parker, Beppe. Marini hasn't left. Well, not of his own volition.'

They stand there, waiting.

'I am not authorised to say anything.'

Beppe intervenes.

'Then it must be bad. Bad stuff.'

'Well...'

'Please, Mr. Wilson. He was very angry with me, I must know if it is my fault.'

'It isn't, Parker. It isn't.'

He lays his briefcase on the floor and insert his hands in the pockets of his slacks, staring at the floor. He really loves these two, their endearing cheek, their inseparability.

'Marini has been arrested. For shoplifting. He was stealing food from his local supermarket. For his family. He's been taken to the Carcere Minorile, awaiting trial. It'll take some time here. He's admitted to it anyway. He said they were hungry, that's all. He's not coming back. Can you keep your mouth shut? Please.'

Stunned, they nod.

'Yes, Mr. Wilson.'

'Thank you, boys. I've always known something wasn't right at home. His mother is ill and his father a violent alcoholic. I tried to warn the office of the Headmaster but everyone is very reluctant to poke their nose into family affairs here. They didn't want to know. I gave him some money but with my teacher's salary I'm not exactly flushed with cash.'

They walk to the courtyard and perch themselves on the wall, staring at the tiled floor. Beppe is first.

'Boy, that's shit. He was dirt poor after all.'

'I feel awful.' He wipes his eyes with the palm of his hand.

'Don't cry. They'll ask you why.'

'Can we do anything?'

'Nope. No use, mate. He's been nicked.'

'Why didn't he look for a job? Can you work at sixteen here?'

'Yes. But perhaps he wanted to study. I think he wanted to teach. Man, with that temper, I don't know.'

He leads Parker away as he can't hold back the tears. All that gold.

Like most Italians, Beppe exudes an air of confidence not necessarily matched by his internal contradictions. He's happy most of the time, his smile sunny and infectious, but he can become obstreperous when in a brooding mood. We are a breed of our own.

Every few Sundays, Beppe is unavailable. He gives no excuses for the planned disappearances and Parker never questions them, until curiosity kills the proverbial feline.

Ice cream pit stop by the walls of Piazzale Michelangelo on a sunny day of May is a place like any other for a good old nag.

'You don't have to tell me.'

Beppe takes a large slurp at the cone, while staring ahead at the view of the city.

'But you want to know.'

'Well, yes. But you don't have to tell me.'

'I don't keep secrets from you. You are me and I am you. This is just a bit difficult, that's all.'

'Ok.'

'Now I have just made you even more curious.'

'Yep.'

He almost finishes the ice cream in big gulps, Parker noticing his nervousness. He disposes of the wafer cone by throwing it into the bushes.

'On some Sundays, I go to mass.'

'To mass?'

'Yes.'

'Didn't know you were a Catholic, I mean, a practising one. I know you all are. My mum is one.'

'Well, kind of. It's complicated.'

'Why a secret though? I don't have a problem with that. Why should I?'

'I said it was complicated.'

He jumps off the wall. On the walk down to the Arno, Parker has an idea.

'I'll come with you. One more thing we can do together. And not a wicked one for a change.'

Beppe laughs.

'Oh. I like our wicked things.'

'So do I. I meant...'

'I know what you mean. But we do lots of other things. Come on, our friends can't get enough of us. I'll think about it. Do you mind?'

Parker might not be able to resist doing anything his friend might demand, but, in his insecurity, he remains unaware that Beppe is as besotted as he is, falling asleep while holding Parker's hoodie tight against his chest, smelling his sweet scent, dreaming of him every single night.

'Half past ten, in front of the Duomo.'

'The Duomo?'

'Yes, that's where I go.'

He finds it strange. Why the Duomo? Santa Croce or Santa Maria Novella are much nicer churches, and why not one near his home? He goes along without giving too much of a thought. It's Beppe. His Beppe. He can't possibly do anything wrong.

Once inside, Beppe crosses himself after dipping his fingers in the marble holy water stoup. Parker doesn't know what to do and he resolves to do nothing and just tag along. He has never even crossed himself.

They walk down the south aisle and Beppe takes a seat just behind the first column away from the huge altar. Parker, noticing the empty row extending all the way to the nave, points at the chairs in a whisper.

'It's all empty, we can move along.'

The specks of coal open still, with a sting of reproach.

'No.'

Parker looks ahead in silence but can't help it.

'But the row is...'

'I said no.'

The mass is boring to the point of suicide, Parker fighting hard to avoid nodding off. When the incense is sprinkled around he's unable to stop sneezing. He's only kept awake by Beppe's odd behaviour.

Beppe sits upright, from time to time sticking his neck out. He peers at the altar and then returns to his position. He is quiet and sits still most of the time. He doesn't participate in any of the prayers and doesn't take communion at the end. If anything, once the service is over, he grabs Parker's arm and quickly drags him out of the church via the side entrance.

They walk in silence, both aware that Beppe's strange behaviour has created a crater of wondering between them. What was that?

And that is Parker's first question, one that Beppe ignores outright. Once they are near the place where they have parked the Vespa, Parker can no longer hold it in.

'I don't understand. Why hiding behind the column? And why hiding at all? We were in a church. And why go? You didn't do any praying, didn't take communion. You just sat there, peering out like a thief behind the column. I know you crossed yourself with the holy water but...'

He gulps when Beppe turns. The angry face. He has never seen him so angry. So upset. He freezes.

'Shut up! Just shut the fuck up! It is none of your business, ok? Why did you want to come along? Couldn't you keep your nose out of this one? You don't have to know everything, ok? I told you it was complicated. You come here and think this is all a bloody fairytale. We have a lot of shit to put up with, but you live in your fantasy universe, thinking that we are all carved out of a Botticelli painting. Just... I don't know... leave me alone... just... fuck off!'

He sees him shaking. He has just shouted at his Parker, and

sworn at him. He wants to die. He has hurt the human being he loves most in the world. He feels sick. Parker is unable to move and, not knowing what to say, he lowers his head.

'I'm sorry. You are right. I've been a nosy git. I am so sorry.'

Beppe swings on his legs, turning his head left and right, before staring at the pavement.

'My place.'

He hands the spare helmet to Parker with determined force and revs up the Vespa with a sharp turn of the throttle. You want to know? You will.

They take their shoes off, Beppe relieved to read a note by his mother informing him that she is on call at the hospital and that lunch is ready in the fridge with a spare portion for Parker.

He throws the note back on the table and heads for his bedroom, not a word exchanged.

'Sit there.'

He points at his bed. Parker obediently sits on it, crossing his legs and holding his ankles.

Beppe opens up his laptop and starts googling stuff, followed by Parker's wondering eyes.

He then turns the computer in his direction without a word of explanation. Parker adjusts his spectacles and looks at the screen. The picture of a handsome man, perhaps in his late forties or early fifties occupies half of the screen, the other half taken by a Wikipedia biography. He wears what it seems to be a black shirt with red buttons. His greyish hair is tidily combed under a red cap. Parker just reads the top of it, before the screen is moved away by Beppe.

'*Cardinale Francesco Maria Lambertenghi, Arcivescovo di Firenze.*'

Parker looks up with an inquisitive stare. *And?*

Still silent, Beppe comes closer holding the laptop by his face, Parker still very confused. He moves closer, his face now cheek to cheek with the photo. After shifting his gaze left and right, Parker lifts both hands to his mouth, his eyes on stalks.

'Fuck!'

Beppe returns the computer back to the desk and lowers his head, staring at the rug.

'You got there.'

A long spell goes by without a single word being spoken, Parker afraid of having stumbled on such a huge story, feeling he has no right to intrude. Beppe squats cross-legged on the floor, still staring aimlessly at the rug.

The first few words breach a dam.

'I found out about a year and a half ago. The Archbishop was invited to my Scuola Media and my class was chosen for his visit, speech and blessing; we had the best grades. Normal, everyday stuff here. I was in the third row of desks. We stood up to listen to his speech. He started with warm and nice words, without reading notes. After about ten minutes, his absent gaze fell in my direction and couldn't move away. He started stammering and losing his way in the speech while wiping sweat off his forehead with his handkerchief. Between every other word he couldn't stop looking up in my direction. I felt uncomfortable and started shifting left to right, nervously playing with a pencil I had kept in my hand. I had no idea of what was happening and my classmates were wondering too. I feared they would suspect some foul play, you know the reputation of some of these guys.

'He managed to finish the speech and gave his blessing in a hurried and trembling voice before literally flying out of the classroom, still visibly agitated. The first question was obvious: what was that? But I had no answer while assuring everyone that nothing had happened in the past, worried that people would start accusing him of stuff he had never done. I hardly knew then who the Archbishop of Florence was. Never been much of a Catholic myself.

'I walked home in a trance. I couldn't take those searching eyes off my mind. I had never met the man and yet something had started to creep in. Something I could not put my finger on.

'When I arrived home, mum was at the hospital, like today. I crashed on my bed and fell asleep for an hour or so. When I woke up I went to the bathroom for a pee and looked at myself in the mirror. I felt my heart coming up my throat, almost jumping out of my mouth. I fixed my eyes on the glass and slowly touched the edges of my jaw, the cheekbones, the eyebrows. No. It can't be, I thought. This is madness.

'But I ran to my mother's study and started opening all the drawers with a sudden fury. I was swearing at myself, at God and all the saints. The anger, the sudden, suspicious anger. I felt I was going crazy.

'The drawers revealed no papers, letters or photographs. Nothing. I moved to her bedroom and everything from the drawers flew out in a rage. I opened the bottom compartment of her vanity table and saw a picture: a few students on their graduation day at the faculty of Medicine. I looked closer and saw my mother in her younger days, smiling, the rolled up *Laurea* in her hands. Next to her was the then Bishop of Siena. Very close to her.

'I pulled the compartment off its hinges and lay on her big bed. I took the letters out and read them all; it took me the best part of two hours. At the end I had cried so much I could no longer distinguish the words.'

Parker hasn't been able to move a muscle.

'She found me asleep on her bed, holding the letters to my chest. She hugged me. She had wanted me to tell me for a long time but had never found the courage. She said she had always been so afraid to hurt me and the lie that my father had left for America before my birth had been the easiest path to take. We cried together until we fell asleep on her bed, late in the night.

'I don't blame her for anything. I have always loved my mother. But something had broken and we didn't know how to put it back together.

'I don't blame him either. People fuck. We do.

'Their correspondence told me the whole truth in chronological order. Their affair first, the love messages, the fear of being discovered. Then my birth, by a single parent.

'He has followed my life step by step. The letters assiduously enquired about my progress at school, asking if I was getting into any trouble, worrying when mum informed him I wasn't well and had missed class. Every communication ended with a plea for more pictures and more information.

190

My first steps, my first day at school, learning to swim, my first communion. His words were so loving but invariably laced with sadness and regret. They tore me apart.

'He has paid for this apartment. He pays for almost everything, out of a secret account. The hi-fi, the guitar. The Vespa is his last anonymous present. Mother earns a good salary and doesn't need it but I think guilt is driving him.

'I've never been sure whether on that day he had been afraid of being discovered or agitated by seeing me for the very first time in the flesh. He must have known that it was my school but his staff probably chose it for the visit and he couldn't get out of it. I remember smiling at him when he first turned his head and that probably caused an earthquake he couldn't stop. I remember now that his hands were shaking.

'We haven't told him that I know yet. Perhaps we never will. He might panic and fear that I'll do something stupid. On the days he's due to say mass in the Duomo I go and sit behind the column, careful of not being seen. I look at him every now and then, shifting back in a hurry if I suspect he might be turning in my direction. That is the closer I can get. I might be your Telegonus, but I will never be allowed to sail for Ithaca.'

'But... can't you...'

'No. I cannot. He is a cardinal. And the Archbishop of the city. A big shot. One day, who knows, he might be Pope. When it happened he was a bishop. The scandal would ruin him. His career would be over. Like any big shot, he has powerful enemies who would be only be too happy to discover a skeleton in the closet. And I am that skeleton.'

He finally looks up at Parker.

'In his last letter, he told my mother how happy he is that I have found such an amazing friend. To love and be loved by. My mother sent him a picture of us, you know, the one we took at the opera, in our bow-ties. He told her we are a pair of handsome young men. She now keeps him updated on our progress at school. Like we were brothers.'

He lowers his head again, the knot in his throat choking his voice.

'He said he's very proud of me.'

The silence is thick with the debris of such an explosive discovery, an orange sky intruding in the enchanted microcosm that their bedroom has become.

Parker stares at his beautiful friend, the fragments of his hero shattered on the floor.

'But how do you feel? I mean, knowing that you'll never be able to even meet him?'

Beppe drags himself up onto the bed and lies beside Parker who slides along behind him. He wraps him tight with his arm, hearing his choking efforts to hold back the sniffs. He takes Beppe's shaking hand in his. The amazing friend. To be loved by.

'It kills me.'

VI. Sacellum Sixtinum

As with all the decisions taken by the corrupt and inept papal administration, the order to return to the capital at the onset of winter had been a disastrous one.

The journey is slow and beset by inclement weather, the passes on the Apennines blocked by snowstorms and gusty winds. Two weeks have gone by and progress has been slow.

Farnese has long despaired of the corruption and incompetence of the *Papa Re*.

Cardinals, archbishops and officials alike are daily occupied with court intrigues, siphoning money away from the already much impoverished papal possessions and vying for honours and power.

The young Prince had always been a sharp critic of the way state affairs were run. However he soon realised that change would have been impossible without some kind of revolution which the apathetic subjects of the dominions were unlikely to organise, let alone win.

He had a taste of the entrenched state of affairs when he had tried to point out the faults to his father when merely fifteen years of age, receiving a vicious beating as a reward, compounded by accusations of being blasphemous and possessed by the devil.

To get away from the putrefied stench of the capital he had become a Commander, trying to improve at least the battle skills of a ragged and hopeless army.

The problem is that it is hardly an army in the proper sense of the word. Mercenaries from the four corners of the continent fill the ranks, making communications near to impossible and desertion for better paying kings or princes inevitable.

When battles are won, Ferdinando and Agnolo regularly fail to prevent their soldiers from burning down entire cities while killing, raping and maiming their inhabitants.

On this difficult journey, Fino endures long days wrapped up as warmly as he can in the cart, the rain dripping through the moth-eaten covers, the rations of food smaller and smaller as hunting becomes more and more difficult. At least he's not marching and Farnese, Agnolo and Lionello take turns in checking up on him. The summons from Rome came from the highest of places.

On departure, Farnese's page had paraded in front of Lionello holding the bridle of a decent mare, offering no explanation at all.

In thanking the Prince, Lionello had humbly pointed out that he would have preferred to march like his now fellow comrades. Farnese had patted his shoulder with a hint of affection.

'Oh, but they aren't. Aides-de-camps need a horse.'

He then left it to his page to explain what an aide-de-camp was.

Fino becomes the mascot of the regiment. He likes the soldiers. Some he understands, others not so much, but he has brought some papers and charcoal with him and starts drawing them in several poses. That makes them laugh and when around the fire in the evening they all thank him and sneak extra rations in his bowl. One evening Lionello finds him asleep between the arms of a burly Scandinavian mercenary who has wrapped him in a thick fur hide, while signalling with his finger over his lips to be quiet and not awake the 'little scribbler'.

The climatic conditions improve a great deal once they leave the mountains behind them. The march to Rome is now on flat ground, though still muddy and through poor roads.

They enter through Porta Flaminia, and after having left the men of their regiment in their barracks, Farnese and Lionello escort the cart until they reach the walls of the Vatican. They stop in front of an imposing iron door, the round handle in the middle bigger that Fino himself.

Fino jumps off the cart with his sack of possessions - he had to leave the trunk behind - and turns around to bid his farewell.

Farnese, absent-mindedly nods while Lionello trots closer.

'Good luck, my friend. Look after yourself.'

'Good luck, Lionello. Thank you for everything.'

'Done nothing.' He winks and smiles while shaking the bridle. 'Bloody wuss.'

He hears the knock resonating through an empty space inside and after a good ten minutes the huge door creaks open, revealing a priest of about twenty, perhaps a seminarist.

'I'm Serafino. Fino da Ferrara, as I'm called now.'

The young man offers no reply while letting him in and closing the door with a loud slam, jolting Fino out of his tiredness.

He walks behind the priest through a long corridor, the ceiling so high and dark, he cannot discern whether there are any frescos on it.

Once through a few cold and empty rooms, they reach a wooden door. The priest lets him in first.

'That is your bed. Bell at six. Mass at seven. Don't be late.'

'What's the punishment for being late?'

The priest frowns.

'Punishment? This isn't an orphanage. You and the other boys are apprentices. We are not allowed to beat you. Although some of that lot would deserve a good thrashing.'

Fino sits on his bed. It feels rather comfortable after all those nights in the cart or between the arms of burly mercenaries.

'You stink.'

Fino sniffs his shirt.

'Sorry, we have been travelling for nearly a month. Hard journey.'

'Any clean garments?'

Fino shakes his head and the priest joins his hands together in a huffing prayer.

'Follow me.'

He takes him to another room where some rudimental basins for the boys to wash are built in the unpainted wall. There is also a rather dirty wooden tub in the middle. The young priest kicks a scuttling rat away.

'Animals of the devil. Bath is once a week, same water for all you boys. With your arrival it's now seven of you brats.'

He hangs a huge metal bucket full of water in the fireplace.

'Exception for you today, as you stink like a boar on heat. Get in there.'

Fino undresses and jumps in the freezing tub, though he sighs in happiness when the warm water is splashed on his head by the priest while filling the tub. He then throws a bar of rough soap into the tub for Fino to pick up.

'I'll find some clothes for you. The boys do share anyway. Most of the time you'll be wearing your working tunic anyway. The Master doesn't take well to slacking.'

Before he leaves, Fino calls him out.

'Thank you, Father. I'm not a brat. I'm sixteen.'

He dons the work tunic and, all cleaned up, sits back on his bed, ready to fall asleep. Just as he is about to doze off, the young priest reappears through the creaking door and makes a gesture to follow him.

They walk through long and empty corridors again, though different from the previous ones. How big is this place, Fino asks himself, while realising that, except for the young man, he hasn't seen anyone else yet.

The priest turns back to him.

'Remember the way, I won't be taking you to the chapel every day.'

He opens another wooden and creaking door and Fino is ushered into a vast chapel, though one bereft of any altars or chairs.

He finds himself behind two rows of easels. Six boys of

various age are immersed in their work in stony silence. The chapel walls are lined with scaffolding all around, stairs and ladders allowing access to several levels.

He notices a huge wooden table in the corner laid with paints, powders and brushes. He's taken aback by the extraordinary abundance of material.

As the door slams back, the boys turn in unison. He stands there, not knowing what to do, unsure of whether they know who he is, though he is clearly meant to be here.

'Good day to all.'

No one replies and they all quietly turn back to their easels.

One of the boys in the front row leaves his position, walks up one level of stairs and calls out.

'M-maestro! M-maestro! D-Da Ferrara is h-here.'

He hears the steps resonating between the walls of the chapel. They are slow, sharp and determined. He moves forward and stands in front of the first row. The man now parading in front of him looks vaguely threatening. His tunic is very fitted, covered in paint, the eyes hollow and searching, the beard jungly and profuse, the hands big and holding his hips in a challenging poise.

'So. This is Da Ferrara. Fino da Ferrara.'

He bows.

'At your service, sir.'

'You certainly are, young man. Now, I am told that you have spent the last year or so painting frescoes in some god-forsaken hamlet in the north.'

'Yes, sir. My Master was Jacopo da Cremona.'

His disdainful laugh is as booming as vicious, the sneering from the boys equally contemptuous.

'What has the good city of Cremona done to deserve such an inept imbecile, I will never know. Hope you haven't un-learned anything mastered under Mastro Filargiro, that good man.'

'I finished two panels in the cloister, sir.'

'Probably the only two not deserving a good dose of solvent.'

Fino doesn't reply, well aware of Jacopo's talentless ineptitude, though still uncomfortable at the callous derision it elicits.

'Very well. These reprobates are your fellow apprentices. You'll get to know them in good time. They will undoubtedly inform you of my revulsion to laziness and lack of concentration. Everyone here works hard.'

'Yes, sir.'

'To work then.'

Fino turns and slowly scans the rows of easels. He finds an empty one and positions himself in front of it, though he notices that a semi-finished work is already on it. He turns and sees the stammering boy shaking his head.

'Th-that isn't y-y-your place.'

He looks at Buonarroti who theatrically waves his hand, pointing at a ladder on the left hand side.

All the boys are watching him in silence. He walks over and sees a huge panel on the first level, painted cream white.

'Word has preceded your arrival, Mastro Fino. That is your panel.'

Fino gulps.

'It's very large, sir.'

'And?'

He gulps again. Now very frightened. Michelangelo Buonarroti allows no dissent.

'What would you like me to paint, sir?'

'Your choice. Take a good look at the other panels. You don't want to replicate any scene. Let me know.'

He looks back at the boys and sees their open mouths. Mastro Buonarroti loudly claps his hands.

'To work now!'

They dive back into work. Fino starts walking around the vast room.

After a tour, he tries to find a subject. He has never been told to choose a scene, he has always been told what to paint. He moves under the main scaffolding, the one which leads to the ceiling.

'Sir. Sir.'

The stammering boy walks behind him.

'Y-You have t-to shout. I-It's v-very high.'

Once Buonarroti has descended the stairs, Fino is reduced to stammering himself, the man scares him.

'P-Perhaps, s-sir, Cain and Abel? I haven't seen any panels with that subject.'

Michelangelo looks around and nods.

'Sounds like a good idea. They are not my work, these panels. You might have noticed that.'

'Yes, sir.'

He walks up the ladder and starts taking in the size of the panel. He moves around to find the perspective but when he touches it, he freezes. He walks back down to the stammering boy. He's not sure why but he is the only one who has talked to him.

'The paint is not entirely dry, I can't draw on it yet.'

He notices the other boys turning their heads at each other with suspicious, fearful looks.

'H-e had m-me paint o-over it. I-It was a w-work by M-messer Bramante. B-but they d-detest each other.'

'But it's still fresh.'

'H-He knows. H-He is t-testing you.'

Fino moves to walk away but the boy grabs his forearm, his small, cerulean eyes pleading.

'D-Don't a-argue with him. P-Please.'

He had fallen asleep before dusk, the exhaustion having the better of him. He had heard the chattering and banter of the other boys for no more than five minutes before passing out still in his tunic. He had been left in that position for the whole night.

After a quick wash among riotous splashing, breakfast turns out to be decent fare. The milk is warm and so is the bread. There is fruit, butter and some slices of crostata di mele, which are raided by the other boys before Fino can even get near them.

When he's up on the scaffolding he touches the panel and he's relieved to feel that it's finally dry. He walks down to the table for some charcoals.

He thinks intensely in front of the white canvas, then walks back to the other side of the chapel, using his hands to size the perspective. The boys are staring at him and notice that he's not using the brush in his hand to take measurements.

He stops drawing for a moment and turns his head

towards the easels. All the stalking eyes brusquely lower and hide behind the canvasses.

Only the stammering boy keeps looking at him and for the first time he notices his breath-stopping beauty. The flaxen long locks, the rosy, almost blue complexion, the sky blue small pupils, the thin lips, gently protruding forward when negotiating the next stammer.

During the break, after he has finished his bread and cheese, he walks up to the boy's canvas. A voice distracts him from his perusal.

'Y-you can be h-honest.'

'I... well...'

'I-I know.'

Fino points at the nose of the Archangel Gabriel.

'Perhaps, if you... well... he's supposed to look at Mary... I don't know...'

'It's a m-mess. I'm n-no g-good.'

'I didn't say that. What is your name?'

'L-Lorenzo. C-called *Lorenzino*.'

'Da?'

'Da n-nothing.' And he darts an explanatory look at his canvas. Fino extends his hand.

'Friends?'

Lorenzino smiles warily, his eyes rolling left and right, as of checking the reaction of his fellow apprentices before shaking it.

'F-Friends. S-Sorry if it t-takes so l-long to t-talk to me. N-No one ever s-speaks to me. T-they lose p-patience.'

'Your looks are not of our race, if I may say.'

'No. A m-mercenary from t-the lands w-where the snow

n-never melts. M-Mother too.'

'Where are they now?'

Lorenzino opens his arms in resigned wonder. Perhaps back among tribes of flaxen hair.

He sits back on the stool, before Fino makes to return to his panel.

'W-We have h-heard about you. B-Be careful.'

Cain and Abel start to take shape on the canvas, Fino working with both charcoals in his hands, using his thumbs, turning back to gaze at Lorenzino.

After supper he sits on his bed, updating his diary. He raises his head and scans the small dormitory. Some boys walk about, some play games with dice and marbles. The boy in the next bed lies on his back, munching a piece of bread.

'He doesn't sleep in the dormitory.'

Fino turns.

'Where does he sleep?'

The boy sits up and with his index finger points at the ceiling.

'I don't...'

'Don't play stupid. You've seen his canvas. He has no talent whatsoever. He can't paint to save his life. This is Mastro Buonarroti's workshop, we are here because we are the best of the land. Well, until your arrival, that is. But there are other ways to survive in this wretched city.'

'That is harsh. He only needs to make a few corrections.'

'Liar.'

The boy comes around and sits by Fino.

'I'm Maturino. *Maturino da Firenze.*'

'You know my name.'

'It's on many lips.' He takes a bite of his bread. 'He's his property. That's why he's still here. Don't even think about it. He's untouchable. We can be passed around between princes and cardinals like lambs to the slaughter but Lorenzino is his. And his only.'

'I wasn't thinking that way. I like him, that's all.'

'All the same. I've seen your early drawings on the panel.'

'What do you think?'

He lays a switchblade knife in Fino's hand.

'I think you might need this in the future.'

The young priest was right, this isn't an orphanage. A few rats aside, it is relatively clean, the beds comfortable and the portions at supper abundant, the food fresh and nutritious.

Fino asks Maturino if they are allowed to go and see the city and again it is explained to him that he's not imprisoned, they can come and go as they please, though Mastro Buonarroti considers even a few idle hours as wasted.

'The Lord doesn't like us working on Sundays, Maturino.'

'The Lord doesn't think he's Michelangelo.'

He immerses himself in his work and it starts to absorb him, the size of the panel no longer intimidating him. He works hard, jumping on and off the stairs to walk to the other side of the room to check his progress.

On the third night, while he's sitting on the side of his bed, updating his diary as usual, a swarthy, round-faced boy in a night shirt parades in front of him.

Fino lifts his head, his eyes wide.

'I'm Caramuele. *Caramuele da Pescara.*'

'Where is Pescara?'

He hears Maturino's voice, muffled by the bread which he always seems to be munching.

'In hell. Where it belongs.'

The boy ignores him.

'I'm the best apprentice here.'

Another intervention between the bread-munching.

'Second-best now.'

He ignores him again.

'You are the new boy. You will please me as the rules have it.'

Fino doesn't understand, until the boy walks over to the last candle flickering on the wall and blows it off. Then returns to the bed, lifts his night-shirt and, by grabbing Fino's locks with both hands, he makes his entry. Fino gags but he has no strength to push him away. Caramuele gasps and spends himself after only a few thrusts, excited by his new trophy.

Fino falls on the floor coughing and spitting, while Caramuele walks away. Maturino hasn't moved.

Every night he has to endure the same ordeal. On the third, hearing him crying himself to sleep once again, Maturino comes around and sits by him.

'You can say no. He's just a bully. Where is the knife I gave you?'

'I... I am not very good at... these kind of things...'

'Lord. Very well. Leave it to me.'

At the big breakfast table Maturino takes his place beside Fino and, after drinking his milk, he lays his dirty napkin on the table. Then he starts touching and weighing the apples in the big wicker basket in the middle. After selecting a few he lays them in the middle of the napkin and closes it up with a tight knot. Fino watches this odd preparation in silence.

Silently he walks to the other end of the table and stops behind Da Pescara.

'Caramuele.'

Da Pescara turns and the swing is so sharp and violent that he falls immediately onto the floor, his hands holding his face in pain. The priest in charge of the refectory moves to separate them but a blade flickers in Maturino's left hand, the right still holding the sack of apples.

'Go away, we are not your charges.'

Da Pescara moves to fight back, but Maturino swings the sack of apples in such a confident and strong fashion, Caramuele is catapulted to the other side of the room. The boys have stopped eating, Fino is speechless.

After hitting him a third and fourth time, Caramuele's lips are bleeding and so is his ear, the eye socket already purple. He gives up trying to fight back and pleads for mercy. Maturino unties the knot and the apples rumble over Caramuele's head, rolling away to the four corners of the refectory. He folds the knife close.

'Wank yourself dry like everyone else.'

He turns and with a few steps he's back at Fino's side with Caramuele's plate. He places in front of Fino while still munching on his bread.

'You can have Da Pescara's apple tart today. He's not hungry.'

After a few days, Fino collects all of his chalks and walks over to Lorenzino.

'I have finished the drawing, could you show me which paints and powder I am allowed to use? I don't want to use Mastro Buonarroti's by mistake.'

There is no answer. One by one all the boys leave their positions and slowly walk to the panel, their jaws dropping one after the other.

Fino joins them and, puzzled, shows the palms of his now multi-coloured hands.

'What?'

Maturino turns, clocking Fino's wondering gaze.

'I've never seen anything like this.'

They hear the steps, slow and determined as always.

'What's the meaning of all this?'

'M-mastro F-Fino has f-finished the d-drawing, sir.'

Buonarroti turns and freezes. He says nothing while walking up the scaffolding and slowly scanning the whole scene. He turns and from atop the ladder he shouts in an angry voice.

'Very well, you have seen it. Now back to work.'

Once on the floor he stands in front of Fino in silence, his hollow eyes scrutinising him. Then he turns and kicks a can of paint with hysterical force against the wall, the contents leaking out onto the floor. The boys scamper back to their easels terrified. Fino stands there, perhaps understanding a little, though exhausted. Everyone always seems to be so angry with him.

Lorenzino, Fino and Maturino go to town on a Sunday afternoon. They have attended mass and had lunch in the refectory. Buonarroti has given them an afternoon of freedom, the nights far too dangerous anyway.

They saunter along the uneven streets of the crumbling city. Once in Campo de' Fiori, they squat on the edge of a fountain, sharing the cannoli siciliani purchased from a street vendor.

Lorenzino is silent. He is very self-conscious of how long a conversation can take with him, so he only says the minimum necessary.

Maturino's curiosity has the best of him though.

'You didn't take any measurements, didn't you?'

'No one ever taught me how.'

'That's because they saw you didn't need to learn how to take them.'

'Why does Mastro Buonarroti always correct everyone's work when he does his round but never comes up to check my panel?'

Lorenzino and Maturino stare at each other.

'The eyes of Abel roll exactly as they should. The arm of Cain, his sinews. There are no mistakes in it. Not a single one.'

'That can't be possible.'

Maturino touches Fino's forehead with the tip of his finger.

'What's in there scares me.'

Fino stares at the cobbles of the square.

'Sometimes I feel like I'm an anomaly of nature. Some kind of monster.'

Lorenzino finishes eating his cannolo and cleans his lips with his paint-stained hand.

'H-e does c-check your p-panel. At n-night. S-some nights

I d-don't see h-him until the m-morning.'

Fino stares at Lorenzino.

'At night?'

'Y-yes. I h-have heard him c-cry.'

Michelangelo's rounds are sought and feared at the same time. He easily points out the mistakes and explains to the apprentices what to do, but when some of the works are below standard he explodes in a rage.

Fino regularly sees him hitting some of the apprentices with a slap to the back of their heads. Once he is shocked to witness a fit of anger as he smashes a canvas over the head of a boy, then drags him by his hair to the front of the class to expose him as useless and lazy. After such a scene Fino had climbed down the ladder and had carefully freed the crying apprentice from the painting around his neck, everyone astonished by such careless defiance.

One day, at the end of the afternoon, Buonarroti sends all the boys back to the dormitory as usual. While they are collecting and tidying up their brushes and paints, they hear him shout from the top of the tower.

'Not you, Lorenzino. You come up here.'

Faces turn to each other in worried wonder.

Lorenzino climbs one set of stairs then stops, shaking and holding the handrails tight.

'M-maestro. I'm a-afraid of h-heights.'

'Nonsense! Close your eyes.'

Tentatively Lorenzino makes it to the top while trying not to look down.

Buonarroti positions himself behind him and with his

hands on the boy's cheeks, he points his face to the very top of the fresco. The hand of Adam isn't finished yet.

He keeps Lorenzino in that position for a minute or so, then he grabs the brush he had prepared for the last few brushstrokes and passes it in the hand of his charge.

Lorenzino is trembling.

'N-no. M-maestro. P-please, no.'

'You can do it. Look at the hand, the way it's bending, the flesh. Look at Adam's body, how it connects with his arm, the extension. Look closely. You can do it, Lorenzino. You can.'

Lorenzino positions himself under the hand and tentatively starts to paint Adam's finger.

But the curvature is hopelessly wrong and he also misses the right angle of the hand.

He drops the brush, and as it tumbles down between the scaffoldings, he starts to sob. Michelangelo turns him around and hugs him tight, holding his head with his hand.

'I-I am s-so sorry, M-Maestro. I-I am s-so sorry.'

'Never mind, Lorenzino. Never mind.'

He kisses his locks and his forehead. He has tried. He has tried so hard. But there is nothing there. Except for love perhaps.

The mild winter makes way for the Roman spring, the bright, fresh light now filtering through the high windows of the dormitory and the chapel.

The apprentices can now linger in the courtyard before the Vatican gardens, eating their lunch and running after an improvised ball made of old rags. They might be masters-in-waiting but still young they are.

Despite the oppressive presence of Mastro Buonarroti, Fino has greatly enjoyed working on the panel. The progress has inspired awe in Maturino, Lorenzino and other good-hearted apprentices while making Caramuele green with bile.

Abel is all but finished and his body is gently turning to face Cain: pearl white, the ribs, muscles, the limbs and Abel's foot exactly where they should be.

Neither brothers wears any garments and, as always with Fino's men, they are breathtakingly beautiful.

The afternoon escapades to Campo de' Fiori for a cannolo or two have become routine, the three lads enjoying each other's company. When together, Lorenzino's stammer eases quite considerably; perhaps it's all in the fear when confronted with his Master's irate judgement.

But one morning, the stool in front of his easel remains unoccupied. No one has the courage to enquiry why and about one hour later he appears.

He walks to the easel with his head lowered as much as he can, his flaxen locks arranged in such way to cover almost all of his face.

No one says a word, though Fino walks down the ladder and approaches him.

He keeps staring at the floor.

'Lorenzino, are you well?'

'P-please, go a-away.'

'Away?'

'D-don't make it w-worse.'

'Worse? What shouldn't I make worse?'

He lifts his head as discreetly as he can, hoping to hide it from his fellow apprentices. The socket of the right eye is slowly changing from purple into a deep blue. The eyebrow has a cut which hasn't entirely stopped bleeding, and his upper lip is swollen. Fino looks through the opening of his shirt and can discern further bruises.

'H-he came b-back drunk l-last night. When i-it happens, he l-loses it and he t-takes it o-out on m-me.'

Fino is not sure he can control his anger but Lorenzino grabs his forearm.

'P-please. N-not y-you.'

'Not me?'

At lunch Lorenzino disappears to see someone who can treat the wounds.

Maturino perches himself on the garden wall next to Fino, munching his loaf of bread as usual.

'Awesome idea painting Lorenzino as Abel. And making him twice as handsome. As if that was necessary.'

'Why is it a problem? We all need a model.'

'You imbecile. He thinks you are lovers. He has beaten the shit out of him before but that was some work. I'm surprised he hasn't given you one. But you were ordered here by the Pope himself. Even Michelangelo knows where to stop, I guess.'

'But we aren't lovers. That's a lie.'

'I know. But he doesn't. And Lorenzino is black and blue. Well done, Messer Fino.'

'It's all my fault.'

'Well, no. But the Master is a little crazy. And now insanely jealous. Learn to live with that. For the sake of everyone. Your panel is driving him mad. Now that it's almost finished the perfection is starting to show and he's realising that he can't match it. It is an extraordinary piece, my friend, and he's terrified. He has forbidden visitors to the chapel. He is afraid someone will see it and talk.'

'But I just like to paint. I care not for fame and money. I'm happy painting, that's all.'

'Yes, I've noticed. But they don't know that. They don't know what to do with you. They are worried that they will lose all their commissions.'

'But it's just me. I can't paint everything or everyone. That is crazy.'

'Their fears might be irrational, but real nonetheless.'

Fino thinks for a few minutes and then he recalls what he heard from Maturino's mouth and wants to double-check in disbelief.

'The Pope?'

'Yes. But don't get too comfortable. He's weak and propped up by the men from the north. He almost never comes to see the chapel. I've seen the Master shouting at him. Be on your guard.'

Despite Buonarroti's veto, a few days later two Helvetians slam the door to the chapel wide open and Pope Julius does indeed enter, followed by Cardinal Barbarigo, his Secretary of State.

All the apprentices are immediately down on their knees, heads bowed. He walks by them giving to some the opportunity to kiss his ring.

The Cardinal shouts at Michelangelo who slowly walks down all the ladders.

When in front of the Pontiff, he neither kneels or bows. He just places his hands on his hips.

'Good day, Your Holiness.'

Barbarigo is incandescent.

'Messer Buonarroti, such insolence...'

Pope Julius waves the Cardinal into silence.

'We are by now inured to the arrogance and insouciance of Messer Buonarroti. The Lord will see to his repentance in due time. In the meantime, He must be pleased to be painted by him. We guess.'

Michelangelo smiles sardonically, sending Barbarigo apoplectic. The Pope moves over to Fino's panel. He stands silent for a good ten minutes before turning to the apprentices.

'Who's Fino da Ferrara?'

Fino stands up and bows but the Pope hardly moves. He whispers something in the Cardinal's ear before making a move towards the exit.

He extends his hand in front of Lorenzino who tries to kiss the ring without lifting his head.

'Look up, my child.'

Pope Julius sees the results of the beating and closes his eyes in despairing resignation. Cardinal Barbarigo is about to lose it with Michelangelo but he is once more waved into silence by the Pontiff who performs the most regal of turns.

'Messer Buonarroti. We turn a blind eye to sinful lust when we believe some true affection might lurk behind it. But we are most vexed by unwarranted cruelty to innocent creatures.' He looks up at the ceiling. 'Try painting Our Lord without displeasing Him.'

Buonarroti bows. He has already hugged Lorenzino to near asphyxiation. Asking forgiveness. Begging him not to flee. Reassuring him that it will never happen again. Lorenzino very well knows that it will. And yet he was the one comforting his wayward Master.

The approaching summer ushers in warm evenings and nights suffused with the scent of Mediterranean pines. Fino and his fellow apprentices sometimes loiter aimlessly along the gardens, talking nonsense and mocking each other's work.

Tonight Fino lingers a bit longer. Perched on the wall outside the dormitory, he looks up to the starry sky, as always wondering what will happen in his life, still missing Ludovico.

One by one the high windows of the chapel light up, glowing with the flickering gleam of hundreds of candles.

He waits until they all shine like golden frames dotting the dark blue sky. Then he makes his way through the long and deserted corridors leading to the chapel, still somehow mindful of breaking rules which do not exist. As Maturino had remarked, they are the best apprentices of the land. One day people will bow at their entrance.

He slowly pulls the door open and enters the chapel. As he walks towards his panel, he sees him on the scaffolding.

He approaches and once closer he notices that he is kneeling down, almost as if he were hugging Abel, his forehead against the fresco, where the face of Cain's brother is turning in shock and fear.

'Maestro?'

Buonarroti turns with a sharp movement. Immersed in his contemplation, perhaps adoration, he hadn't noticed his entrance. Fino spots a half-empty carboy of wine on the table. Michelangelo slowly walks down the ladder.

'Messer Fino. What brings you here at this hour?'

The speech is slightly slurred, the eyes bloodshot.

'I saw the candles lighting up.'

'Bright enough to admire your work.'

'Maestro. We aren't lovers. Please, don't beat him up again.'

Buonarroti approaches him. When close, Fino smells the breath, reeking of cheap Frascati. Michelangelo grabs the hems of his shirt with closed fists.

'Which accursed corner of hell sent you? Which vengeful demon dispatched you here?'

'I... I just paint, sir. I'm not doing any harm. Why are you so angry with me?'

He takes hold of Fino's lithe wrist and starts dragging him along towards the paint and powder table. Fino tries to resist. Michelangelo turns and his face is suddenly less than an inch from his.

'Be still. And know that I am God.'

Beside the blasphemy, applying the quotation to himself is a clear sign of derangement. One that sends shivers down Fino's spine.

He's dragged all the way across the room. He's not sure whether he should start screaming for help. Buonarroti slams his wrist onto the table, holding it with the strength of a mad man. He grabs a cleaver used to cut solid rolls of powder. Before lifting it all the way above Fino's hand, he turns to him, the eyes flaming red now.

'What if you couldn't draw my Lorenzino anymore? What if you couldn't plaster your divine inspiration on any wall anymore? What if... what if you couldn't "just" paint anymore?'

Fino shuts his eyes. He can't free himself and by the time the cleaver falls with a loud thud, he has already fainted.

The morning after, Mastro Buonarroti takes Fino along on his round of the apprentices' works. Fino stands silently behind him but when they reach Caramuele's easel, Michelangelo steps aside and with his hand theatrically gestures to him to favour them with his opinion. Fino gulps and obediently peruses the painting.

'I... I can't find anything that needs correcting.'

Buonarroti grabs Fino's by the scruff of his neck and almost slams his face into the canvas.

'That is a lie. Are you not good enough to spot the mistakes?'

Caramuele smells the bitter scent of revenge.

'Sure he is, sir. He's been telling everyone that he is much better than you by a long way. He's told Monsignor Barbarigo that his panel is a masterpiece and your ceiling rather third rate. He has written to Prince Torlonia and his wife is going to cancel your commission for her portrait. They all want Fino now. He struts around telling everyone that he is the new Master. Better than da Vinci even.'

Lorenzino, frozen on his stool in the front row turns, his eyes welling.

'I-it's n-not t-tr...'

But he has no time to finish the sentence. He never has.

The last grain of sanity which had prevented Buonarroti from disabling Fino for life leaves him, the rage uncontrollable. The backhand is sudden, sharp, and so violent, Fino falls over Caramuele's canvas, hitting the floor with his head. Before he can even attempt to get up, the blows are raining fast on his face, on his chest, in his stomach. He tries to drag himself away but Buonarroti chases him and the kicks land on his body and then on his chin. Blood is starting to flow across the floor.

The boys are paralysed with fear. Maturino tries to restrain him but he gets shoved away with a forceful blow. He's about to get his switchblade knife out but first he shouts at Lorenzino.

'Get help. Anyone. He wants to kill him.'

Lorenzino runs through the corridors until he finds two Helvetians playing dice on the steps of another chapel. He grabs their sleeves.

'P-please. C-come quick. H-he's k-killing him.'

The two guards look at each other perplexed.

'Was passiert? Killing? Who's killing?'

Lorenzino cries while still pulling at their sleeves. The two guards, not having anything better to do, run after him, daggers in hand.

When they enter the chapel, Fino is lying on the floor, possibly unconscious, Buonarroti shouting obscenities at him, almost wailing, still hitting him. The boys are frozen, except for Caramuele who stands at the back, arms folded, a satisfied grin on his face.

One of the Helvetians takes hold of Michelangelo's arms and pulls him away, shouting at him in German to stop.

Lorenzino kneels over a lifeless Fino, then turns to his Master, the crying making his stammer hopeless.

'Y-you h-have k-killed him.'

Maturino kneels and checks Fino's heart and neck as he was once told by his family doctor.

'No. He has not. Run to Barbarigo, get help.'

The sound of riding boots bounces off the grey and dark corridors leading to the dormitory. At the head of the four guards, a tall man, perhaps in his early thirties, marches ahead with confidence, his deportment revealing aristocratic stock, the flaxen locks a northern lineage.

When in front of the dormitory door, one of the four guards slams it open with assured force.

The boys stand back as the four soldiers enter and position themselves on the side, guarding the entrance of their Commander.

The young priest who had welcomed Fino on his first day in Rome walks up demanding an explanation. The Commander takes his long gloves off and disdainfully waves him away.

'Joachim von Hasenbach, Margrave of Hasenbach. Guarantor of the Holy Father's safety. And yours. Make way or else.'

The priest and the apprentices retreat in fear. The guards are armed to the teeth, knives and swords at the ready.

He approaches Fino's bed and stops by it, silently looking at his injuries. He has just woken up and he is confused at seeing a tall and imposing man in the best of finery staring at him. The cerulean eyes meet Fino's for a longer moment.

The Margrave says nothing. He turns around and gestures to his guards to follow him, leaving the apprentices and the priest frozen in consternation.

The Helvetians guarding the entrance have no choice but to let the Margrave through the huge double door leading directly into the pontiff's study. When facing Pope Julius, he neither kneels, bows nor kisses the ring.

The Pope waves away Cardinal Barbarigo's customary protestations at such insolence, knowing very well that his illegitimate claims to temporal rule are only made possible by the authority of the men of the north. The recurrent carnage and pillage guarantee that no one dares to stand up to the papal writ.

'Margrave, we were expecting you.'

The guards and the two pages arrive in the early morning, when the rest of the boys are in the other room, washing and preparing for the day ahead.

The guards stop by the door, while the two pages wake Fino up and wrap a blanket around his shoulders.

'Wir müssen gehen. Schnell.'

Fino has no strength to resist. He has no idea what's happening and he only manages to utter three words while pointing at his bed.

'My diary. Please.'

One of the pages looks under the bed and finds it. He darts a questioning glance at Fino who nods to confirm. Wrapped in the blanket, with the diary close to his chest, he is marched to the back gate. It's still dark, the morning fog making everything hazy. He has enough time to recognise the Margrave, on his horse, imparting orders to his lieutenants. There must be a full regiment, he thinks, all on horses, swords and spears at the ready.

This time there is no cart. One of the pages opens the door of a black carriage, a gold and light blue coat of arms engraved on one of its windows.

He slumps into the red velvet seats, wondering again what is happening to him. Who are these people? Where are they taking him? He hears the men shouting in some Germanic language. The two pages are in the opposite seat, one of them holding a basket, some bread sticking out from under the cover.

Von Hasenbach shouts and the convoy starts to move. The carriage jolts ahead, surrounded by the Margrave's cavalry. Fino lifts himself up and peeks through the back window. The fog has started to lift. He sees him bursting out of the gate, still in his night gown, Lorenzino behind, holding him back, trying to plead for reason.

Then he sees von Hasenbach drawing his sword and pointing it at his throat, while holding the bridle of his horse with confident force. The exchange is brief, Buonarroti now on his knees, perhaps crying, Lorenzino trying hard to pull him away. Von Hasenbach's sword is back in its sheath and he canters away.

One of the pages tucks Fino further in the blanket. Acknowledging the frightened look in his eyes, he passes a flask of water to him with a smile.

'Keine Sorgen. Du bist in Sicherheit jetzt.'

VII. Rossini Spritz

Where have two years gone? Parker has sailed through them, fired up by his growing confidence in the language. With the unmissable swear words vocabulary now fully established, he has occasionally started to lose the 'c' in front of a few words, creating some sort of Tuscan-American accent which has Beppe in stitches.

Larry and Elizabeth have been frequently summoned by the eccentric teacher of Pittura e Disegno to talk about Parker's future.

After a slightly embarrassed start, Tommy had welcomed Beppe with all the reserved warmth he was capable of. When they told him that they had been conscripted into their basketball team, Tommy's eyes had flashed with men's herd complicity and he had wasted no time in throwing a ball at Beppe. The ensuing game had sealed the bond.

Building a temporary basketball court in the back garden had proved complicated.

Everything in the house has to be temporary. The ambassador in Rome is near the end of his term and Jeff's summons to the Oval Office have become a weekly recurrence. According to Steven, Michelle loves his colourful ties. When Larry mentions the possibility at dinner times, Parker goes all silent and broody. Being away from Florence and Beppe is an option he's no longer prepared to entertain.

When Larry had enquired with the superintendent of the building, the reply had been respectful though tentative and slightly reproachful of American insensitivity.

'A basketball court? Signor Henderson, you'll understand, Palazzo Hasenbach is under the protection of the Ministero delle Belle Arti. The gardens are historical, there are statues by Canova all around them. I mean, a basketball court...'

In the end they managed to have it built by promising to remove everything before leaving the post. The superintendent had been on the verge of fainting every time one of the builders even walked by one of the sculptures, trotting nervously after them while wiping his forehead with a visibly soaked handkerchief.

The previous summer hadn't been one of life-ending separation. The Hendersons had decamped to Viareggio, where they had acquainted themselves with the quintessentially Italian phenomenon of crowded yet eye-wateringly expensive private beach establishments.

Like every summer Beppe and his mother had travelled to the Ligurian coast to spend their holidays in the quaint seaside town of Portovenere, where she had bought a spacious apartment after Beppe's birth.

When Beppe had heard the Hendersons' choice of destination, his fists had shot to the sky.

'Yes! Not a long drive with the Vespa. And you'll come and visit too.'

The Vespa had stayed in Florence though, his mother not too happy at Beppe travelling on state roads. It hadn't stopped their insatiable thirst for each other's company and they had kept travelling back and forth by train.

Beppe's secret is safe with Parker but he hasn't attended mass with him again. That is his friend's 'thing'. The 'American' in him pushes for finding a solution to every given problem of the world and beyond. From time to time he conjures up schemes which could help Beppe to have some sort of rapport with his father. But he never reveals them to him. Beside the language, he's starting to learn that in his adopted country certain problems aren't meant to be solved. Ever.

Parker has news about their second summer and they aren't good.

'My folks have gone opera maniacs. They are taking us to Pesaro. They want to go to the Rossini Festival.'

'Man, that's far from Portovenere.'

'Yep.'

Beppe holds him in his arms, distractedly kissing his neck, smelling the mellow scent of his hair. The four o'clock cuddle. After homework. Parker's favourite time. When he melts.

'Mother has a new man.'

'How do you feel about it?'

Beppe shrugs.

'He's cool. A colleague. We can fall ill as we please now. This apartment is like a hospital ward.'

Parker laughs but he turns sharply to face him with an exciting idea.

'What about... what about coming with us? For the whole holiday? They will want some romance. You'll get in the way.'

A flash of possibility in Beppe's eyes.

'Will your parents let me?'

Parker's shoulders drop.

'Don't be daft. They adore you.'

He gets his phone out and furiously starts texting.

- mum. Can I go on holiday with the Hendersons? -

The journey is fun. Squeezed in the backseats of the Range Rover, Tommy, Parker and Beppe decide to be dead stupid when not playing games on their iPads.

Tommy had loved Parker's answer when he had asked him about Beppe.

'We aren't a couple.'

'What are you then?'

'More than that. Much more.'

Olivia has flown to Montana to meet Jack's parents. She had joined her family in Viareggio the previous year and she had enjoyed her first foray in the country immensely. Montana, of course, will be different. Very.

The villa is an art deco two-storey building almost in the centre of town and only two blocks from the beach. The garden is surrounded by a tall hedge and the first floor sports a sizeable terrace with a restricted view of the Adriatic Sea.

There is a surplus of rooms to choose from and after the main en-suite bedroom inevitably goes to Larry and Elizabeth, the choice is between two rooms with a double bed and one with two single beds positioned along the walls.

Tommy points the latter to the boys with a wink.

'Let's not make it too official. And I don't want to hear it.'

Parker and Beppe laugh. As if they'd need a double bed for

their wicked games. A floor will do. The beach, the garden. Who cares where?

They have reserved two places with loungers at the Bagni Excelsior, the most expensive establishment in town. Everything that can be seen by the achingly elegant members is matt white and marine blue, including the polos of the students working through the summer as beach attendants. The crowd is positively upper-middle-class and vaguely international, the festival attracting punters from all over the world.

The first day Tommy changes into his trunks in their private cabin to go for a swim and strolls along the boardwalk that leads to the shore. He literally parts the waters of the Red Sea and the second day he ambles along with a new girlfriend, leaving a posse of very disappointed young ladies trailing in his wake.

Parker and Beppe continue to exist in their self-absorbed universe. The villa comes with bikes and the second day they cycle all the way to Fano. They first sit on the low wall separating the pavement from the beach, feet in the sand, slurping an ice cream, before running to the sea and riding the waves for hours. It's a crowded free beach and they dive to attempt a silly snorkelling snog which fills their mouth with salty - and possibly heavily polluted - water.

Free of consular workload, Larry develops a sudden passion for cooking and family dinners on the terrace at sunset time are a chaotic and uplifting experience. Parker and Beppe are allowed a glass of wine or two.

At night they stay in their respective beds. Fun is out of the question and Beppe explains why to a disappointed Parker.

'With your wailing? You are kidding me. You'll wake the whole family up.'

They sneak back to the house a few afternoons. Beppe shuts the windows and keeps his hand on Parker's mouth most of the time. It makes Parker giggle hysterically.

But, as Beppe had pointed out, they are 'hot' and, now seventeen, even more so.

They try as much as they can to avoid the flirting, but the 'in' crowd wants them, well, 'in'.

The clique is unashamedly well-bred, hailing from the four corners of the peninsula. Every gang, whatever its social status, has a leader and this one seems to have gone overboard. They actually have a king and a queen. They are the ones approaching them first. They casually slump into the soft sofas of the beach bar next to Parker and Beppe with a confident *'Ciao'* and that is it.

The boy is apparently nicknamed *Il Surfista* - The Surfer. And he looks like one. Painfully fit, six packs, blond but tanned, his hair curly in some sort of afro way, the eyes a deep blue. A series of colourful and studiously threadbare bracelets wrap both his wrists. A smattering of sand seems to always grace his wiry limbs. His girlfriend, Cinzia, keeps waving her long blond hair around her slight, sinuous body. They are so beautiful they almost hurt the boys' eyes.

Parker is always eager to get another local idiosyncrasy under his belt.

'Why is he called The Surfer? There is no surfing here, the waves are about a foot high.'

Beppe laughs. He loves it when Parker is confronted with Italian madness.

'He looks like one. How you look is what counts. What you do is incidental.'

Either way, the pair seem to like the boys a great deal and Cinzia wastes no time in providing a long list of her friends who wants to go out with them. Parker and Beppe look at each other and worry about what to do to stem the tide.

The Surfer (they will leave Pesaro without ever learning his name) is a keen basketball player and the ensuing afternoon games get the girls off their back for a while.

With Tommy out with his new girlfriend and the boys now perching themselves on the benches of the *passeggiata* nearly every given evening with a crowd of almost fifteen, Larry and Elizabeth have the opportunity to enjoy a few romantic evenings for themselves, trying the best restaurants in town.

The Surfer and Cinzia exude the confidence bestowed on children of major gods, and they aren't stupid either.

'Boys. Come on. Game is up.'

The rest of the gang has left. Nearly midnight and they have sneaked to the front of the beach. The Surfer rolls up two joints of hashish and passes one to the boys. They are all lying on their backs, counting the stars, hearing the small waves crawling up the shore, nearly reaching their bare feet.

Parker lets Beppe do the talking.

'What you mean?'

'There is only one thing we can mean.'

'Ok.'

'You ain't no friends. When you look at each other. That ain't friends' look. No way.'

They stay silent. Then Parker finds the courage.

'Is that a problem?'

Cinzia sits up. She wraps her hands around her hair and shifts it behind her shoulders. With her lithe fingers she takes the joint away from her lips and exhales an eastern-scented cloud in the warm, humid evening air. She passes it on to the Surfer. Every one of her moves reveals a confident, elegant sensuality. A few days earlier Beppe had found himself having thoughts.

'Don't be daft. Of course not. You two are dead sweet. We girls were the first to suss it out. Boys are always slower.'

The Surfer sits up.

'Hey. Speak for the others. I told you the first day.'

Beppe sits up too.

'The first day?'

'Yes. I was wearing my Speedos and Parky kept looking at my cock.'

Parker springs up in outrage, coughing after an overconfident puff.

'I was not!'

'You were.'

Beppe laughs and turns to him.

'You do look at cocks.'

'I do not!'

'Chill out, Parky, I don't mind. I have a nice cock.'

But they can't carry on. The joints are kicking in and they are laughing too much. Too loud. Too happily.

Every time he puts his muscular and tanned arm around his shoulders, Parker worries about his reaction showing through his trunks. The Surfer always wants him on his team when they play basketball and when he scores the hugs are tight. He always feels the defined abs rubbing against his flat, still boyish stomach. Every time he calls him 'Parky', he melts.

They talk about it: slouched on the garden's old hammock, Beppe holding Parker's head on his chest, his hand through his now longer hair (a summer rebellion).

'He's not gay. He's kind of pan-sexual. And vain as fuck. He's loving it that you are drooling all over him like a puppy. I think Cinzia finds it hilarious.'

'I'm not "drooling" over him.'

Beppe's look allows no dissent.

'Ok. I am drooling over him, sorry.'

'Hey, we don't do jealousy. But he won't have sex with you. He's playing. Don't know. Maybe he'll let you suck his cock.'

After the first week the routine is well established. Lying about on the beach in the morning, lunch in the garden, nap, back to the beach and the basketball court to sweat it all out under the afternoon sun.

But this afternoon a quiet boy who hadn't exactly warmed to the gang's new acquisitions, throws the ball back to the Surfer with unnecessary force.

'You play with those two faggots. I'm out.'

Parker and Beppe freeze. And so does the rest of the gang. They hadn't bothered to come out to the rest. They had assumed that if the royal couple knew, the rest would too. Cinzia stands by her boyfriend in one of her expensive-looking bikinis, her beautiful eyes murderous.

The Surfer remains calm and starts bouncing the ball on the floor.

'You have a problem with some of our friends?'

The boy points to Parkers and Beppe.

'No. I have a problem with those two cocksuckers.'

The Surfer swirls the ball on his index finger. The skill. Cinzia has the expression of someone who is about to eat you for breakfast, lunch and dinner. With a bottle of Chianti.

'The word is "gay". Unless the twenty-first century has bypassed you, mate.'

Beppe comes forward.

'We'll go. We don't want to cause trouble.'

The Surfer turns to him, the ball still swirling on his finger. How does he do it?

'You two go nowhere.'

The boy's younger brother jumps off the wall, visibly embarrassed.

'Bro, you're being a dick. They've done nothing to us.'

The Surfer passes the ball to Beppe.

'The boys play.'

The young man folds his arms.

'You're turning into a faggot too then?'

The Surfer turns to Cinzia who smiles and winks back. *We had wanted to do this from day one anyway.*

She walks over to Beppe who drops the ball when he feels her arms around him, her soft tongue inside his mouth, her hand in his hair.

Parker has no time to enjoy the shock. The Surfer has his muscular arm around his skinny waist and the slow, deep kiss prompts his eyes to close while he feels the rugged palm of his hand caressing his neck. Not knowing what to do, he wraps his hands around the Surfer's waist, feeling the rock-hard ribs. On some days, in one of his endearing efforts to look 'native', Parker has taken to wearing Speedos on the beach. Luck has it that today he's back in his baggy trunks.

The jaws around them are still on the floor when the royal couple detach themselves from the stunned boys, the Surfer turning his grinning smile to the unhappy friend.

'The world has just turned upside down, hasn't it? It's never black and white, mate. We just pretend that it is. Too complicated for you perhaps?'

He turns to the gang.

'Parker and Beppe play with us. You are free to fuck off if you like.'

They all follow, some putting their arms around Parker and Beppe, 'Parky' walking in a state of trance. What was that?

The boy's brother hesitates a little then follows them, not before briefly turning back to his now very angry sibling.

'Bro, you're an idiot.'

On the way to the court the Surfer walks by Beppe while bouncing the ball with the usual skill. When he opens the gate of the court, he turns to him with a big smile.

'You're a lucky man, bro.'

'What?'

He throws the ball at him, before starting to run.

'Parky is a damn good kisser.'

This time Tommy can't get out of the opera nights and the concerts in Piazza del Popolo. Larry had wanted to keep their presence 'incognito' but had made the mistake of booking the tickets through the consulate.

As a consequence the mayor and other local dignitaries have invited the whole family for a cocktail party in the Town Hall and a post-performance late dinner. Not only is Tommy bored to death but he had to endure a whole afternoon of shopping with his mother and the two boys for Oxford shirts, deck shoes and preppy slacks. Elizabeth had put her foot down.

'No, Tommy, you can't wear shorts and trainers. The mayor has invited us for dinner.'

'No chance of a burger then.'

Parker shakes his head. They might have left America but America will never leave Tommy.

When all together no one seems to question the presence of an Italian boy and everyone assumes they are all brothers. Parker is over the moon at the organic inclusion.

During another sunny lunch however, it happens.

Larry has prepared a big bowl of salad and a big *tagliere* laid with a vast selection of charcuterie. He proudly walks out of the kitchen door and when he's at the table he sits in front of Beppe. Then he grabs the salad bowl with both hands and passes it to him.

'Beppe, you start with the salad.'

The wine. The sun. The rays filtering through the pergola. The banter. The stories. The laughter. The incessant artillery fire of affection from all sides over what is turning out to be the most extraordinary holiday of his life. The muscular arms handing over the salad. The bulky Breitling watch on the left wrist. The confident oozing of virility.

The elation trips him. And it comes out in the most silent of moments. As it always does.

'Thanks, Dad.'

And for Beppe the sun disappears behind a dark screen.

The embarrassment cuts the midday heat in bitter slices of pain. Tommy's bruschetta is still between his fingers, half-way to his open mouth. Larry and Elizabeth exchange worried looks. Parker shuts his eyes.

Beppe is still holding the salad bowl. No words come out. He stares into the bowl for a few seconds before getting up and running inside.

They need a few minutes to recover. Elizabeth takes hold of Parker's forearm before gently stroking his fringe.

'There is nothing to be embarrassed about.'

Parker is still staring at his empty plate.

'I know him. He feels humiliated.'

Tommy is finally munching on his bruschetta, the only damn thing which vaguely resembles a burger. Or perhaps not.

'What's the problem, bro? Beppe is family now.'

Larry pats his shoulder.

'Parker. Are you ok?'

'He left his mother before he was born. He went to America and never came back. He doesn't even know who he is.'

Elizabeth lowers her head while still holding Parker's arm.

'That explains it. I guess.'

Parker nods.

'He probably thinks he has offended us all. And that he has embarrassed himself. They are not very good at losing face here. I'll go and talk to him.'

Larry folds his napkin on the table and makes for getting up.

'Hold on, son. Since I was the target of his Freudian slip, I'll be the one to fix it.'

He leans on the door frame, hands in the pockets of his shorts, the polo soaked in sweaty patches, the fringe still rebellious despite the middle age.

'Going anywhere, Beppe?'

He stops packing his holdall for a second before answering. Then he continues to throws t-shirts and socks in the bag with renewed anger.

'Home.'

'This is your home until the end of August.'

'No, it isn't. It never was. I'm a stupid fool. An idiot.'

'That is a heck of a lot of insults you hurling at yourself, young man.'

'I'm so sorry, Mr. Henderson. At the table. I wasn't thinking.'

'There is nothing to apologise for. By the way, do you think Parker is going to be happy to see you leaving?'

'At least I won't be here to steal his family.'

'Steal? You're not stealing anything. We love you, Beppe. We all do.'

He stops packing and starts shaking.

'You don't have to. I deserve nothing.'

'Nonsense. Incidentally, your mother gave us the responsibility of looking after you for the holiday. I'm not sure I can let you go.'

He turns to face Larry, now severe, his arms folded. Beppe's specks of coal are glistening, desperately gazing for a flash of authority.

'I suppose I need your permission, Mr. Henderson.'

'You do. And I'm not giving it to you.'

'You're not?'

Larry shakes his head.

'Then... I will have to stay.'

Larry nods. He's got him.

'Come on. You must be hungry.'

Larry's arms open up like a haven welcoming a vessel lost in a raging storm. Beppe runs into them. He feels one hand patting his back, the other stroking his long locks, the strong biceps holding him.

The sobbing is muted. His face is buried in the sweaty polo, the manly waft from Larry's chest raising up through his nostrils. Seventeen long years. And now he knows. This is what it feels like.

The intoxicating melancholy of the hazy summer. The long morning swims, the sand in Beppe's long black curls, the smell of sun cream on his smooth, now tanned back. The dream Parker finds himself joyously trapped in.

They nap every afternoon, after the riotous, Renoiresque lunches, either embracing in the hammock or loosely holding hands while slouched on separate loungers.

When on the hammock Parker buries his face into Beppe's neck, the sea and all its scents in one tiny patch of velvet skin.

He had spotted his mother at the window one day, holding a coffee mug and not pretending to look away.

The day after, he had dispatched Beppe to the bar to get a snack after their morning splash and had sat by her, still dripping water from his now very long hair.

Larry and Tommy had disappeared for a windsurfing session. Time was short, Beppe could return any moment.

'We only hug, Mom. We have been very good.'

Elizabeth had sat behind him and had started to dry his hair. When almost finished she had wrapped him in the towel with a tight embrace and had kissed his head.

'This is getting too long, any thought about visiting a barber?'

He had whispered it. Without turning to look at her. Not even sure she could hear him. The feel of her slight arms around his torso, the softness of the towel.

'Love you, Mom.'

After the heavenly naps, Parker gathers his drawing material and cycles along the long sandy stretch between Pesaro and Fano. He has found a beach bar whose owner lets him stay for an hour or two, working on his drawings. Beside purchasing a few cans of coke, the man seems to think having an artist at one of the tables might attract the curiosity of prospective punters.

The sunny beach landscape is almost finished, then he will move on to Fano, to draw some of the old buildings perhaps.

He feels the presence behind him and turns. The man is calmly sipping an espresso while concentrating on Parker's work. His sunglasses shield an angular face rounded by a hint of grey beard. The Panama hat sits over a leonine mane of grey-black hair. The white linen shirt is loose, open along his chest. The tan perhaps hides an older age but at first sight Parker reckons the gentleman must be around fifty.

Without introducing himself, he points at a detail on the canvas, his finger only an inch away from it.

'The crest of the wave. That one needs to be lower. The perspective.'

Parker faces the canvas again and corrects it.

'Yes. That's much better. I knew you could do it.'

He turns again, shielding his eyes with his hand.

'I'm Parker.'

'Antonio. And that is a hell of a drawing, young man.'

Parker stands up.

'Hang on a minute. Antonio del Mare? "The" Antonio del Mare?'

'I live in hope that there is only one of us.'

'Oh my god, sir. I know you from the interview in the Washington Post. You had the same hat in the picture. You have three works at the MOMA. And one at the Tate in London.'

'That's me.'

'Wow. I don't know what to say.'

'Oh, words are an awful thing for us painters. Our soul is all in there.' He points at the drawing. 'Carry on while I order another coffee. Would you like one?'

'Yes please, signor del Mare.'

Larry and Elizabeth have enquired with the owners of the villa whether they are allowed to throw a party for their children and their new friends. The villa is furnished to the highest of standards and the couple initially pull a face, though they relent upon the promise that it will only be on the terrace and in the garden. With the daily temperature never falling below thirty degrees, that is certainly not a problem and they announce it to the young things.

After a quick round of messages, the count stands at thirty and rising, making Larry and Elizabeth gulp. Perhaps they hadn't realised how popular the three boys were. The first thing they do is to make sure all the rooms have keys to be locked with. Seventeenth-century lamps, tables and consoles disappear from the hallway and the stairs connecting the garden to the loggia.

One of the boys at the beach is local and has a full DJ paraphernalia complete with glittery ball ready to be unleashed on the unsuspecting neighbours.

Parker and Beppe work all day putting up long cables of light bulbs above the garden and the terrace. Their parents arrange the catering and drinks. Beppe reassures them about the beers.

'We don't really get drunk-drunk. Tipsy perhaps, but getting smashed is a no-no. You lose your cool and that's anathema to us. The girls run a mile and the shoes get dirty.'

At dusk the Vespas and the bikes start clogging the pavement outside the entrance of the villa. The DJ boy is all ready, playing soft disco at low volume while the first guests straggle in.

Amid a sea of fitting shorts and colourful Lacoste polos, the dancing commences, then the flirting and a bit of drinking too.

Parker and Beppe mingle, Larry and Elizabeth help the caterers while keeping an eye open for possible disasters, though everyone seems to be on their best behaviour and having a great time.

The Surfer and Cinzia are at the top of their already dizzying glamour, gliding through the crowd, dispatched on earth by Apollo and Aphrodite, bottles in their hands, the confidence of resplendent creatures in their smiles.

The Surfer leans against a table and another boy joins him while watching the ravers.

'How come Parker and Beppe are such good dancers? I can't move to save my life.'

The Surfer laughs and taps the chest of the boy with the top of his hand.

'They are gay, you dumb fuck.'

Gone past ten and everyone is sweaty, tipsy and so overwhelmingly happy. But you can be happier, the Surfer and Cinzia know.

Cinzia discreetly tiptoes towards the DJ boy and whispers in his ear.

'It's Parky and Beppe time.'

The boy turns all the lights off except for the blue ones and the garden is suddenly sea and sky all in one. He takes a record kept on the side and places it on the turntable, then slowly mixes the playing track into the new one.

Yes, you're *The Greatest Dancer.*

Parker and Beppe love the song and continue to dance facing each other. What a summer.

Cinzia slowly positions herself behind Beppe and starts following his rhythm, their bodies merging.

The Surfer is behind Parky. His little Parky.

Beppe feels Cinzia's fingers gently sliding into his.

The Surfer does exactly the same with Parky and soon his lips are on his neck, kissing it, lightly biting it.

Parky squeezes the Surfer's hands. The ecstasy.

The Surfer starts biting his ear. When his tongue dips inside it, Parky fears that he's about to faint.

Then a whisper. That soft, deep voice. Neither a boy nor a man yet.

'Close your eyes, Parky.'

Cinzia repeats the instruction to Beppe and the sea of blue lights vanishes from their eyes. And it's dark. Their beautiful dark.

They push them closer, while playing with their necks and their ears. They are now so close they can feel each other's breath blowing on their faces.

And their lips and tongues have nowhere else to go.

Cinzia and the Surfer hold them for a brief moment. Then they detach themselves.

Parker and Beppe's arms reach for each other's hips and slide under their polos, feeling that smooth, sweaty skin.

And it's out. For everyone to see. As it should be. As it should have always been. So normal, so natural. So fucking awesome.

They slowly open their eyes and remember where they are. But the panic is brief. The crowd is dancing around them, toasting the pair with their bottles of Peroni, cheering, crying, loving every single minute of it. Their first public kiss.

Parker's glistening pupils wander over to the end of the garden and spot Tommy in the corner, an arm around his summer fling. He's staring over. He has seen everything. Parker demurs and waits. A nod perhaps, a wink, a smile even.

Tommy takes his phone out of his pocket and taps a message in.

Beppe's phone vibrates in his back pocket. He reads the message and then shows it to Parker.

- look after my little bro -

Antonio del Mare's agent had seen the colour of the greenback when the MOMA had contacted him. He was well aware of their financial firepower. The New York Times and the Washington Post had published a rave review of his works and as a result of the deal, his villa on the hills south of Pesaro is a rather stunning abode, perched on a cluster of rocks, the vast terrace beholding breathtaking views of the Adriatic. At sunset it makes you almost weep in awe.

The interior is messy - he is a painter - but tastefully and expensively decorated. Paintings of fellow artists are to be found on the walls, sculptures dots corners and corridors.

In the summer months he works mainly on the loggia, overfilled ashtrays everywhere, empty bottles of Barolo and Amarone under the loungers, dirty glasses left festering even by the toilet bowl. The cleaning lady does her best but he is an artist after all. Money won't buy you tidiness.

Parker enjoys the hour or so spent at the villa immensely. He cycles to the bottom of the hill then climbs up the path for fifteen minutes.

They have espressos and soft drinks - del Mare tries not to be drunk in Parker's presence - and the tutoring is on a level he has never experienced.

Del Mare has plenty of canvasses and material and he gets Parker to start on the long coastal landscape visible from the loggia.

Parker also gets a full rundown of the arcane workings of the art world. When he asks his new mentor whether he should experiment with abstract, he catches del Mare's smirk.

'Not before you are established as a landscape or portrait artist. The thing is, critics might understand your work but, unless you've proved that you can paint "normal" stuff, the public will sneer. You know, the types who go to the MOMA and blurt it out loud: "My ten-year old can do that!". Well, why the fuck hasn't he?

'Picasso and Dalì did all that before going beautifully bonkers. And now everyone drools over their late periods. But they could fucking paint. Picasso's portraits of boys and horses were sensational work. But of course, now it's Guernica here, Guernica there.'

Checking on Parker's painting. He's not lying in his praise, the talent is genuine and his company blissful.

Too blissful.

While leaning over to suggest an alteration, he smells the sweet scent of his body, the ripples of sweat dribbling along his neck.

His lips land on the nape, his hand on Parker's open shirt, his fingers lightly stroking his nipple.

Parker freezes and shuts his eyes, his innocent trust in mankind evaporating in the searing heat.

In the time it takes him to recover from the shock and regain the power of speech, del Mare's hand is already on his belly button, confidently heading south.

'Signor del Mare. Please, don't do that.'

The hand stops and disappears behind Parker. He feels the lips detaching from his neck.

Del Mare walks to his huge desk and lights a cigarette before walking outside and standing by the bannister, looking away.

Parker is at a loss of what to do. He likes del Mare and his tutoring has been nothing short of sensational. He feels he has learned so much. But everything seems soiled now, contaminated.

He gets up, walks to the terrace and stops behind him, thinking of what to say. After a minute of silence, he speaks up, the voice knotty.

'I... I don't feel that way, Maestro. I'm so sorry.'

'How presumptuous of me to expect that you would.'

'It's not the age.'

'No, of course. It never is. You're a polite young man, Parker. Most would have used fists rather than words.'

'It doesn't bother me, I'm not angry with you.'

'No. I know you aren't. The only person angry with me right now is myself.'

He turns around. The sunglasses cover the watery eyes, burning at Parker's unbearable handsomeness.

He exhales a white cloud before stubbing the cigarette out in an overflowing ashtray.

'Please, leave.'

'Can I come tomorrow?'

'No. Never come back here, Parker. Hell hath no place for pure souls.'

He lowers his head. He genuinely holds no ill feelings.

'If it's so important to you, I can let you...'

Del Mare shuts his eyes. The agony.

'Please, go.'

Once alone he returns to his desk and starts working on a letter. He walks to the post box and then returns to the the beach bar where he met him first. The amazing drawing, the gentle poise, the serene smile, the vulnerable innocence. When he finishes the espresso, he strolls back to the villa.

He grabs his dressing gown and ambles slowly towards the terrace. He lights a cigarette on the way, taking in the peaceful dusk, the mellow scent of the pines down below.

He wears his young, toned body and nothing else when he steps out onto the terrace. He lights a cigarette too and perches himself on one of the loungers. Fully exposed.

'It's an extra fifty for breeding me, you horny old goat.'

Del Mare doesn't move.

'Your vulgarity is only matched by your impossible beauty, Rocco. Both rather grotesque.'

'What the fuck are you taking about?'

'I wasn't anticipating an understanding.'

'Blah, blah. It's fifty, you old cunt. My hole is full of your stuff.'

Del Mare inserts his hand into his right pocket with despondent force, huffing. The fist holds a crumpled bundle of fifty euro notes. He throws them behind him, in Rocco's direction.

'Fetch. You despicable hump of devilish flesh. Fetch.'

The strong breeze lifts some of the notes across the bannister, landing them between the branches of the pine trees.

'Are you fucking nuts?'

Rocco scrambles to gather as many notes as he can. He

has no pockets to put them in so he keeps hold of them with both hands.

'Disappear into the lowest circle, you handsome vermin. One where even Dante and Virgil would be loath to ever enter.'

Rocco mumbles while retreating inside, holding the notes against his chest.

'You've lost it old man. I'm out of here.'

The peace. That is all he wants now. *Pace.*

He walks back inside and picks up Parker's unfinished painting. He had left it behind: '*Without your help, I wouldn't be able to finish it, signor del Mare.*'

He weeps over it. The youth he never had. When life wasn't an option and all the feelings were kept safe inside him. Exploding every day. Every night. And nothing could happen. And nothing ever happened. The tides of history have come too late. Now only gold will buy that shiny, glittering hour. False love dwelling in the embrace of despising, handsome sewage. The cruelty. The inhuman cruelty.

He acquired this remote abode to come and live with his memories. But his past has failed to shine a bright light on his present and every dawn brings nothing new, just more and more regrets.

He places a record on the turntable and walks back to the terrace. Dusk is turning into a blazing orange sunset, soon to be drenched in crimson blood.

He leaves the dressing gown on the floor and steps onto the bannister.

Let the jagged edges of the rocks greet the end of my days. Let the emerald limbs of the pine trees be my eternal bed.

Let them.

When I am laid, am laid in earth,
May my wrongs create
No trouble, no trouble in thy breast;
Remember me, remember me, but ah!
Forget my fate

And he flies. The pungent, salty breeze. The squally wind in his face. How suffering starts and how it ends. And the life of an idiot in between. Signifying nothing indeed. Hard and impossible. The sins all but invented. And never forgiven by the men who create them.

VIII. *And then we emerged to see the stars again*

The eyelids flicker a few times before he can discern the surroundings. The first thing he notices is the four poster bed and the emerald velvet drapes gracing its corners. The room is spacious and richly decorated. The four walls are covered in oak panels and paintings of vaguely Flemish origin hang on them in orderly fashion.

The rays of an early morning spring sun slash through the iron grilles of the narrow windows.

He lifts himself up, almost disappearing between the fluffy pillows. He checks the bedding and he can feel it's all linen of the highest quality, embroidered with coats of arms. His night gown is also soft and for the first time in his life not grating against his tender skin.

He looks at his arms and inside the night gown. There are still some bruises and cuts but they are on the mend. He still feels exhausted and he's about to close his eyes again. The regiment's doctor had given him a strong potion - the only thing he can remember right now - and he slept the whole journey. To where he still doesn't know.

The hidden door in the oak panel in front of the bed opens slowly and the two German pages enter on tiptoes, one pushing a trolley. They smile, they always smile.

'Frühstück, Meister Fino.'

'Fru...?'

'Breakfast.'

He makes to get up but the first page gently pushes him back and fluffs the pillow up behind him. The second page carries a big tray and skilfully positions it in front of Fino.

The fare is something he had never had before. Freshly baked warm bread, jams, cakes, milk, honey and pastries which release a heavenly aroma.

His big brown eyes are wide open demanding an explanation. One of the pages makes a gesture indicating him to wait and leaves the room. He's back soon after, followed by an older man of perhaps fifty, elegantly dressed, carrying a big and decorated leather folder with several papers between the thick covers.

He approaches and tells the pages to leave the room. Then he grabs a heavy wooden chair and sits by the bed, laying the folder on the oversized side table.

'You'll have to excuse my Italian, Messer Fino. I have tried my best to learn it over the past year. Unlike Ludolph and Statius, who do nothing but giggle. They are a bit silly and frivolous but loyal and hardworking. Once in Florence you'll have a new valet. One you can understand.'

'A valet?'

'Please, eat you breakfast, you've been sleeping for days. You need to recover your strength.'

Between a bite and a sip, Fino stares at the gentleman. The long beard is fastidiously trimmed, his attire elegant but sober, the northern way.

'Allow me to introduce myself, Messer Fino. Bartholt

Dormettingen, Chief Secretary and Treasurer of His Excellency, the Margrave of Hasenbach.'

'With your forgiveness, Your Excellency. Where am I?'

The old man smiles.

'I'm no "Excellency", Messer Fino. Of course you don't know. We are in Arezzo, guests of the Albergotti family. The von Hasenbachs have strong connections with them.'

Fino's hunger is returning and he eagerly dives into the pastries.

'You are now under the protection of the Margrave and your abode in Florence will be Palazzo Hasenbach. You'll be given a valet and private apartments. That is the will of His Excellency.'

Fino is speechless, though even if he had the words, his mouth is full with the sumptuous breakfast.

'I never had a valet.'

'Of course not. His Excellency is a generous man, however the summons to Florence comes directly from Messer Piero de' Medici. We had been inclined to leave you with Mastro Buonarroti for a while before rescuing you. His workshop hosts the best apprentices of the land and we had concluded that it would have been beneficial to your development. But Messer Buonarroti's temper precipitated events. We feared for your life.'

Fino turns and looks at the dusty rays.

'He's an unhappy man.'

'That is very benevolent of you. He almost killed you.'

'He wanted to cut my hand off.'

The Secretary freezes, his eyes open wide in amazement.

'That we were not aware of.'

'How am I to repay the Margrave for his generosity?'

'His Excellency does not anticipate a recompense, Messer Fino. But you won't be idle, that is as sure as the air we breathe.'

He sees the puzzled expression and grabs the folder from the side table.

'These are your commissions. The requests are from the four corners of the peninsula though some from the northern lands have started to pile on my desk. I was tempted to give them priority in chronological order but, with your permission and as a sign of gratitude, the portrait of Piero de' Medici's consort should be your first work. She is in the most fretful of moods at the thought of meeting you in person.'

'Me?'

'Mastro da Ferrara. We are aware that you've been kept in the dark about your sudden fame. Your name is on the lips of princes and dukes. I daresay kings maybe.'

'But... I just paint.'

'Just?'

'Is she a beautiful lady? I always wanted to paint a beautiful lady. I'll do a profile perhaps. Or I will let her choose. What do you think, sir?'

'I think I am glad to see the enthusiasm returning. Regarding the monetary aspect, I understand that you're rather disinterested in it, am I correct?'

'Yes, sir. I never had a ducat to my name.'

'We have taken the liberty to set up a trust fund for you. With your permission I will manage it, though everything will be in your name.'

'Thank you. Could you send half of my earnings to my family?'

'Half?'

'I know it isn't much, but they need it for the Osteria. The best hare in the world, sir.'

The Treasurer smiles.

'Messer Fino, we will do whatever you ask, however I am under the impression that you are not familiar with the level of remuneration your art now commands.'

He fishes out a contract from the folder and shows it to a shocked Fino.

'That can't be true.'

'That is for the portrait. I will come to the frescoes later.'

The German pages have deposited most of the trunks on the floor and left. Fino looks around the spacious room on the second floor. He leans out of one of the windows and takes the landscape in. He can see the Duomo and Giotto's bell tower. The Arno is dotted with barges and small wooden boats, the men sailing in them shouting at each other, maybe arguing or just advertising their wares.

A cloudless day. Perhaps he will go for a walk. He hasn't been told when he will meet Piero de' Medici's wife. He's thinking about the portrait. It's already in his head, without having even met the model.

He's not sure what to do though. Should he unpack the trunks himself? He doesn't even know what's inside.

The door hidden between the tapestries opens with a sharp turn and a young man of perhaps the same age of Fino literally jumps in the room, like a court jester but with more dignified pose. He bows with grace, bringing his right arm to his chest.

'Maestro. Allow me to introduce myself, sir. I'm Billo. Your new valet.'

Fino sits on the bed, his hands holding his knees.

'Billo?'

'Camillo. But I'm known as Billo. From Naples. Or thereabouts.'

'I've never had a valet.'

'It's a nice thing to have, sir. I'll take care of everything. I'm so happy to serve a young master.'

A streetwise, earthy aura surrounds young Billo: lean, rebellious curly black hair, powder white complexion, alert eyes and a mischievous Vesuvian grin. Fino likes him immediately.

'Can we be friends?'

Billo starts to open the trunks and walks in and out of the adjacent room where garments and shoes are obviously stored.

'Ehm... sir... that isn't quite possible. I'm your servant, sir.'

He notices the expression of dejection on Fino's face.

'But... I can become... your *confidante*...'

Fino springs up and off the bed.

'I like that, Billo. Yes. Let me help you with the trunks.'

Billo stops him with his hands up.

'No, no, no, sir. You don't "help" your valet. You don't do anything. I do everything. That is the way it works. The barber will be here soon for your hair and I will arrange a bath. In the meantime, you could explore the loggia upstairs. It has been set up as your workshop over the summer months. All for you.'

'For me?'

Billo carries on with his chores. Fino walks up the staircase and reaches the loggia. The panorama of the city takes his breath away, he will definitely paint that. A table is already there with materials and a few easels of different sizes lie against the wall. He feels overwhelmed and realises that he still hasn't met his benefactor. He returns to the apartment and sees Billo carefully laying an evening outfit on the bed. The hose are flaming red, the doublet embroidered in gold, the sleeves black velvet.

'One of the best I could find. For tonight. The Margrave has invited you for supper. Just the two of you.'

He winks.

'Billo...'

'He's such a handsome man. Not even thirty yet. The most engaging manners. The short beard is soft, the lips so thin as to be almost invisible, the eyes the colour of a summer sky, hands that know how to caress...'

Fino observes the raptured state in which Billo describes his master and coughs as a way of breaking the spell.

'I'm so sorry for the liberty, sir.'

Fino frowns.

'How do you know about his hands? I mean... the caresses?'

Billo reddens and makes for the door.

'I'd better prepare the bath.'

He almost tiptoes while following Billo downstairs. Before opening the door and announcing him, the valet arranges Fino's blouse and hair, dusting off the last specks of fluff from the velvet sleeves. Then he stands in awe.

'You're perfect, Master. So handsome.'

He turns and open the double door, announcing him.

Joachim von Hasenbach sits at the end of a long, heavy table at the centre of a large room, the four walls almost entirely covered with tapestries.

Fino feels overwhelmed by a luxury he has never experienced and unsure how to behave. He possess natural good manners but the formalities of the aristocracy feel daunting.

He resolves to bow without saying anything. After all, he's in the presence of a Margrave.

Von Hasenbach signals to the servants to bring some wine to Fino.

'How is young da Ferrara this evening? I do hope a full recovery is imminent.'

Fino panics. He has no idea how to address him and he forgot to ask Billo. He plays safe.

'Much better, Your Majesty, I am confident I will fully recover.'

Von Hasenbach smiles.

'Majesty? You give too much credit to my lineage, my dear boy. We are a small principality, though we are proud to contribute to the safety of the Holy Father with our men. The best soldiers of the empire.'

'I am ever so sorry, I have no idea how to address you. My parents run an osteria near the city of Ferrara. I'm a peasant, sir.'

'That is no longer correct. You are a painter, and one with plenty of admirers at the moment.'

'I don't know how to thank you for your generosity,

sir. You have been very kind. I so look forward to my commissions.'

'Let's drink a toast.'

The supper is delicious, the fields and farms of central Italy providing all sorts of high quality meats, game and fresh vegetables masterfully prepared by von Hasenbach's chefs.

The warm evening allows them to climb the stairs and stand in the loggia, taking in the cityscape, the street torches slowly being extinguished by the night watch.

The Margrave has looked at Fino intensely all evening, Fino shyly turning his gaze away at every long, languid stare.

'Mastro Fino. I feel I must confess I am very fond of you. Such fondness set its roots when I attended your bedside, after you were savaged by that monster.'

'I am so grateful for being rescued, sir.'

'I am in no way demanding a reward. I am hoping such fondness might find a way to your heart, Mastro Fino. But you're under no obligation. I want to make that clear.'

Fino breaths in the cool evening breeze, elated by the unhurried courtship. He turns and kisses the Margrave on the cheek.

'I feel my heart will soon make way for your fondness, sir. With your forgiveness, I do feel overwhelmed by the events.'

'Of course. Time is on our side. You'd better have a safe and tranquil sleep tonight, Mastro Fino.'

He gently takes Fino's hand and kisses the palm before retiring. Fino walks to his apartments to find a fretting Billo, preparing the bed and his night gown.

'Is my master going to visit His Excellency's bedchamber tonight?'

'Billo! His Excellency has been most kind and I am very fond of him. In due time our hearts will cross the same path.'

He claps his hands in contentedness.

'You will make such a fine pair. Resplendent.'

'Billo...'

When he's introduced to the Medici extended family, he has the first taste of his new celebrity status. Everyone wants to meet him, ask him about his work and commission more for themselves, their wives, chapels and mistresses.

The Treasurer has come along as he has rightly guessed that Fino's non-existent business sense might induce him to promise work for which he has no available time.

Piero de' Medici's consort is a refined, good-hearted lady and takes to her young new painter with motherly affection. Once finished, the portrait is a sensation, her features astonishingly realistic, the light grey eyes angelic and intriguing at the same time. Once it is shown to Mastro Sanzio and Messer Rucellai, they dissemble and pretend to praise the work. Once away, Mastro Sanzio explodes.

'I told you to keep that pest away from me!'

'Mastro Sanzio, he's under the protection of von Hasenbach. The Medici are very close to his family. What do you want me to do?'

He's about to faint. He raises a hand to his heart, as to feel the palpitations.

'That portrait. Oh Lord. I have never seen anything like that. We are ruined.'

The morning is golden, the Arno translucent with specks of diamond reflections along its placid currents. Billo is attending to the final touches for the breakfast trolley, its sumptuous fare laid on a white cloth with brocaded hems. He claps his hands with authority to Ludolph and Statius.

'Everything has to be perfect this morning. You two part the drapes and I will wheel the trolley in. Then we will set up for breakfast on the loggia. Be ready with the morning gowns.'

He opens the door and when the light filters through the iron grilles of the windows, he sees von Hasenbach holding Fino in a tender embrace, without their night gowns, both still asleep.

They slowly turn and the first thing Fino notices is Billo's beaming happiness at such a serene tableau. He had himself lovingly set Fino in the Margrave's bed, as nature had made him, his skin caressed by the soft linen sheets while waiting for him. Billo had left with a wink.

'The Margrave is the best of lovers.'

And the first kiss had melted Fino's senses, the night turning more and more wonderful in the small hours. And no pain. Just ecstasy.

The second commission is a fresco in the Strozzi's chapel. And then another portrait. And a landscape.

Winter is setting in, and life as a protégé of the Margrave and now successful artist couldn't be more blissful. They have long strolls along the Arno, conversations about Fino's works and passionate nights in the Margrave's bedchamber, the light emanating from the fireplace making their cheeks glow while they hold each other in tight embraces. Von Hasenbach will at some point return to his northern possessions and to his family. He reassures his ward that he will be warmly welcomed as the court painter by his consort and his children. Fino is not so sure though, besides the fact that at such a young age he has already been dispatched to different places at the behest of anyone with the whim to summon him or even abduct him.

Von Hasenbach and Fino have been invited by Piero de' Medici to a dance at Palazzo della Signoria. Billo and the German pages commission their garments from the best tailors of the city and both look dazzling tonight, the Margrave beaming with happiness. He's in love.

In preparation, Fino has been taught a few dances and he has applied himself to the task conscientiously, not wanting to disappoint von Hasenbach.

Signora de' Medici's portrait is displayed in its full splendour in the grand hall and a stream of admirers flows incessantly along. When Fino is introduced to them, they elegantly bow, making Fino very uncomfortable. He still hasn't got used to that kind of deference and it unsettles him.

The great and good of the city are no fools and think nothing of referring to Fino as 'his' painter when conversing with von Hasenbach. Signora de' Medici is motherly to both. Every time she meets Fino, she kisses him on the cheek, turning his still baby face crimson. When they met for the first modelling session he couldn't help remarking how strikingly beautiful she was and that he was so excited and honoured for the commission. Signora de' Medici had smiled with affection and intimated to her husband to guarantee him his family protection and patronage in case von Hasenbach had to leave the city for the north.

But the Fates are blind and possibly find it tedious when life is set up to be fine and fair. It won't do.

Piero de' Medici takes Fino by his arm and gently drags him to a group of gentlemen in a corner. They are holding silver goblets of wine, perhaps discussing the fraught politics of the peninsula.

The ruler of Florence turns to Fino.

'Someone is very eager to meet a great artist. Gentlemen!'

They all turn and Fino feels his heart in his throat.

'I believe you might already be acquainted with His Highness, Prince Ludovico d'Este, Duke Alfonso's special envoy to our court.'

Now on the cusp of manhood, Ludovico's features are more striking than they ever were. The blond curls are shorter, the contours of his once baby face more angular, the eyes a deeper blue, darker than the night waves of the Tyrrhenian sea.

The garments are sumptuous, black and silver, the sleeves a wavy silk. He holds the silver goblet with the elegance and confidence of a grown man.

Fino bows, old feelings and dark foreboding mixing in his exploding head.

'Mastro Fino and I were apprentices in the same workshop, Your Excellency. Of course my talent was and is non-existent. Messer Fino, you cannot possibly comprehend my happiness in being re-acquainted with you.'

They are left alone and the fire re-ignites with wild fury, their gazes fixed on each other.

'I have promised a dance, but I'm sure the young lady will have a friend to pair you up with. Have you mastered the moves of the Allemande?'

'I have, Your Highness.'

'I forgive you the deference. I will make you know that in private I won't tolerate it.'

Fino lowers his gaze. The privacy will come at a cost and it will be betrayal. While they dance, they keep crossing past each other between leading the young ladies, their eyes meeting at every turn, their hearts jolting at every touch of hand.

Fino's eyes wander for an instant, just enough for his gaze to settle on von Hasenbach, standing in a corner of the room, observing their manoeuvres. Billo is beside him, his hands behind his back, his expression vaguely resentful.

They walk along the Arno, followed by Billo and the two German pages, the silence deafening.

'I believe that what I witnessed was love, Messer Fino.'

He feels his eyes welling up.

'Sir. We were fellow apprentices and much younger.'

'That is not an answer. Were you lovers?'

Fino's silence is as good as an answer.

'As I stated clearly before, you're under no obligation...'

Fino turns, von Hasenbach notices the tears.

'I won't betray you, sir. You have been immensely generous to me.'

'Hardly a declaration of eternal love.'

Once through the hall of the palace, von Hasenbach and

his two pages head in the direction of his apartments. Fino
calls him out but the reply is cold and sharp.

'Forgive me, Messer da Ferrara, but I believe your heart
and mind are frightfully occupied tonight. No serenity would
blossom from our coupling in such circumstances. I wish
you the best of sleep.'

Once in the room he dives on the bed crying his eyes out.
Yes. He is still in love with Ludovico. He always was and
Ludovico is on the other side of the river, waiting for him.
But tonight his heart is bleeding for his protector, the kindest
of gentlemen who loves him with all his heart and knows
that his affection is unrequited.

Billo is ready with the night gown.

'His Excellency does not deserve such a slight.'

'I haven't done anything, Billo.'

'But you are in love with the Prince and you will.'

The move to the Medici residence, where Ludovico is a guest,
is painful, Fino ravaged by remorse. The Margrave hasn't bid
him good-bye. He has hardly seen him in the day preceding
the move.

He falls into Ludovico's arms and days go by before they
can finally savour the bliss of their love.

Time heals. At the onset of spring the two young men are
at the apex of happiness. Their nights of passion under the
thick, soft bedding of Ludovico's regal bed are a never-ending vortex of untrammelled sensations; the youthful banter
after the athletic tumbles flow into the late hours until their
eyelids flicker shut.

Between the overflowing commissions, Fino finds the time

to start working on Ludovico's portrait, promising that it will be his best work ever.

And it is. And so are the frescoes. And the landscapes. And the altar pieces. Begging letters land daily on the desk of Herr Dormettingen, magnanimously allowed by the Margrave to continue to look after Fino's affairs. Every prince, duke and powerful family demands Fino's services. And one day a missive marked with a blue and gold fleur de lis appears in the hands of a royal courier. The Treasurer has difficulty in finding the words to announce the request by the King of France to the flabbergasted young man. The Dauphin is demanding Mastro Fino da Ferrara to be made court painter, the courtiers still unsure whether because of his talent or just because he wants him to visit the royal bedchamber.

It's wonderful. Almost unreal. Overwhelming. And dangerous.

The steps resonate among the oak-panelled corridors of the palace. Every time he walks by one of the large windows he barely notices the flaming sunset painting the canals in vivid orange brushstrokes. He lunges towards the heavy door at the end of the last recess, the one leading to the private quarters of the Doge.

Without knocking and without his page to announce him, he bursts into the room, jolting the old Treasurer and his young apprentice out of their chairs, dropping their quills on the ledgers they were intent on working on.

They both look at him with their eyes wide open, though the old man was indeed expecting him.

'Mastro Vecellio. Please... come in.'

He throws his brocaded velvet cloak on a chair and stands in front of the large desk, the young apprentice looking up, his lips parted in astonishment.

'I am here to demand an explanation, sir.'

'I dare to say that you are. And rather forcefully, it seems.'

He plants his hands on his hips, the gaze menacing and scornful.

'My agent has informed me that the advance for the portrait of His Excellency's consort has not been paid. Care to explain why?'

The Treasurer turns to the apprentice to demand a letter. The boy is stunned and has to shake himself out of the shock before shuffling the pile of documents on his smaller desk. Once he's found the paper he passes it to the Treasurer.

'Ah, yes. You see. His Excellency has informed me that his serene consort has expressed the firm desire to be portrayed by this young new painter, let me see... ah, yes, I believe he goes by the name of Fino da Ferrara. Yes, that's him. Do you happen to know him?'

Vecellio can barely contain his anger.

'Of course I do. No one seems to be talking about anything else. Da Ferrara here, da Ferrara there. It's tiresome.'

'Well, it might be so. But the Doge makes it quite clear in the letter that he wants his services. Though I believe him to be rather on the busy side at the Medici court.'

'This is utter nonsense. I am a Master. My artistry is sought by kings. By emperors!'

'I am in no doubt that it is. Though not by the Doge any more, sir.'

He slams his hands on the desk, leaning forward.

'This is an insult too far.'

'I am deeply sorry that you feel that way, Mastro Vecellio. As His Excellency's Treasurer I do not take such decisions, you would understand. My trade is accounting, I am no expert in yours, I'm afraid.'

'Tell your Doge that I will be leaving Venice soon and will not set foot in this city ever again.'

'I will report your wish, sir.'

He grabs the cloak and makes for the door. He slams it behind him with angry force, again jolting the Treasurer and the apprentice on their chairs. The old man darts a resigned look at the flabbergasted young man and opens his hands wide.

'Artists...'

The boys bow one by one as Torlonia ambles past their easels, disdainfully glancing at their works, haughtily towering over them, oozing entitlement and pomposity.

He halts his stroll by Lorenzino and lifts him up by grabbing the lapels of his tunic, his face now close to his.

'Call your Master, you stammering whore. Before old age will be upon us, if possible.'

Lorenzino, who by now is so used to everyone's casual abuse he barely registers it, moves to the centre of the chapel and does as he's told.

Buonarroti descends the ladders and stairs with his usual slow steps and presents himself in front of the Prince.

'Your Highness. What brings you here?'

'Maestro. We were of course interested in following your progress. And checking the standard, since your next project is supposed to be the chapel of our residence.'

'Supposed?'

'Yes. Supposed.'

He moves towards the side of Fino's panel and turns to Buonarroti. He takes his gloves off.

'We understand you had an apprentice here. And that he left. Or was abducted. Or whatever, that is not of interest to us.'

'You must be mistaken, sir.'

Torlonia notices the murmur among the boys behind their easels.

'Perhaps I should ask your charges, they seem intent on conferring among themselves.'

'You will receive the same answer.'

'We will. We are aware of your reign of terror.'

'These boys will be masters.'

'If they survive you.'

He moves to the ladder and, after darting a suspicious look at Michelangelo, he starts to climb the steps. When on the platform he turns to the fresco.

'Fine work. Do you concur?'

'The best Messer Bramante can come up with. I do not rate his capabilities as you do perhaps.'

Torlonia leans over the railing and frowns.

'Messer Bramante?'

'Indeed.'

With a sharp turn he stares at the boys who have been peering from behind their easels. He shouts at them.

'Messer Bramante?'

They hastily retreat behind their easels, pretending to go back to work.

'Messer Buonarroti. We are aware that artists do not sign frescoes as they do with paintings, are we correct?

'You are, sir.'

He draws his sword and with a theatrical sweep he points at the landscape behind Cain. The tip of the blade lands on a precise spot.

'Except Mastro da Ferrara, of course. He's cleverer than you give him credit for, Messere.'

Buonarroti stalls, visibly furious.

'We have had the pleasure of enjoying the generous hospitality of my good friend Duke Alfonso many times over, sir.' He turns to face the panel. 'That is his castle. The seat of his family right in the centre of the city of Ferrara. Now, why Messer Bramante would paint such an abode, we wonder.'

'You'll have to ask him.'

'We intend to. In the meantime, allow me to reflect on your next commission. Our residence would gain in status if the ceiling of our chapel were to be painted by young da Ferrara.'

He descends the stairs while replacing the sword in its sheath. Without acknowledging Buonarroti he walks towards the door but he stops next to Lorenzino. He grabs his jaw with his hand and inserts his thumb in his mouth, holding his tongue down, making the boy gag and cough. The Prince's face turns to Michelangelo.

'Does your catamite stammer when you ravish him? Or when you flood his mouth with copious amounts of your seed?'

Lorenzino is choking, the Prince holding him down.

'Take your pick of the others. Leave Lorenzino alone.'

He lets go of him and he tumbles on the floor, holding his

throat with both hands, crashing his easel down alongside him.

'Never mind, boy. Your painting is worse than the pox.'

He kicks him in the stomach and Maturino, who never had Lorenzino's resilience to torture, leaps on the Prince. The blood spurts in every direction. The nobleman's screams become louder and louder at every furious stab, Maturino's rage and shouts almost inhuman. Lorenzino begs him to stop but he can no longer contain so much repressed fury. Alerted by the commotion and Torlonia's screams, two Helvetians barge into the chapel and restrain Maturino. Lorenzino is crying, not for himself but for his only friend, who is taken away by the guards, his short existence soon to be ended by the Holy Tribunal. One way or another it was always bound to happen. There is only so much one can take.

The letters keep landing on his desk. The ones from Raffaello tinged with hysterical panic, the missives from Mastro Vecellio invariably laced with vexed contempt. Da Vinci, the ethereal aloofness of his genius never abandoning him, hasn't written to complain but Buonarroti knows that he is on the verge of having his commission withdrawn by the King of France. The Parisian court peremptorily demands da Ferrara to be brought to the capital, regardless of the fee. The Doge has dispatched the ablest of his ubiquitous ambassadors to the Medicean seat, the funds at his disposal unlimited. At every reception the envoy takes Fino aside, trying to lure him to the Serenissima with ever bigger offers.

He leaves after supper to walk to the tavern. Lorenzino, fearful of another thrashing, begs him to stay sober. The narrow streets are dark, prostitutes, fraudsters and murderers free to roam the nearly lawless eternal city.

He's wrapped in his cloak, constantly looking over his shoulders. Then he sees an unshaven giant of a man approaching. He's covering the lower half of his face with a black cape. His boots hit the cobbles with confident force.

'Sir?'

'Go away, I have nothing to give.'

'I'm not begging. You see before you a man of the sword.'

'A thief?'

'A man, rather, who for a consideration will rid you of a rival. And you have one.'

'Who?'

'Mastro da Ferrara. Presently in Florence.'

'Heavens! How much would you charge?'

'Such a celebrity would cost a little more.'

'When must the price be paid?'

'One half before the deed is done, the rest when the mission is accomplished.'

'How do you ensure secrecy?'

'At night. In the streets. A simple stab and he's dead.'

'I understand.'

'Not a sound is heard.'

'I understand.'

'Here is my sword. Can it serve you?'

'Not at the moment.'

'So much the worse for you.'

'What's your name?'

'Sparafucile, I am called.'

'A foreigner?'

'Burgundian.'

'And where, to arrange the commission?'

'Here, every night.'

'Go then.'

'Remember. Sparafucile. At your service.'

IX. Book of Revelation

Almost winter. The last before the end of their long spell at the Leon Battista Alberti. Beppe will be heading to the faculty of Architecture, Parker hasn't made up his mind yet.

The rain never seems to stop. The days are grey, mist and drizzle lending a melancholic drowsiness to both.

They stop on the school steps before heading to Il Forno di Pugi next door for the after school snack. It's raining and they are just about to raise the hoods of their jackets to cover themselves for the short hop.

The street turns blue. The flashing lights blind them while they hear the screeching brakes of the Carabinieri's Alfa Romeos blocking the narrow roads surrounding the school.

They can't go anywhere so they follow the scene. The cops leap out of the cars and jump on a boy with his head covered by a dirty hood.

When the hood is lowered they see him, his eyes red and watery, the black and purple shades of addiction around them.

Before he's led to the car and shoved inside by a hand on his head, he has the time to clock them and they shiver. The resentful, scowling glare is still the same but there is an added anger, veiled with desperation and resignation to a catastrophic fate, perhaps an exhaustion from the relentless demands of toxic addiction.

It was the Headmaster who had tipped off the Carabinieri. He had tolerated the dealing for a while. He had tried to talk to him and convince him to seek help while begging to stop selling to the boys of the college.

It hadn't worked and one day a boy in the third year had collapsed in the corridor, twitching and convulsing, his eyes rolling upwards. By the time the ambulance had arrived, he had been declared dead at the scene and the exasperated Headmaster had named the culprit to the investigating officer.

If it is proved that he was the dealer of the fatal overdose, he will probably get life and will leave jail perhaps an old man. The chances are that he will never make it and will be the next one twitching and convulsing.

His last look will stay with Parker and Beppe forever. It spoke of unendurable hell. The life you have. The life I will never be able to live. Your golden, beautiful families, your money, your beauty, everything that I will never have, now that I am inside a police car, being taken to a place where I will be beaten, stabbed, perhaps raped. Where I will punch more and more holes in my ravaged forearm. And then one day I'll be twitching and convulsing on the the floor, while you are driving around in your Vespa, kissed by the Tuscan sun, the breeze through your wavy, soft hair, on your way to university, a career, and yet more money, more comfort, more of everything. You beautiful, unbearably happy young things.

Marini. Born in the gutter, he never even had the chance so much as to glimpse the stars.

Too cold now for painting outside. The loggia has been cleared of all his tools and he has relocated to the library room. It is on the same floor, warm and cosy. The light filtering through the big window is perfect for painting and the old books on the shelves release a musty, ancient scent.

He's finally working on Beppe's portrait. Occasionally Beppe sits for Parker but he's found himself a bit behind with his homework and has decided to stay at home to catch up.

Parker doesn't mind. He can concentrate on the details and, after four years, Beppe's features are sculpted in his mind and heart.

He walks downstairs to the kitchen to grab a Coke from the fridge and returns upstairs. He decides to take a break and slumps in the big armchair in the corner, the floor-to-ceiling shelves all in view, Beppe looking at him from the almost finished portrait on the easel.

He's about to doze off when he hears footsteps. He gets up and walks into the long corridor.

'Tommy?'

'Bro.'

'What's up?'

'I did a stupid thing and told this German professor at my school about this old place. He wants me to pick an old book from the collection, read it, and write an essay about it.'

Parker slaps his forehead, genuinely sorry for Tommy.

'Man, that sucks.'

'Yeah. You know me.'

'I'll do it.'

'Good bro, but he'll rumble me. I'm shit at these things. You ain't.'

'Let me help you pick an easy one.'

'Awesome.'

They start removing dusty tomes, Parker slowly perusing their contents to find an easy subject for his poor brother.

The collection is not exactly Mills & Boon and Parker is starting to despair: science, astronomy, poetry in old Italian, pamphlets in Latin and Greek. Tommy picks out a small book and hands it over to Parker after a quick look.

'That's handwritten, no good.'

Parker riffles through the pages before distractedly laying it on the table.

'Looks like an old diary.'

Tommy has had enough and leaves the task to Parker who promises to embark on slower and more accurate research.

He keeps opening the books, now worried that his brother's Italian will never be enough to understand the titles, let alone the contents. Parker has also mastered Latin well, to the satisfied surprise of his professor who never misses an opportunity to point out to the rest of the class that young Henderson never had the advantage of the similarities between the two languages (Italian kids are incredibly lazy with Latin as we mistakenly believe that we don't need to study it. We cheat and just slap the genitive *'orum'* or the nominative *'ae'* at the end of Italian words thinking that it'll be alright. It isn't.)

He interrupts the search when his eye falls on the book on the table. Handwritten?

He picks it up, slumps back into the armchair and dives in with fearless concentration. The calligraphy is neat and clear, elegant, possibly the hand of an artist. When evening falls he's still deep in the dog-eared pages.

Whenever he's home alone he runs up the stairs, works on the portrait, then spends the rest of the time studying for the Esami di Maturità or reading and re-reading the diary.

And suddenly a page. He lifts his head to look at the wall. He reads it again before getting up and fixing his stunned gaze on the portrait. He stoops to closely examine the lower right-hand corner. His eyes flick back and forth between the page and the picture, his breath hostage to the implications of what he thinks he might have discovered.

One early afternoon the bell rings. He hesitates for a while until he remembers that no one is home and runs to the door.

The postman demands a signature and reminds him that it is urgent and should be in his father's hands today.

'No worries, I'll walk to the consulate across the river, he's in meetings all afternoon.'

He stows the diary away and starts strolling over the Amerigo Vespucci bridge, reaching the consulate in no time.

The guard knows him and informs him that his father just went out.

'I thought he had meetings all day.'

'Not sure, but several days a week he always goes out at three. For about two hours or less.'

'Several days?'

'Yes.'

'Do you know where he goes?'

'He has never said.'

'Thank you, here is the parcel, urgent apparently.'

Beppe is hugging him from behind, talking softly into his ear.

'He's not having an affair. You are paranoid.'

'Where does he go almost every day? And at the same time for two hours?'

'Could be anything. Work. Some American citizen who needs help and assistance.'

'He's the Consul, not a clerk. He doesn't get involved in minor stuff, unless it's important.'

'Well, maybe it's important. Stop thinking about it, I can hear your brain cells exploding. Your Dad loves your Mum, he's not cheating on her.'

Parker goes silent for a little while then turns, facing Beppe.

'Would you come with me to check?'

'You mean following him?'

'Yep.'

'That's crazy. You should trust him a bit more.'

'Please.'

He's always unable to say no to Parker and the next day the two impromptu detectives are found hiding behind the corner of the consulate, waiting for his father to appear, Beppe shaking his head at the madness.

And just about after three he does indeed leave the consulate and starts walking at a good pace along the Arno, followed by the two boys, hopping from corner to corner, baseball hats and sunglasses, in the hope of not being caught in their embarrassing pursuit.

He walks for a good fifteen minutes until he reaches a tree-lined boulevard where he finally stops at the door of a building and rings the interphone.

Parker turns around.

'Let's go and take a look at the names.'

Beppe's face is white, though in the excitement, Parker fails to notice his friend's sudden discomfort while he's dragged away by his forearm.

'There's no point, we wouldn't know any of them anyway. There's a bench over there, let's sit down and think it over.'

They walk to the bench and sit down, Beppe staring at the pavement. Parker turns to him.

'Are you ok? You seem strange.'

'What? No, no. I'm fine. Well, it can be anything, as I said. Work, most probably.'

'Maybe. Perhaps we should check if he comes to the same address every day.'

'We're not going to do that, Parker, come on.'

After a a brief, thoughtful silence, he turns to Beppe with a light frown.

'You know, it felt like you didn't want me to look at that interphone before. And you went a bit pale.'

'Nonsense.'

'You dragged me away. Why don't you want me to look at the interphone?'

'You're making things up.'

He jumps up and in seconds he's crossing the boulevard, swerving between cars, the drivers swearing at him, Beppe shouting at him to stop.

He gets to the interphone while Beppe waits on the bench, still staring at the pavement, waiting for him to come back with questions. Lots of questions.

When back, it is Parker's turn to go pale, his hands shaking. He nervously walks up and down in front of the bench, his hands in and out of his pockets.

He's afraid to ask, as if he wants to delay the reckoning. After more walking up and down, he comes to a stop in front of Beppe.

'Please tell me that it's not what I think it is.'

But Beppe stays silent. He's in shock too.

'No. No, no, no. This isn't happening. It is not true. Not my Dad. This is not true.'

'It could be a coincidence. You know, it happens.'

But he doesn't believe it himself and it shows. Parker's eyes are welling up. He covers his face with his hands. Beppe hugs him tight.

'You're making assumptions. What if there is a perfect innocent explanation to this?'

Parker detaches himself and, as if having remembered something, points his finger at Beppe.

'Wait a minute. You didn't want me to look at the names because you knew that Mr. Wilson lives there. How do you know where he lives?'

Beppe turns away. With his hands in his pockets he shrugs and stands by the bench, looking guilty.

'I do.'

Parker grabs his arm to turn him around.

'How?'

They sit back on the bench.

'The year before you arrived. New, good-looking teacher starts and I got myself a massive crush; I went a bit mental. Started flirting, pestering him, almost stalking him and doing stupid stuff like loitering naked around him in the swimming pool changing rooms and so on.

'He was either ignoring me or trying to push me away but I was relentless in my chase. He gave in and we had a brief affair. In the afternoons I came here for a couple of hours and made love. But he's not into boys. He's still a boy himself actually and it didn't really work. Besides, I could tell he was dead worried about being caught. I was fourteen at the time. Please don't say anything to anyone. He's a good guy and he'll get into a hell of a trouble if this comes out. My crush had evaporated by then anyway and he's clearly into older men.'

Parker drops his head, now both staring at the leaves flying across the pavement.

'Like my Dad.'

'We don't know that. Perhaps they are talking about your school progress.'

'What progress? In English? And every day?'

Beppe ruffles his locks and wipes his face with the palms of his hands.

'Man, I wasn't expecting this.'

'I don't understand, he's married Mom and they had us. How can it be?'

Beppe sighs.

'You're kidding me, right? Don't know about in your neck of the woods but here it has always been the case. They marry, have children, live a "normal" life and have their fun on the side. The further south you go the worse it gets. It's a bit better now but your father's generation had it tough, you can't know what he has gone through and maybe this has just happened. And we are still not sure. It might be a lady in the same building where Mr. Wilson lives.'

'Would it make it any better?'

'I guess not, I don't know.'

Suddenly Parker lets his face drop in his hands.

'Mom. Oh my god. She's going to be devastated. This can't be happening.'

The winter days go by in a haze. Larry doesn't mention anything though Parker notices some changes. He seems withdrawn and worried. In the end, desperately wanting to know, he plans a little stratagem. Without notice he walks into his father's study with his easel, a blank canvas and some brushes. Without an explanation he sets up the easel and then turns to his father who sits at the desk wondering what this is all about.

'What about a portrait? Perhaps standing at your desk. Would you pose for me?'

'Well, sure, son. What gave you such an idea?'

'Mr. Wilson's birthday is coming up. Perhaps I could give him your portrait as a present.'

Their eyes clock in silence and the confirmation Parker needed is in his father's tears. He sits down and without anger he blurts out a simple fact.

'You've got to tell Mom and Tommy, Dad.'

Tommy hasn't turned for the last thirty minutes. Lying on his bed, he either stares at the wall or shuts his eyes, hoping that all this will go away once he awakes from this terrible dream.

Parker has sat frozen on his bed, looking at his brother, feeling somehow guilty for what they are, now two of them in the family. One too many, he feels.

'I'm so sorry, bro.'

'You are?'

'Well, you know, for belonging to the same tribe.'

'Don't be an idiot.'

They hear a knock on the door and not knowing whether it's their mother, father, or both, they shout to tell them to come in.

Elizabeth opens the door with a slow nervousness but also with her usual composed calm. She comes in and, on the way to one of the chairs at the desk, ruffles Parker's hair and gently caresses his chin before sitting down.

She holds a rectangular white box tied up with a light blue ribbon and she place it on the desk with a delicate movement. Tommy hasn't turned but Parker's guilt has the best of him.

'Mom, I'm so, so sorry.'

Elizabeth stays silent for a little while, as if reflecting on what she's about to say. Then she clasps her lithe hands together on her lap and starts talking in a soft voice, while looking at the parquet floor.

'There is a lot you don't know, boys.'

Tommy finally turns, Parker can't tell whether he has been crying or not. That would be a first.

'There is?'

'Yes.'

She sighs and takes a deep breath.

'When I was about Parker's age, I attended a party organised by some classmates at my High School. I went there with a girlfriend and it was a good party, a bit of drinking and some light drugs, the usual teenagers' stuff. When nearly everyone had left, my girlfriend and I stayed a bit longer and downed a few more shots. Lots of the boys had stayed behind. Without realising, we were slowly lured upstairs where more boys had squatted with a couple of girls.

'But it was different upstairs. No one was wearing any clothes and we could hear the noise of some action from one of the bedrooms. We instinctively tried to turn back and leave but there were too many of them and they started to insist on us staying, first with words, then by physically dragging us to one of the bedrooms. Intoxicated by alcohol and drugs, we were unable to put up a resistance.'

She doesn't turn to her sons. She feels their stunned gaze upon her.

'After an episode like that, I developed a mental and physical revulsion to men. All men. I went to university and perfectly nice students started flirting with me but I pushed everyone away and remained withdrawn.

'One day I clumsily spilled my coffee in the canteen and a gentle-looking young man helped me to clear everything up. We started chatting and somehow I didn't find him threatening. There was something about him which inspired trust and, above all, safety.

'We started dating and even after a few weeks there was no insistence on his behalf to go all the way. He remained gentlemanly and caring.

'We fell in love and started to make plans for the future. But he felt he had to be honest with me and reveal that there was a side of him which refused to go away, no matter how hard he had tried.

'I listened carefully and without judging his predicament.

Despite his inclinations, he told me that he was genuinely in love with me. And that is still the truth.

'Those were different times. There was a terrible epidemic and men were dying in droves. That scared him away from the temptation to try out his orientation. He also wanted a family, children and a safe and happy life for me and, above all, for you. He loves all of you as much as I do.

'Mr. Wilson has offered to break up and leave Florence. They are in love but he cannot bear being the family wrecker.'

She looks at them first before continuing.

'I said no. There is no point. We have been defying nature enough as it is and nature always wins in the end. The arrogance of us humans in wanting to make people do what they are not supposed to. There will be someone else, or even if there isn't, your father will be an unhappy man for the rest of his life. I won't allow it.'

The pause is long. She allows the boys to take it all in before carrying on. She slowly turns and grabs the box with both hands, carefully placing it over her knees. Then she starts undoing the knot.

'That night had consequences.'

She lifts the lid of the box and places it back on the table.

'Those consequences could not be wished away. As you well know, your grandparents on my side are devout Catholics and disposing of the result of such an act wasn't an option.

'I was sent to Toronto to stay with family friends for nine months.'

She places the open box on the floor, Parker and Tommy can discern some large photographs inside.

'This is Jimmy. Your brother. Well, half-brother. I had to give him up for adoption to the family who took me in. In order to receive news and pictures of him, I had to promise not to ever contact him or reveal the circumstances of his birth. I agreed. After all I didn't and still don't want him to know that his father is one of those boys. He's married now and still lives in Toronto. They already have three children.

'I decided to marry your father when I revealed the whole story to him. I was expecting him to get up and leave. Instead he said that he loved me even more and that he would have helped me as much as he could to forget. That, of course, is near to impossible but he has been a wonderful husband and father. I'm asking you not to be angry with him.'

She stands up and quietly strolls out of the room. They stare at each other, Parker in tears. Then Tommy tentatively grabs the box, takes a picture out and shows it to Parker. He smiles.

'He takes after you, bro.'

Parker looks at the picture and suddenly remembers that his brave, wonderful mother is alone downstairs and he springs up. He runs down the stairs and they hug so tight as to be almost one.

Winter brings fog, some snow and a pervasive sadness while the process of working things out takes its course.

On a sunny day in May, he climbs up the stairs to the loggia and takes the painting down from the wall in the library. He takes it in for the last time before wrapping it in a velvet cloth. Then he grabs his phone and books an appointment.

He strolls over Ponte Vecchio for the short walk to the Uffizi. The secretary lets him in and he takes a seat in one of the armchairs in front of the over-sized Renaissance desk, admiring the frescoes covering the four walls of the office of the Director General. He lays the painting, still wrapped in the cloth, against the other chair.

When the Director comes in, he stands up and greets him with a handshake.

'So, young man, my secretary informs me that you have something for us.'

'I do. Do you have an easel?'

'Yes, I think I have one in this cupboard, let me see.'

He walks to the cupboard and fishes out an old easel. Helped by Parker they set it up by the desk.

Without further explanations, Parker unwraps the painting and carefully positions it on the easel. The Director puts his glasses on and walks closer.

'It's a da Ferrara, sir.'

'Da Ferrara? Ah, yes. Quite a minor, not many works are left, heaven knows what happened to them. The few we have are quite remarkable though. Always thought that strange.'

'It's a portrait of Prince Ludovico d'Este, finished while he was in Florence as a special envoy of his uncle. Fino da Ferrara was his lover. The signature has been scratched out. You can see a small amount of damage on the lower right-hand corner.'

'How do you know all this?'

'I do.'

The Director silently inspects the painting. Then he grabs a magnifying glass from the desk and carefully examines the details.

'How did you get hold of this?'

'I can't reveal that, sir.'

'Mmm, would you mind waiting here for a moment? We have a few experts to whom I would like to show this find.'

'Yes, sir.'

He walks at a fast pace to the restoration labs and calls out a couple of men in white aprons. They walk across the long corridor with visible excitement; when they get to his office he slowly opens the door while turning back to the experts.

'Gentlemen, I do believe this to be an authentic find. The boy wouldn't say where he found it, but I want your opinion on this and...'

He scans the big room and turns to the men with a puzzled expression.

'Where has he gone? He said he was going to wait.'

One of the men positions himself in front of the easel.

'He left the painting, Signor Direttore.'

'So he has. That's most odd.'

He walks back to the desk and presses a button on the interphone.

'Signorina, has the young man left a name, a telephone number or an address?'

'Nothing, signor Direttore, he just walked out.'

He turns to the men in astonishment.

'I don't understand, if it were authentic he would be entitled to a big reward.'

One of the experts lifts his head from the canvass.

'I might need further checks, sir, but this looks authentic to me. It is a da Ferrara.'

What is money? All the gold on the surface of the planet? Nothing, when you are almost eighteen and you are in love with the most wonderful boy in the world. And he loves you too.

And you are strolling along the Arno, hands in your pockets, straw hat and a beaming happiness radiating from that effulgent smile.

He crosses Ponte Vecchio, buys himself an ice cream and keeps heading home. His home, in his beautiful city. What is money indeed?

Fino's work will be where it belongs, where everyone will be able to see the genius, the mastery.

He keeps walking while slurping the ice cream. When he gets in front of Palazzo Hasenbach he stops and thinks about all the events past and present. And what the future might hold.

His beautiful family is in trouble. He loves them all, now perhaps even more. He will try his best to help them, without fear, without judgement. Because it's Parker. 'Parky'. And unlike too many of our fellow men, he's made of sunshine.

X. Santa Maria Novella

'TRENO IN ARRIVO AL BINARIO 3. SERVIZIO FRECCIAROSSA IN PARTENZA PER ROMA TERMINI. CARROZZE DI PRIMA CLASSE IN TESTA'

'That's me, guys.'

They start walking along the concourse, fending off a crowd of hurried fellow passengers. Clouds amble above the platform's long roofs on this crisp day at the onset of summer.

His new rucksack is humongous but he's going to be travelling for the whole of the holidays and, despite its size, he still had to tie a pair of spare trainers on the outside. Larry points at them with a cringe.

'Your fellow travellers are not gonna like that. You know what the Italians are like.'

Parker raises his eyes.

'They are clean, Dad, have a sniff.'

'Not gonna do that.'

They are by his carriage, Parker drops the heavy bag on the pavement and turns to them.

'Well...'

'This is going to sound a bit weird, son, but if you're going to have fun, make sure it's safe.'

'I thought the point of having two Dads was to avoid all the nagging?'

Larry frowns.

'Your Mom never nagged you. That's unfair.'

'Not as much as Mr. Wilson, yeah.'

James smiles.

'I guess you'll never call me by my first name?'

'Nah, too much fun. But, well, I suppose you're not my teacher anymore so maybe when I'm back?'

'I'm counting on it.'

Parker winks.

'Wrong answer, now I'll want to keep you guessing forever.'

'Remember, your card has a high limit, I know you won't go about spending it but if you lose it, call us right away and we'll sort it out. Try not to lose you passport. And call regularly.'

James turns to Larry.

'And I'm the nagging one.'

'If I run out of money, I'll sell my body.'

'Very funny. Anyway, better not miss the train. Good bye, son.'

Parker hugs him and turns to James who presents his right hand in the most friendly and polite way possible. Parker looks up with a cheeky frown.

'Oh, fuck off, Mr. Wilson.' And draws him close in a tight hug.

He stows his rucksack in the luggage rack and comes back to the door. Larry and James are standing there. In awe. The

Capostazione thoroughly checks the platform and fires off a long and piercing whistle. He must be quick.

'I'll tell you something if you promise not to cry like two old queens.'

They nod.

'Love you both.'

He taps on the window with the palm of his hand and disappears inside.

The fields of Lazio appear through the window, dry and wavy. He has gone through southern Tuscany glued to the glass, reflecting on the last few months of his life, his gap year ahead of him.

After an amicable separation, Elizabeth had settled in Boston with Tommy while Olivia continued her studies at Princeton. Perhaps she had lived either in fear or in the expectation that this moment would one day finally arrive and she had left in sad resignation, still in love with her husband.

Tommy never warmed to the Italian lifestyle and it's highly unlikely he will ever leave American soil again. He had locked himself in a titanic struggle with the language and got badly defeated; after four long years, the Florentines still had to politely ask twice or even thrice in order to understand what he was trying to say. Beyond ordering a Coke or a pizza (and a goddam burger), he had found the grammar and the array of different pronouns fiendishly difficult and in the end he just gave up. If the subjunctive had been a man he would have murdered him. Outside the International School he had made no friends. The Italians talked too much and hugged and kissed at every god-given encounter; Parker had to explain to him that the boys were neither gay nor latent homosexuals and that was the way they interacted, but for Tommy excessive contact was tantamount to a near death experience.

He loves his father too much to be angry and resentful but the sense of betrayal hasn't gone away and as much as he had tried, he had found it impossible to even speak to Mr. Wilson, whose sense of guilt shot up every time Tommy was anywhere near him.

Larry and James were trying to live happily ever after but theirs was no easy fairytale ending All that baggage kept getting in the way. They hadn't moved in together and the reasons for Larry's separation from his wife were kept as secret as they could be. Jeff was made aware of it and had reassured him that a future ambassadorship was still on the cards; the current administration was very favourable on LGBT matters. When he had put down the phone, Steven had seen the pallor on his face and had calmly continued to fix a couple of strong Dry Martinis on the terrace of their Provincetown villa, while avoiding Jeff's gaze.

'Larry has come out, hasn't he?'

'You knew?'

'Jeff. One day you'll have to learn to lift your head from that goddam desk of yours and for once in a while look at people. At what they do. How they move. What they say. What they don't say. What perhaps they should say. They can have a thousand wives and a million children. Or play basketball until they turn blue in the face. It's there. All over them. In their eyes. Desperately looking for help. You just never see it.'

He had handed over the Martini and clinked the glass.

'That is why I see it for you. How's young Tommy?'

'Not that good, from what I heard.'

'Never underestimate the storm raging inside people who say nothing, Jeff.'

Parker had decided to stay behind. And he will never leave. He's planning to apply for citizenship. He will miss his Mum and she will miss her baby. The tears never seemed to stop when she finally left. Larry has promised to finance all the air fares. The visits will be frequent.

But America has lost all meaning to him and his Italian now sports some rather sophisticated syntax and turns of phrase which makes Signora Boiocchi turn in wonder.

He has passed his Esami di Maturità with flying colours. His 'c's have now disappeared and the aspired Tuscan 'h' comes to him naturally, weirdly merging with a lingering American accent. Beppe finds the mix unbearably sexy.

He was asked to enrol in the prestigious Accademia Delle Belle Arti. When he had received the letter of invitation he had called them to book a date for the interview.

'What interview, Signor Henderson? You have been accepted. We received a letter from Maestro del Mare. The day after the tragedy. A glowing recommendation, I may add.'

They were a bit shocked when he said that he was going to take a year off. There's no gap year tradition in Italy.

Beppe too was a bit surprised at the gap year decision. Not out of jealousy but for the same reasons as everyone else.

The exchange under Mr. Wilson's home and the smashing

of too many Pandora's vases had cracked an otherwise pristine sheet of glass. Every time they look at each other through it now, their eyes have to dodge wedges of growing doubts. As they had never become an official couple, there hadn't been a need for an official separation. In any case they weren't sure whether they wanted one. But Mr. Wilson had felt a frosty breeze between the two boys, still sitting in the front row at adjoining desks.

Sex had continued. In Beppe's room and in many other bedrooms on both sides of the Arno; on their now separate holidays and wherever else gay boys have sex, which is basically everywhere and beyond. They had parted still unsure of what they were and what they were going to become, though Parker had noticed a flash of forgotten happiness when he had revealed his intention to make Florence his future home.

Ten minutes to Roma Termini. He gets up and positions his big rucksack on his shoulders. He walks through the heat to the hostel and in less than an hour he has stowed his luggage in the big locker and he's ambling through Piazza Navona: shorts, sunglasses, straw hat, hands in his pockets and girls turning at every corner.

He has booked a slot in the afternoon for a visit to the chapel. He has a deep, restful sleep, the four-bed dormitory only partially occupied: a French boy leaving in the morning and a taciturn Slovakian one, both more or less his age.

He doesn't take the smaller rucksack he has packed with him. He walks all the way to the chapel with just the small diary in his hand. He regrets not having taken something to cover it up. It is and looks like an antique and he's now afraid someone at the Vatican might question him. Italians can be paranoid about artwork theft. Perhaps because there is so much to steal.

While his fellow visitors concentrate on the frescoes on the vault, he discretely veers left and stops in front of the third panel in the row. He opens the diary and his head starts flicking up and down from the pages to the fresco. He turns to check if anyone is noticing his weird behaviour; he scans the other visitors, trying to spot an art critic perhaps.

The panel is about twelve feet from the floor but he gets as close as possible and slowly peruses the arch of the foot of Abel, the marks and the shading. He freezes at the overwhelming handsomeness of both boys, their snow-white, wiry bodies, the terrified eyes of Abel at the sight of his brother, about to strike him. A masterpiece by Bramante, as everyone in the room believes. He covers his mouth with his left hand, the diary in his right. Then he re-opens it and reads it again. Not that he needs to; he now almost knows it by heart.

14 Giugno 1508, dusk.

I am about to apply the last brushstroke to Cain. Mastro Buonarroti is spying on me from afar. I sense that the other boys stop working when I have my back turned from them. When I'm painting, I feel their eyes on me, perhaps afraid for my safety.

I smell his breath. He's standing behind me. I have to lift the brush from the wall as I have started shaking. Am I about to die? I jolt when I hear him snapping his brush and kicking a stool away with an angry grunt. I close my eyes, expecting perhaps to be hit, dragged away by my hair, beaten unconscious. I am so afraid, but I can't paint any different. Abel shouts at me, as if wanting to warn me.

Parker would like to touch the foot of Abel; that beautiful foot, the sinuous arch, the pale and rosy flesh, the lightly painted dirt marks on its side.

He closes the diary and turns. An usher is indeed noticing his strange behaviour but he has seen worse: art critics can be an eccentric bunch.

Later he strolls in the searing Roman dusk, in a trance. He has seen what no one else sees, because no one else knows. He sits on a bench in Campo de' Fiori and holds the diary tight to his chest, his eyes welling up: *Fino*.

After a burger he returns to the hostel. The French boy has left, though he takes no notice of who is or who is not in the dormitory. He strips down to his briefs, crashes on the top bunk and closes his eyes. Slightly bored and excited at the same time, he turns his dating app on and a bing on his phone is matched by another one across the room.

The Slovakian boy springs up from the top bunk on the other side, his flaxen hair dishevelled, his slavic blue eyes on stalks. Parker springs up too and the boy half-laughs while tapping on his phone.

- horny American twink? -

Parker laughs and nods, the boy lowers his head and continues to tap on his phone, making Parker's bing again.

- horny Slovakian lad. My bunk or yours? -

Parker smiles and opens his arms claiming no preference. The boy jumps out of his bunk in his underwear and socks.

Under the sheets they kiss, the Slavic passion of his hook-up making Parker shiver. He halts the proceedings for a moment.

'What if someone comes in?'

The boy fixes his blue sapphires on Parker's wanting eyes.

'If we are lucky they'll join us. If we aren't, we'll get beaten up.'

Parker needed this. So badly that even the Slovakian boy laughs earthily at his much needed release of energy.

'Man, that was like a bloody lake. Where...'

'Yeah, ok, I know. I don't know where I keep all that bloody stuff.'

But the boy hasn't wiped the flood off his face. Instead he uses it to lubricate a long kiss which makes Parker shiver, while his impromptu lover gasps and transforms the bunk into an overflowing Venetian lagoon.

They remain entangled in a sticky embrace for a while before hitting the showers. While drying himself, the Slovakian boy looks at his watch.

'Shit, my boyfriend is getting into Termini in an hour.'

He plants a quick kiss on Parker's mouth and slaps his buttocks.

'Must run. That was awesome, mate. You're dead cute.'

'I'm Parker by the way, what's your name?'

But the boy has tied the towel around his waist and he's walking back to the bunks.

'And funny.'

It has taken the best part of the day to travel to Chioggia, the efficiency and speed of the Italian High Speed service rapidly dissolving into nineteenth century standards when on regional trains.

This time the hostel is quite full and he gets a bunk in an eight-bed dormitory. He works out the best way to travel to the parish of San Procopio and the next day he hires a bike at the local shop.

The sun blazing down on the plain of the river Po is starting to burn his skin and he has purchased a very high factor sun cream. He rides along the canal. He stops from time to time under a chestnut tree to drink from his bottle of water and rest a little. His smartphone shows thirty-nine degrees. He's amazed that the bike's tyres haven't melted on the sizzling asphalt.

The small village is deserted; lunchtime is not far away and the temperature doesn't encourage outdoor strolling.

He locks his bike to a lamp post outside the church, takes the diary out of the rucksack and walks to the cloister, drying his face and neck with a flannel.

He stands to take the whole fresco in before veering again to the left. He's now standing in front of the first scene.

No one is around and he moves over to the fourth panel. He touches the arms and the chest of St. John the Baptist. He then glides his fingers along the defined sinews; the most beautiful man he has ever seen. A knot forms in his throat while he opens the diary.

23 Settembre 1507

Master Jacopo is a mean man. He used to yell at me but since the incident he has been ignoring me completely. I was trying to save him from being ravished but my gesture has made it worse. From time to time he sneers at me while repeating my words with a disgusted face: 'I come willingly'.

I love painting on my panel but every time he checks my progress he becomes really angry.

It is so lonely here. I miss my family. I miss Filiberto and his little gang. I think they really liked me and he would have beaten Messer Jacopo up, no question. It felt so good to have his protection.

And Ludovico. I dream about him every night. I'm very unhappy here.

He closes the diary and puts it back in his rucksack, someone is approaching.

'Good morning.'

'Good morning, Father.'

Father Gabriele is a slender man in his thirties sporting a neatly trimmed beard. His clerical attire looks immaculate and Parker detects a friendly deportment while he stands there, breviary in his hand.

'I'm Father Gabriele, the parish priest. You seem to have taken an interest in our frescoes.'

'Yes, Jacopo da Cremona will be one of my subjects at the Accademia delle Belle Arti.'

'Where are you from, young man?'

'I'm American, but I have been living in Florence for the last four years.'

'I must congratulate you, your Italian is rather impressive. And you have gained a delightful Tuscan twang.'

'Thank you, Father.'

Father Gabriele gets closer to the fourth panel. He must have passed it a million times but he thoroughly goes over the details.

'You seem to show a particular interest in the first and fourth panel. True, they are possibly the most beautiful of the series. Almost on a different level altogether. It has always puzzled me that in the other scenes his technique became so mediocre. Do you think they are from the same artist?'

'Maybe he had an apprentice, but there are no records.'

'Yes. Everyone has always assumed that the whole work is by Jacopo da Cremona. He remained a minor artist though. He never gained fame.'

Parker lifts his straw hat and dries his forehead with the flannel, sweating profusely.

'Would you like to rest for a bit in the shade? I can offer you some coffee or a cool drink.'

Parker nods and follows him inside the modest house at the side of the church. It's dark inside; windows are open but the shutters are all closed, the Italians' way of keeping their abodes cool through the long scorching days.

Parker sits at the wooden table and leaves his rucksack on the floor. For a moment he absently checks how old the table could be. Perhaps Fino had sat around it.

'I'm going to make an espresso if you'd join me, but first I think you need some water.'

The cups lie empty on the table. Parker likes chatting with Father Gabriele. At one point he briefly considers making him part of what he knows about the fresco but he thinks again. It is a secret between him and Fino, he will not betray him.

'May I use your bathroom, Father?'

'Of course, last door on the right at the end of the corridor.'

Parker slowly walks along the dark corridor. When by the door before the bathroom he distractedly turns his head to the right. A swarthy, eastern-looking young man is making the big bed, tucking the sheets and the covers in, fluffing up the pillows. Aware of being watched, he stops and stares at Parker who freezes for a few seconds. The boy must be in his early twenties. He's in shorts, t-shirt and barefoot.

While still holding a pillow in his arms, he smiles and humbly nods at Parker who tentatively nods back. When he passes the door on the left he sees a smaller room with a single bed made up to perfection, almost as if never used.

When he returns to the kitchen, the young man is at the sink, washing up the cups and the glasses. Father Gabriele stays silent for a while, Parker not sure what to say or what to do. He's not uncomfortable, both men have an aura of vulnerability around them.

Father Gabriele puts his hands together on the table, almost like in a distracted prayer fashion. He looks at Parker a few times before resolving to speak.

'Ruslan is my verger. He has been with the parish for almost a year now. He's from Chechnya.'

Parker turns his head to look at him. For the first time he notices a long scar on his left cheek.

'He was discovered and hunted down by the men of his village. He was tortured, and it's a miracle he's still alive.

They slashed his cheek and broke his leg, that's why he limps. He couldn't receive any medical care so it just healed the wrong way. I used some of my savings to pay for reconstructive surgery; they sodomised him with a variety of sharp objects. He nearly bled to death. The story of his escape is a tale of wanton desperation. A long journey through the lowest and darkest circles of a Dantesque inferno.'

While Parker ponders the extraordinary story he has just stumbled across, Ruslan has grabbed a chair and he now sits beside Father Gabriele, holding his hand.

'He's also deaf in one ear, because of the beatings.'

Ruslan turns to Father Gabriele and smiles keeping his lips sealed. His eyes are redolent with gratitude. Love perhaps.

'This is a rural little neck of the woods and people are very conservative. Perhaps they know but no hatred has ever come to us. I have taught him some Italian and he's an enthusiastic learner. He's no idle boy. He does a daily round of the old and lonely ladies and they love him. He sits and chats with them, makes them coffee, goes shopping for their groceries and helps them to walk from their pews to the altar to receive communion. They have an ingrained tradition of respect for their elders where he comes from. Sadly also one of violence and intolerance.

'His application for asylum has gone through, the Bishop of Chioggia himself put a good word in for us. You must be familiar with our way of moving things forward by now. All he asked in exchange was our total discretion. I would like to think it was tolerance but I guess they are just short of priests. Ruslan has no issue with that and he has also become a Christian. That pleased the Bishop no end.'

Father Gabriele smiles and squeezes Ruslan's hand.

'I don't know why I'm telling you all this. We can't talk to anyone about us, nor of the way we live. Not of the way we love each other. We have never held hands in the presence of a stranger. You struck me as a kind young man when I met you under the portico. That's all.'

Parker gently nods in silence, his eyes glistening.

'Ruslan is in a good place now. Safe. Loved. The screams at night haven't gone away and I doubt they ever will. But at least when I hold him they stop. He still doesn't understand what has he done to be hated so much.'

They walk him to his bike in silence. While pedalling away, he turns and waves. Father Gabriele has his arm around Ruslan's shoulder, their intimacy about to retreat behind the humble discretion guaranteeing their survival.

He is exhausted when he returns to the hostel. He crashes in his bunk for a long nap. At about five he wakes up and goes for a long, regenerating shower before hitting the pathways along the canals. After treating himself to a Coke at a quaint Café, he walks away from the centre and finds a deserted path along a quiet waterway. He sits on the bank with the diary in his hands, the blazing sunset blinding him.

Time to let him go.

He stares at the diary and starts to understand how everyone tries to live their lives the way they want and hardly anyone ever succeeds. We are made by what happens to us.

His father's secret, all those years. His mother knowingly marrying him, after a fateful and bruising encounter with the bestiality of humankind. His half-brother. The brother he will never meet. Signor del Mare, ending his implacable, crippling lust like a mythological hero. Mr. Wilson, the Peter Pan who will never grow up. Cesare Marini, who perhaps wanted to become a teacher and is presently languishing in some rotten jail, possibly overdosing on the very same shit he dishes out to desperate fellow drifters. Father Gabriele, sheltering a terrified cub from the cruelty of his fellow men, running amok in a medieval hellhole. Beppe. Sweet, handsome Beppe, who has humbly accepted that he will never be allowed to step anywhere near the man who gifted him with his life.

And Serafino. *Yes, Fino da Ferrara.*

He kisses the cover of the diary and his hand lets it slowly slide into the placid waters of the canal with a silent splash. It drifts away. A gust of wind flutters the pages until they become too sodden to float. When it sinks, a golden ray squeezes between two houses and strikes his face. A sudden brushstroke. He shuts his eyes and lets himself be swathed in its warmth.

It's love. Of course it is. *The Love which moves the sun and the other stars.*

'DER ICE-ZUG AUS VENEDIG KOMMT AM GLEIS 6 AN. ERSTE-KLASSE-WAGEN VORNE.

Nürnberg's temperature is several degrees lower than the sizzling Italian one and he is leisurely strolling towards the hostel, the trainers still dangling from the back of his rucksack.

He spends the following morning visiting the city after a lazy breakfast at the hostel cafe, chatting with fellow young travellers.

In the early afternoon he walks to the Gemäldegalerie. He reaches for the floor plan and darts towards the Italian Renaissance room.

Among several Mantegnas, Lottos and Caravaggios, he finally finds the two paintings he was looking for.

He stops in front of the first one and he sees him. The boyish, white complexion, the shirt crumpled and unbuttoned, revealing a smooth, bony chest. One nipple is on show, pale and flushed. The long black locks wave disorderly along the round, baby-like contours of his face. The expression is angelic but the smile is veiled with sadness and dejection. The only surviving self-portrait, in oil.

He moves on to the second painting and it is much bigger, though unfinished. Soldiers playing cards in the courtyard of Hasenbach castle, a changing of the guards happening in the background. He gets closer and notices how breathtakingly beautiful all the men are, some shirtless and basking in the midday sun.

He turns his head back to the self-portrait and sees a young man in a t-shirt, shorts and sandals looking at it, pushing back his ruffled flaxen hair at regular intervals.

The youth turns and their eyes meet.

'Findest du es nicht merkwürdig?'

'I'm ever so sorry, my German doesn't travel further than *"Guten Morgen"*.'

The young man smiles.

'Sorry. Where are you from?'

'I'm American, currently living in Florence.'

'Ah, that explains the interest in this room. You have been standing in front of these two paintings for nearly twenty minutes now.'

'Yes.'

'What I was trying to say is that I find it strange that he didn't become a master. I'm no expert but anyone can see these works are way above everything else in this room.'

Parker turns his head back to the painting. A powerless, hesitating anger.

'They didn't let him. He was better than any of them. Natural talent. A true genius. But also a threat. A threat to their unchallenged supremacy. He would have eclipsed them all and they could never allow that to happen. He was an unhappy boy.'

A frown.

'How do you know all this?'

Parker shrugs.

'I do.'

The German boy extends his hand, Parker shakes it.

'I'm Udo. Nice to meet you.'

'Parker... as in my first name.'

Ludovico sits pensively at his desk. His page has just delivered an envelope without the name of the sender. He recognises the coat of arms as it is his own: the House of d'Este.

He toys with the missive, fearful that the Duke might be recalling him back to Ferrara. Away from Fino.

Dear Nephew,

There is no time for niceties. Your dear friend, the young painter, is in grave danger. Men of no scruples are on their way from Rome and they mean harm. They are cunning and have safe-conducts with the papal insignia. Even the Medici would not have power to stop their murderous quest. They are dogs trained to kill for gold and will not betray their client for bigger rewards. Even if you succeed in stopping these henchmen, others will follow.

Be on the alert, they cannot be too far away.

Your aunt,
Lucrezia Borgia, Duchessa d'Este

Nothing escapes a Borgia. Or their spies, connections and court informants. People whom we believe cruel and insensitive might not be such. They might just need the mask to protect themselves. Sometimes they'll be the ones to run to our aid, and for no specific reason. Perhaps because you are family. Or perhaps because they have always secretly loved you but could never afford to admit it in public.

She hadn't failed to notice the brooding melancholy constantly veiling her nephew's gaze. She had visited Mastro Filargiro's workshop and had demanded to be briefed on its causes. Upon learning that a young and gifted painter had been summoned to the Medicean seat, she had pestered her husband until he had consented to dispatch Ludovico to Florence as his envoy.

Duchessa Lucrezia. Bending this world of men to her formidable will.

Ludovico drops the letter on the floor and walks to the window. He scans the narrow streets, alert for the cantering noise of horses, looking out for shady characters.

He calls for his page and sends him to Piero de' Medici to ask for an audience.

They are walking side by side, in silence. Parker turns and looks at Udo, detecting an eager lust. Yes. A coffee and a cake. And then a slow kiss. And they will take off each other's clothes. And it will be it. Another one. Another meaningless one. German, Slovakian, Korean. The next one just a little less exciting than the previous, the mystery dissolving in the hazy fog of routine, day after day, night after night. Until only the aridity of mere hydraulics is all that is left to satisfy the compulsion.

Parker abruptly stops, Udo turns in wonder.

'I... I don't think I can come to your place.'

'Why not? Something wrong? Have I offended you?'

'No, no. You are... well, you are cute, but...'

Parker takes the phone out of his pocket and juggles it in his hand, embarrassed but suddenly happy.

'But I have a call to make. A very important call.'

'I can wait.'

'No. Not while I make this call, sorry.'

Udo's face shows disappointment, yet he's a polite young man. He doesn't get angry.

'I think I understand. Someone back home?'

Parker nods and they part with a little wave of their hands. He dives into his phone.

'Parker? Hey, Great to hear from you. How are you

getting on?

'Me? I'm fine. Actually, no. I'm more than fine, I'm so happy. Dead happy.'

Beppe detects the knot in his throat. He can almost see the welling eyes. He knows him so well now.

'Parker? Are you ok? You seem a bit agitated.'

'I'm coming home, Beppe. I'll be on the train tomorrow.'

Beppe pauses while frowning in wonder.

'You are? Why? So soon.'

'I... I don't know. I just want to. I need to.'

The courtyard is almost flooded. It has rained all day and it doesn't seem to ever stop. The convoy is all ready. Trunks, provisions for the long journey, a big box with Fino's works. The Margrave is in his saddle, holding another horse by the bridle, imparting final orders. Billo is on a horse too, next to him.

Ludovico and Fino descend the staircase and stop under the portico, sheltered from the rain. Fino is slightly uncomfortable in his riding boots. He has haphazardly learnt to ride and this will be a long journey.

He turns to Ludovico but they have no tears left. The Prince takes his hand and kisses its palm.

'All we seem to ever do is part.'

Fino nods.

'You will be safe with the Margrave. He is very fond of you.'

'But I won't be happy. Not without you at my side.'

'They are determined to prevent you from ever painting again. Sign your works with a false name and find clients solely on German lands. Beware of visitors from Rome enquiring about your work. Fino da Ferrara no longer exists.'

He can only nod again. He turns and sees von Hasenbach and Billo staring at them, well aware of their pain.

Fino turns back and they hug, kissing each other on the cheeks, their hands through their long curls, sobbing.

Once on his horse he nods to Hasenbach to start moving. The Margrave lifts his hand and the convoy slowly sets off.

Fino turns and sees him for the last time, out of the portico, drenched, dejectedly waving his hand. He tries to sculpt the image in his mind while he canters away yet again to a new life. A life without Ludovico.

They are a few miles from Porta San Miniato. Sparafucile raises his hand to stop the small convoy. The old man on the cart pulls the bridle and the two horses stop with a loud whine. He scans the area. It's late afternoon and the dusty trail is deserted. Heavy clouds far in the horizon threaten a thundering summer storm.

'This will do. Good man, unload the trunks. Gentlemen, time to change.'

The old man unloads the wooden trunks and the four men start to undress while jesting around the velvet and silk garments overflowing from the trunks. Sparafucile snatches a leather doublet from one of his men.

'The one with the Holy See coat of arms is for me, you pig.'

Once finished dressing up, they vaguely resemble four Princes of the Church, though Sparafucile has to adjust a few sleeves and feathered hats on the graceless bandits.

The old man approaches, his hands rubbing each other in avaricious expectation.

'I think it is time for my reward, sir.'

Sparafucile stares mockingly at his men and laughs out loud.

'It most certainly is, you filthy *Giudeo*.'

Before the insult has even finished leaving his disdainful lips, blood is gushing from the old man's throat. He clutches it in pain, rapidly falling and expiring on the grass.

'As if I'd leave witnesses trailing in my wake. Damn fool. Throw him on the cart, send the horses away, burn the whole lot. In haste, gentlemen.'

Ludovico walks towards his wardrobe. He opens it and starts searching for Fino's working clothes, the ones with marks of paint. He changes into them and throws Fino's cape on his shoulders. Once he has donned his hat, he unlocks a drawer of his desk and takes out Fino's diary. He leans over the desk and carefully takes down his portrait. He lays it on the desk and starts scratching out the signature with a penknife.

Once across the long corridor he stops by a heavily framed mirror. He stares at himself in silence, preparing to die. So that his beloved will live. What is life without Serafino anyway? An empty shell of no joy, marred by never-ending regret.

It's late and the streets are deserted. He keeps close to the walls of the buildings, furtively checking for anyone following him. After a few turns, he reaches the entrance to Palazzo Hasenbach.

It has been empty for days now, but he encounters no problems in being admitted by the keeper once he discreetly reveals who he is.

He climbs the steep stairs. The kitchens and the servant quarters are deserted, almost everyone has left with the Prince.

He slowly props the framed painting against other covered artworks left behind by von Hasenbach. Perhaps one day, someone, here or somewhere else, will hang this masterpiece up on a wall again. But right now they don't just want Fino dead. They will try to destroy all of his works. He finds a small gap between the thousands of old tomes on the shelves and inserts the diary into it with nervous care.

He covers the lower part of his face with the cape and leaves the building, scanning the street left and right to check for the mercenaries.

Porta San Miniato. He has handed the Holy See safe conduct to the hapless, terrified guard. It's dark, but even in daylight Maestro Buonarroti's forgery would look almost authentic. The white and yellow seal might have been stolen. The young man kneels as he spots the same seal on Sparafucile's blouse. The mercenary snatches the paper from his hands and half-turns to his fellow guards.

'Make way. Open the gates! I have no time for your kneeling.'

The night watch throw themselves against the walls of via Ghibellina as they sight the four horsemen galloping noisily and at speed through the city, their swords and daggers bouncing at their side, the clatter of horseshoes on the cobbles waking the good citizens of the Tuscan capital.

Fino wakes up in a sweat. Trembling. Due to the heat they have retired in the royal bed without any nightshirts. The Margrave is deeply asleep, exhausted by his recurring nightly passion for his charge.

He silently jumps out of bed and walks to the open window. Despite the heat he is shivering. He leans forward and looks out on to the courtyard of the castle; a few soldiers idle around, playing a cards game.

The thud of the boots is getting close and menacing. Ludovico keeps looking behind his shoulders but sees no men. Yet they are there, daggers in their hands, turning corners, hopping from one side of the street to the other.

He blows the torch out; he won't be able to see where he is heading to but neither can they. He turns the corner of a narrow street and hides himself in a doorway. He kneels and crosses himself, asking forgiveness.

But the thumping noise is getting closer, he can almost hear their whispers now.

Fino's tears have started to mark his cheeks, he's not sure why but something is happening. Away. In Florence. To his beloved.

Sparafucile is first. The blade thrusts through Ludovico's chest. He falls in silence, still covering his face with the paint-stained cape; they must not see, they must not find out.

Sparafucile's henchmen move in with glee, until all their weapons are crimson, dripping with Ludovico's blood. He falls on the pavement and crouches away, still hiding his face.

The pain in Fino's chest is sharp. He grabs the gold pendant around his neck and it seems warm. He leans against the window, staring at the soldiers.

The Frecciarossa slices through the Apennines, in and out of tunnels. Parker's head is against the window, half-asleep. Upon the booming exit from yet another hole through the mountains, he suddenly awakes and by instinct glues his nose to the glass, the palms of his hands leaving fingerprints on it. He sees them: four horsemen, furiously galloping north, their leader delirious in affronted rage, the reward now immaterial. He has been deceived. No one deceives Sparafucile.

He cries out while banging on the glass.

'Stop them! Someone stop them!'

He turns and acknowledges the staring eyes of his fellow travellers. Embarrassed, he slowly lifts his hand with a tight-lipped smile.

'Sorry. Just a bad dream.'

'What are you doing up Fino? Come back to bed.'

He walks back and lies sideways with his eyes open, staring at the wooden bedroom door. He feels von Hasenbach's arm around his chest, stroking his nipple with his thumb.

'Have you been crying?'

'Yes.'

He kisses his neck, holding him tight.

'You have nothing to fear here.'

Fino grabs his pendant again but now it feels cold and he closes his eyes in pain rather than sleep.

Beppe's Vespa negotiates the traffic around the Duomo with the usual Italian flair. Once in front of Santa Maria Novella, he locks the moped, walks up the front ramp and strolls inside the station holding the helmet in his hand. A scorching summer day and his usual Stan Smiths, khaki shorts and dark blue Lacoste, his long black wavy locks sweaty from too much time spent under the helmet.

'SERVIZIO FRECCIAROSSA IN ARRIVO DA MILANO AL BINARIO 4. CARROZZE DI PRIMA CLASSE IN TESTA.'

The flaming red carriages gracefully slide along the platform, stirring more searing heat in their wake. Beppe is standing there, helmet in his hand, the black pupils of his round eyes transfixed. Those glistening specks of coal.

The train comes to a halt and the doors open with a huffing whistle. When nearly all the passengers have alighted, he sees him, his huge rucksack on his shoulders, the dangling trainers, his round glasses, his disarming half-smile.

Parker walks towards him and stops a few metres away, in silence. Beppe smiles with sealed lips while shaking his head.

'My mad American boy.'

He drops his rucksack on the pavement, the smile now full. *You're back, Parker. You're back.*

'My beautiful Italian boy.'

And Santa Maria Novella spins around them in whirling circles. And the crest of a thousand silver waves overwhelms them while their lips meet in the holiest of seals, their eyes closed, seeing everything. The sunshine, the velvety heat, the mellow scent of the Florentine summer.

All that gold.

A few streets from the station Ludovico's life whispers away. Crouched in the doorway, his eyelids flicker shut. His hand no longer tries to stem the crimson flow from his stomach, now finding its way to a drain between the smooth, wet cobbles.

Under the reproaching gaze of the Lord, Mastro Buonarroti sobs haltingly while holding Lorenzino in his arms, the young man's head tilted back, a stream of white foam dribbling out of his stunned mouth, an empty jar of solvent rolled away in a corner.

Presented with an existence bereft of any meaningful future, he had resolved that perhaps all this wasn't for him. All this being life.

Beauty alone is never enough. In the end he had grown tired of having his pride relentlessly wounded by sneers and snarky remarks, his stammer mocked at every given opportunity. While cringing at the painful ineptitude of his drawing skills, every prince or cardinal always ended their passing visits with the same poisonous whisper: 'I wonder when Mastro Buonarroti will dispose of his catamite.'

He had been allowed to bid farewell to Maturino the night before his execution. He had found the courage to be on the scaffold to pray and comfort him, though he had had to look away when the axe fell and his head tumbled into the basket.

And yet he had made the wrong call. He had assumed that when his heart-stopping looks withered - and in absence of any discernible talent - his master would indeed dispose of him. Perhaps with a sound thrashing and in the presence of a younger and even more beautiful new boy.

But his uncontrollable sobbing and desperate wailing perhaps tells another story; behind the toxic mixture of lust and violence, a genuine affection had sprung from Lorenzino's unwavering loyalty and devotion. In the early, fiery years of our lives we frantically seek out an Achilles. Yet in our declining time we can be content with a Patroclus: attending our needs, patiently understanding our ways, tenderly caring for our faltering health, gently warming our shivering bones.

The head turns and, between the tears, his eyes catch Fino's panel, Cain lifting his arm to murder his brother Abel. Or Lorenzino. *Lorenzino the Beautiful.*

Almost as soon as Sparafucile had departed in earnest on his murderous quest, an unrelenting remorse had started to bite. He had frantically scoured the insalubrious vicoli of Rome to find someone, anyone who could gallop after his hired assassin to stop what his folly had instructed him to do. He could only find a boy who, sent on his own and without escort, was duly robbed and murdered not long after leaving the gates of the eternal city. Unbeknown to him, the illiteracy of the bandits had saved him from blackmail or even prosecution. While searching the dead boy's pockets for more silver ducats, the thugs had thrown away the incriminating counter-order.

He turns his gaze on to Cain and freezes. He sees something

no one has ever been able to notice: himself. His hollow eyes. His muscular arm lifting the stone. His wanton rage. Fino had known that only Mastro Buonarroti would have been able to recognise the supreme mastery. His features are skilfully hidden between the wrinkles above the cheeks, dispersed along the open, screaming mouth. Fino had known how Lorenzino's days would end.

He looks up and stares at his creation, the finger reaching for Adam. No human being will ever master anything like this. The world is at his feet.

And so is Lorenzino.

They walk out of the station still hand in hand, their cheeks glowing under the midday sun. Parker flips his head on one side.

'Come.'

They walk to Santa Croce. Once at the main entrance door, Beppe gently detaches his hand from Parker's with a warning smile.

'Not in church.'

He has come to adore Beppe's uniquely Italian brand of Catholicism. Over the past four years Parker has mastered what Protestants have consistently failed to comprehend for the best part of five centuries: it is merely a matter of form. There is no substance and very few of its adherents are remotely interested in the concept.

Mass, pomp, elegant clothes, stunning artworks, rules to be discreetly broken, a tidy home, an old man in a long white dress; and, of course, confessing to the stealing of an extraordinary amount of apples.

An invention. Preposterous and implausible to some, the pillar of all beliefs for others. Take your pick. Alternatively, to call a spade a dagger, a fairytale. And a good one.

They stroll into the cool air of the basilica until they reach a small chapel on the far side of the altar area, forgotten by everyone, tourists absently giving it a pass.

Parker turns and they stand still in front of the two marble tombs. They are quite plain compared to the more sumptuous monuments erected for the great and good of the city. Beppe stoops down to read the plaque on the side.

Ludovico d'Este. Principe di Ferrara 1491 - 1510

Serafino da Ferrara (detto Fino). Pittore 1491 -1510

After being dispatched to Florence as an envoy of his uncle, Principe Ludovico was murdered in an alleyway in mysterious circumstances, perhaps a street robbery.

Fino da Ferrara achieved considerable fame during his stay in Florence, though only a few of his works have survived. Two weeks after the Prince's demise, he was found dead in his workshop in the castle of Hasenbach, his throat slit. The motives of the murder remain unknown.

The Margrave pleaded with Piero de' Medici for the two boys to be buried side by side in Santa Croce. The Medici family complied, in spite of angry protestations by the House of d'Este. The reasons behind the request were never revealed.

Beppe stands still, his eyes fixed on the graves.
'Why are we here?'
Parker shrugs.

'You're not the only one with a secret.'

To Parker's surprise, Beppe takes his hand again.

'They were our age when they died.'

'I know it sounds stupid, Beppe, but I believe... I believe that somehow they are watching over us.'

Beppe turns. Those deep, glistening specks of coal, always searching Parker's soul. He squeezes his hand.

'They are.'

Author's Note

Michelangelo Buonarroti wasn't a monster. At least not one who would think of cutting a fellow painter's hand off or order his assassination. A touch of nonsense is part of the beauty of historical fiction.

He was, however, notorious for a fiery temper and an ever alert eye for potential rivals who could threaten his undisputed primacy among the artists of that period.

He was also primarily a sculptor who rated painting as a less worthy kind of art. It is true that even the pontiff was wary of challenging him. His rage was terrifying and after all Julius II wanted his chapel finished.

He worked hard and was very demanding of his apprentices. He was indeed homosexual, possibly in the hazy meaning of the word at the onset of the sixteenth century. Whether he slept with his charges remains unclear, however the Renaissance ushered in a period of relatively liberal customs (by the standards of that age, of course).

We are often tempted to view the past as a sexless land but that is a misconception. It might have been less visualised because of more formal human interaction, but sex has always played a huge part in how we behave (or, more often, don't).

I've always maintained that a straight man could never have painted a masterpiece as delirious as the Sistine Chapel. As ceilings go, it is as camp as they come.

Nor can we be sure whether Raffaello Sanzio was such a panicking lightweight or Tiziano Vecellio a vexatious and pompous celebrity. In all likelihood they were very nice men.

It's fiction.

I'm not convinced that the violence would have been entirely fictional though.

It is easy to wear the proverbial rose-tinted glasses when strolling along the corridors of the Uffizi, hypnotised by the breathtaking splendour, beauty and mastery of the works on display. Even easier to assume or conclude that these geniuses were mainly mild-mannered and day-dreaming artists whose gentleness transferred onto their masterpieces.

Not quite. At least, not always.

There are plenty of episodes to bore you with (I won't), but for example, Gian Lorenzo Bernini, a sculptor who lived across the sixteenth and seventeenth century, tried to kill his brother Luigi when he found out that he was having an affair with his wife. He went on to order one of his servants to slash his consort's cheek with a razor multiple times. In those times such scars marked you out as a prostitute. Subsequently he had her convicted for adultery. Later, the very same brother caused a huge scandal by raping a young man assisting him in his workshop.

Michelangelo Merisi, known as *Il Caravaggio* was, by all accounts, a murderer on the run. Feisty lot.

These were times of violence anyway. There was hardly any police force and travelling would have been undertaken at your own considerable risk.

Dwellers of the eternal city might have been envious of the vibrant and prosperous life enjoyed by the good citizens of Florence and Venice; yet in both capitals, political murders, rioting and overnight changes of governance were part of everyday life.

That said, the astonishing amount of masterpieces produced across those centuries somehow proves that social and political upheavals can and do create the conditions for flourishing artistic movements. To this day, if you happen to visit galleries around the world, you will still come across minor artists from the Renaissance movement you might have never heard of. The Uffizi Gallery alone could not fit all of its works if it were four times the size of the present building (which is already vast). It pretty much looks like anyone with an ounce of talent had a stab at it, probably lured to the trade by generous patrons.

Perhaps Orson Welles had it right: '*In Italy, for thirty years under the Borgia, they had warfare, terror, murder and bloodshed, but they produced Michelangelo, Leonardo da Vinci and the Renaissance. In Switzerland, they had brotherly love, they had five hundred years of democracy and peace - and what did they produce? The cuckoo clock. So long Holly.*'

There is no fresco depicting Cain and Abel in the Sistine Chapel. However, if you ever happen to be in the Italian capital, the artwork which inspired me is in Villa Doria

Pamphili, high up on the wall of the antechamber to the ballroom.

Only opera buffs will have been able to spot that Sparafucile is actually a character from Verdi's 'Rigoletto'. The street conversation between Michelangelo and the mercenary is an almost exact translation of the one in the opera, with Buonarroti instead of Rigoletto.

Allow me some fun.

My books, present, past and future are 'operatic'. Or at least that is what I am told.

Either way, I'm relaxed about it. And so should you. I write in English (well, sort of), but the contents and the settings of my stories are anything but. We continental Europeans express our feelings and interact in a completely different fashion. There is a special kind of passion and it's rarely understated. Not for us the masterful, elegant restraint found in masterpieces like *Maurice* or *Far from the Madding Crowd*. If I attempted to compete I would probably write a giant pile of trite nonsense (though perhaps I already do).

It would be tempting to pin such characteristics only on Italians but our Spanish and French cousins are equally fiery, the Germans can be languidly sentimental, and the Austrians have at times a rather unsophisticated penchant for a spot of schmaltz. The Russians are, well, Russians.

Italy always had a complicated relationship with homosexuality, and one that bears no similarities to northern European countries. It is unique, in both positive and negative ways.

An essential concept to master, in order to comprehend the almost inexplicable idiosyncrasies around the issue, is the pre-eminence of the family in the national psyche.

We can call it pre-eminent now, but before the turn of the century it was rather all-conquering. It bulldozed everything else to the point that there was hardly any social space outside it. Things are now thankfully changing.

There is a paradox in all this.

Gay rights movements have always found difficult to take off and become fully mainstream. The visibility is just not there. RAI, the national broadcaster, would never screen British TV dramas such as '*It's a Sin*' or '*Queer as Folk*'. It simply doesn't happen.

They would probably pass unnoticed and it's not even censorship in a way. People are simply not interested. They don't want to know.

One of the problems is that, on the surface, there is no problem.

If you happen to discuss gay rights with a non-hostile Italian, the counter-argument is likely to be dismissive: 'But it has never been illegal. Who's prohibiting you from doing it? Who's arresting you?'

And that is true. No one. The fact that it has always been legal (and with a surprisingly low age of consent), means that the battles fought on British soil against criminal charges, clause 28 and the lowering of the age of consent, were largely unnecessary in the postwar republic (I was positively flabbergasted at the British age of consent when I set foot on English soil. Excuse me, but at twenty-one that horse has well and truly bolted and you've already fucked the world and beyond).

The answer to the grievances has always been the same: who's persecuting you? But there is another factor conveniently overlooked: the family. This omnipotent, small - occasionally medieval - nucleus of virulent homophobia.

In the 80s, when I came of age, young men were rarely concerned about being nicked by the Carabinieri while in their cars in the middle of a park, seats reclined, underwear dangling from the rear mirror. The cops would open the glove compartment to search for drugs, warn them of the dangers of being in an isolated place and drive away, the blue lights disappearing between the trees while the boys were already back at it. The police car would be resonating with insulting expletives, sure, but there was no interest in apprehending the randy lads. Besides, there was no law to apprehend them with.

Sadly, this apparent freedom lured many boys into a false sense of security, believing that the legality of it meant it was accepted. It wasn't, and the consequences were dire, at times involving fake marriages, quack doctors and, ultimately, shocking violence. Bear me witness.

Some people would point the finger at the Catholic Church and I agree that its influence has been nothing short of pernicious. Although, beside the eye-watering hypocrisy (the Vatican is by far the biggest gay bar in the world), I'm not entirely sure that without its preponderance, the attitudes would have been much more liberal. As someone pointed out to me once, apart from flags, standards and symbols, nothing has really changed much since the days of the Roman Empire. And nothing ever will.

Beppe's father, the Archbishop of Florence is, like almost everyone else, an invention. In the book, at least.

The character of Cesare Marini is loosely based on Silvio G., a classmate of mine to whom this book is dedicated.

Unlike Marini though, Silvio was handsome and easy-going. He possessed the nordic beauty so often found in the people of the *Lombardo-Veneto*, the northern region which remained under Austrian occupation for centuries before Italian unification. His soft locks were golden, his eyes Teutonic blue and his complexion graced with a smooth Galician paleness.

He was a Communist and so were his parents, his father daily breaking his back in one of the grey and soul-destroying factories dotting the foggy suburbia of what was then a wealthy yet strangely blackened city.

He never seemed to be resentful of the rest of us, a rather tiresome and annoying bunch of upper-middle-class boys with nothing better to do than flaunt the next winter holiday on the slopes of Cortina d'Ampezzo or the summer break on the beaches of Forte dei Marmi. It is impossible for a foreigner to fully comprehend how irritating the boasting, drawling vowels of the Milanese sound to the rest of the country (which, in common with our fellow Parisians, hardly registers for us).

Why Silvio had been packed off to an expensive private college was never really clear. It was a mystery how his parents could afford the fees. Perhaps they wanted to shield him from the political inferno of the state schools of the time, some of them twinned with establishments in hellholes such as Togliattigrad, a dreary Soviet sprawl on the Volga river named after an Italian Communist leader.

We 1960s boys trudged through our childhood and youth in the shadow of the *Anni di Piombo,* a spell of demented, violent terrorist activity by both extremes of the political divide, culminating in the kidnapping and assassination of the then Prime Minister, Aldo Moro. We were trying to have our fun between flying bullets, senseless massacres in packed railway stations and daily knee-cappings. One day a very rich kid in my school disappeared and was duly returned in instalments until there were no fingers or ears left to dispatch back to the family. The law of the time forbade the payment of ransoms.

Aperol Spritz anyone?

Some time after leaving both the Liceo and the country (mercifully the school has since gone bankrupt and the building demolished), I was tracked down and invited to a class reunion.

I didn't go. As a matter of fact I didn't even reply. The deafening sound of silent contempt.

I was however informed by the tracker that Silvio had since passed away, possibly overdosing on heroine, to which he had been addicted for a long time. I felt a sharp pang of sadness. Perhaps I had been hopelessly in love with him over those five interminable years of Liceo; at that age - and in those times - it was impossible to tell.

But I still remember the shaking of his head and his

sardonic yet benevolent smile at being again confronted with rich kids' pursuits he could have never afforded: 'You lot never have to fight for anything.'

Skilfully hidden behind the splendour of its palaces, the lush landscapes of its rolling hills, the cappuccinos dotting the tables of baroque, sun-kissed piazzas and the unrivalled artistic patrimony, Italy continues to be plagued by a dark, sinister heart. At times it seems to vanish, only to later reappear in more virulent and dangerous shapes.

That said, things have already improved (within regional variations) and continue to do so. Despite the resurgence of a fanatic and despicable far-right movement, the attitudes are, albeit slowly, going in the right direction.

The disinterested reserve will endure. But that is not just exclusive to this issue. In Italy the family laundry will never be washed in public. Perhaps it is a matter of taste. Frankly, I've given up trying to come to terms with it. Now I just go with the flow.

So long Holly.

And before you ask.

Yes, my mother bought me a Vespa Primavera on my fifteenth birthday. My summer attire invariably featured an extra-small dark blue Lacoste polo to cover my skeletal chest, khaki shorts revealing skinny legs and, naturally, the ubiquitous Stan Smiths.

But, no. I'm not Beppe. And there was no Parker. That is another story.

Acknowledgements

I so much want to thank my wonderful partner David as my very patient in-house historian, fact-checker, editor and proofreader. The first draft of the book was constantly interrupted by my sudden appearances in his study, demanding clarifications about princes, dukes, Popes, conflicts, Masters of the Renaissance and timelines. He always seems to know what I mean to say. He just makes it sound better.

And, as usual, special thanks to James Essinger of The Conrad Press for once again believing in yet another rather eccentric project.